COA
THE DAMNED

A MONSTER
SQUAD NOVEL

BOOK 3

HEATH STALLCUP

DEVILDOG PRESS

SWANVILLE, MAINE

For Mom

*I wish you could have been here
to read them all...*

1

Dominic DeGiacomo, United States Army Special Forces and Monster Squad operator, had been captured while on an operation in Ohio and spirited away on a trans-Atlantic flight to Rome. He thought he had made his escape when he spiked the vampire escorting him and befriended the pilot. However, the tables were turned on him when the pilot flying the aircraft turned out to be a vampire as well and knocked him silly. Imprisoned then befriended by another prisoner, he was fooled into escaping once more, only to have his fellow escapee turn his own weapon against him at the last possible moment and surrender him to the bloodsuckers once again.

Now he found himself being escorted through a series of passageways and standing in the remains of an old cathedral. Parts of the ceiling had collapsed, walls had crumbled inward and the floor was littered with pieces of blocks and broken bits of statues. He could still see what remained of an altar at the end of the cathedral and he wished that the old legends of vampires burning when they stepped on Holy ground still held true. He'd love to see these ass-hats go up in flames right about now.

He saw a dark figure all but float through what was once a window up and to his left, beyond it and to his right was the courtyard he had spotted earlier during his attempted escape. The sun had just set and the last few licks of color were painted across the sky. Violet hues splattered with streaks of red indicated the final death throes of the day before night took over and somehow, he felt it would be his last day to walk this earth. Dom took a deep breath and rolled that thought around in his head a moment. Yeah, he was okay with it. He could meet his maker knowing that he had done his part.

The dark figure stepped into the cathedral and a wave of energy came off of him that sent the vampires in the room trembling. Dom didn't recognize the vampire, but he assumed he must be the leader from the way the others were reacting. He stood at attention, doing his best to defy the creature that stepped closer to him and assessed him from head to toe.

"Welcome to my city, Mr. DeGiacomo. You may call me Sicarii," the dark vampire said softly.

"DeGiacomo, Dominic, Staff Sergeant, Service Number 243-55-61—"

"Please, Mr. DeGiacomo, I think we are beyond that, are we not?" the dark one asked. "You are my guest here."

Dom gave the vampire a sarcastic stare. "Guest? Is that what you call your prisoners now?"

"I would not say 'prisoner'," the Sicarii answered softly.

"So I'm free to leave?" Dom asked, already knowing the answer.

"I'm afraid not," the vampire replied, a smile playing across his features.

"Then I'm your fucking prisoner," Dom shot back, his features hardening.

The vampire's face hardened in return as he turned his gaze upon him. "I do not take prisoners, Mr. DeGiacomo. Therefore, you are my *guest*. How you are treated from here out…will be determined by how forthcoming you are."

"I have trouble coming a second time. Coming four times is simply beyond my ability," Dom spat. "I'm good, but I'd have to have Viagra to be *that* good." His remark earned him a quick kidney punch that dropped him to his knees, followed by a left cross to the jaw that rattled his molars. He grunted and felt his knees bite into the stone floor as he fell to all fours. "Like I said," he spat, "a *prisoner*."

"Like *I said*, how well you are treated will depend on how forthcoming you are." The dark vampire waited for another smart remark and smiled when Dom didn't offer one. "Excellent. Perhaps now you realize that I only want a little…information." He stepped forward and knelt down beside Dom. "This doesn't need to get physical."

"I ripped the head off one of your underlings," Dom replied through gritted teeth. "You expect me to believe that you're just going to let me waltz on out of here if I play ball with you?"

"A small price to pay to determine your worth." The vampire's face creased into an evil smile that didn't reach his eyes. "Your death would do me more harm than good. I actually need you, Mr.

DeGiacomo." The dark vampire noted the look of surprise on Dom's face. "Oh, it is true, I assure you. I need you to take my intentions back to your people."

"We already *know* your intentions, ass-hat. You're the shithead that keeps setting up the 'good guy' vampires so that we attack them, aren't ya?" Dom shot at him. The dark vampire's face registered a slight surprise. "Yeah, I thought so. See, we already got your number, asshole." Dom pulled himself up to a sitting position. He struggled to breathe. Between the concussion he suffered on the plane and the kidney punch, his whole body was a hurt factory. "Those other vampires already contacted my boss and they're having a sit-down meeting about how to deal with you." He chuckled. "So you just keep on trying to set them up and they'll figure out how to knock you down."

"So you've got this all figured out, do you?" the vampire asked mockingly.

"Oh, yeah." Dom struggled to his feet, the pain in his kidneys letting him know not to be surprised if he pissed blood for the next week or so. "Apparently the 'good guy' vampires only drink blood from live-stock…or something like that. I wasn't really paying attention, to be honest." He caught his breath and worked at his jaw. "But my bosses? Yeah, they're probably going to enter into an agreement with them. The vamps will point out where you fuckers are hiding and then we go in and clean you shadow dwelling blood suckers out." He laughed. "So go ahead. Do your worst. Fuck me up…kill me. It won't matter. Because it's just a matter of time before a whole team of specialists come here and rain down the very fires of hell on your ass." Dom leaned to the side and spit blood on the floor, hoping the smell would drive the other vamps crazy.

The dark vampire stepped back and addressed his minions. "Well, it would seem that our plans have been thwarted!" he announced. The other vampires chuckled or outright laughed. "These human hunters have an ally on their side. And it is US!"

He laughed. The others followed suit, giving Dom the distinct feeling that he was missing something. Something important.

"Go ahead. Laugh it up," he insisted. "But it won't be too much longer and you'll be laughing out another hole in your fucking head. One carved by a *silver bullet!*" Dom spat.

"Ooh! Silver bullets!" The dark vampire cringed mockingly. "Please, no! Not that!" He laughed again and the others laughed harder.

The dark vampire snapped his fingers and one of the minions handed him Dom's P90 carbine and his sidearm. He was still chuckling as he checked the weapons. He selected the Five-seveN handgun, pulled the magazine and held it up so Dom could see that it was still loaded. He used his thumb and extracted all but three bullets and put the magazine back.

Dom had no idea what the hell was going on. The dark vampire chambered the first round and set the safety on the weapon then tossed it to Dom and spread his arms wide. "Feel free to take your shots," he said, smiling.

Without hesitating Dom put two in his chest and one in the middle of his forehead. None of the minions so much as flinched. In fact, they were laughing harder. The dark vampire bent at the waist and held a hand over his wounds. Dom watched the holes smoke as his body simply pushed the silver rounds out of the entry holes and into his hands. He stepped over to Dom and dropped them at his feet. "You may keep them if you wish. Consider them a token of my esteem."

Dom stood there, still holding the weapon in his hand. He bent and retrieved the bullets, slightly deformed, but obviously made of silver. "How is this possible?" he muttered.

"I am the Sicarii," the dark vampire stated matter-of-factly. "It is not just a name." He stepped up to a pile of rubble and sat down. "Now, are you willing to listen to my terms?"

Rufus Thorn, leader of the *Lamia Beastia*, or non-human feeding vampires, had traveled from his island castle in the Gulf of Mexico to Tinker Air Force base in Oklahoma City to meet with Colonel Matt Mitchell, leader of the infamous Monster Squad. The squads, feared by monsters across the globe, had been misdirected by the *Lamia Humanus*, or human-feeding vampires, to inadvertently target the *Lamia Beastia* in the past. While attempting to negotiate a truce Thorn had been made aware of a larger threat, one that would affect mankind on a global level. Faced with this new threat, the *Lamia Beastia* and the human hunters entered into an alliance to face this impending attack together.

Thorn and Mitchell had been discussing tactics for some time in the training room with Laura Youngblood, the executive officer of the Monster Squads. Apollo Creed Williams, Darren Spalding and Jack Thompson, team leaders for the three different squads were also present. Jack had invited ex-Marine Gunnery Sergeant Mark Tufo along as a way to bring him up to speed on everything; much to Mitchell's chagrin. Tufo was one of the original Monster Squad team members when Mitchell ran the teams before it was decided to use the virus found in werewolves to 'augment' the team members in order to increase their reaction times, boost their speed, improve their hearing and sight and multiply their strength.

Thorn listened intently to Mitchell's proposal to use the Groom Lake base in Nevada and he liked the idea to bait the Sicarii to the desert. With wide open areas and few to no structures for the vampires to hide within when they unleashed the UV satellite on them, turning night into day and killing large numbers of vampires in one blast sounded like a wonderful plan to Thorn. He had made it clear to Mitchell that the *Lamia Beastia* revered all life as sacred and they would fight to defend human life above all else…even if it meant their own deaths. As a secondary option, he brought up the religious relics that the Vatican was holding and his plan to send Viktor, his second, to retrieve them.

The Vatican held pieces of the original cross of Christ. One piece was large enough that stakes could be made from it, the other two might be large enough to be made into stakes, but one still contained a nail used to nail His holy body to the wood. Another relic was bloody rags used to clean Christ's body after his death. They were hermetically sealed in a jar, and Thorn thought that if some of the blood could be liquefied or vaporized, it could be used as a weapon against the Sicarii much like mustard gas or silver nitrate was used on lesser vampires. The third and most intriguing of the relics were three of the thirty pieces of silver that Judas Iscariot was paid to betray Christ. If any of that silver was somehow forged into a weapon, even a single bullet, Thorn felt it would be their best bet for affecting the father of all vampires.

Rufus explained what each relic was, its history and their hopes how each could possibly be used. Mitchell liked this approach and called for Dr. Evan Peters, the Monster Squad's resident vampire and techno-genius to take notes and begin devising applications for each of the three artifacts. It was their hope that perhaps Thorn and Evan could work together on the delivery systems while Viktor was gone to retrieve the items and Mitchell would travel to D.C. to gain support for their taking over the Groom Lake base as well as their borrowing the UV satellite for the Vampire Armageddon.

During the whole meeting, both Laura and Apollo tossed in ideas of how they could utilize the Predator drones and high altitude C-130s to both keep an eye on things and to 'bring the rain' when the shit hits the fan. Spalding suggested contacting some of the other supernatural beings they had met to see if they could join in the fray. It was a long shot, but the facts remained, if this Sicarii was intent on taking over the world, odds were he wouldn't rest at simply destroying mankind. He would also see to it that all other creatures were enslaved as well. That included the Leprechaun, the Elves, and the Faeries. They were the three most intelligent and least hostile of the supernatural that the squad had met, yet they had the capability to wage war. Not all were exactly on speaking terms, and they weren't exactly the easiest to reach, but if this was a war to save the planet from a marauding vampire gone loco, they would need all the help they could get.

During the entire meeting, Tufo sat quietly in the back of the room, taking it all in. As the meeting seemed to wind down, he stood up and cleared his throat. "I have a question."

"Of course you do." Mitchell groaned.

"What is it, Gunny?" Jack asked.

"Well, I realize that I'm coming into this a little late in the game, but if I'm gathering this correctly, this vampire that we're about to go head-to-head with…he's like the granddaddy of all vamps, right?"

"*Oui*," Thorn replied. "He is the progenitor of us all."

"Okay. And you say that he was created the day he tried to kill himself when he betrayed Christ, correct?" Tufo asked. "That he is Judas Iscariot."

"*Oui*. This is true," Thorn stated.

"Okay…so I'm following everything right," he reiterated and slowly began to pace. "And he can basically 'call up and control' all the vampires in the world somehow, right? Theoretically through the blood or something, correct?"

"*Oui*. As far as we know," Thorn continued. "But since I did not break the seal on the conscription, and I represent the *Lamia Beastia*—"

"Right, you may be able to fight him off, I follow you on that," Tufo finished for him. "But, back to when this guy was made, okay? At the same time…or about the same time, this Roman guard that stabbed Christ with the spear of destiny… Claudius Maximus Veranus? He would be the granddaddy of all werewolves, correct?" Thorn nodded in agreement. "So…wouldn't he be able to call up *all* the werewolves in the world if he wanted to? Through the blood, or through the howling or some goody-goody supernatural bullshit like that?" Tufo asked.

Jack turned to Mitchell who raised his eyebrows. Jack shrugged.

"If this Roman guy could somehow call up all the werewolves, we might be able to add some serious muscle to this army of ours," Tufo stated the obvious. "And we might just be able to offer a surprise knock-out punch to this Sicarii…you know, just in case Plan A and Plan B happen to shit the bed."

Thorn stepped over to Tufo and embraced him. "*Exactement!*" He kissed Tufo on each cheek then turned to Mitchell leaving the Gunny wide-eyed and in shock. "This is a most *excellent* of ideas!"

10

Jack leaned over to Mitchell. "Maybe this is what Nadia was talking about, eh, Skipper? Maybe me bringing Tufo in with us IS what saves our asses and the world?"

Mitchell rolled his eyes. "Don't go there. Even a blind squirrel finds a nut once in a while."

"Okay then. How do we find this ancient Roman dude?" Apollo asked.

Thorn stepped forward. "I think I know a way."

"I don't think I like this idea," Jack said as Nadia repacked her bags. "You just got here."

Nadia was packing a small travel bag and left the larger part of her luggage stacked away. "It is only for a few days, Jack. I will be back very soon."

Jack looked away to keep from getting upset. "But why you? Surely someone else could go," he stated more than asked.

"My father asked me to do this, Jack. It must be for a reason," she said without looking at him. She searched the room and finally found her hiking boots. Stuffing them into the side of her bag, she finally turned to address him. "Mother will be going with me as well. Father would not send the both of us anyplace dangerous," she said softly, her mouth slowly curving into a smile. She wrapped her arms around him and pulled herself to him tightly.

11

"Your dad doesn't like me," Jack muttered. "I can't help but think he's sending you off just to keep us apart."

"That is nonsense, Jack," Nadia clucked, kissing him on his chin. "Father accepts you. We are mated."

Jack looked down at her, one eyebrow raised. "Something tells me that if we weren't mated, he'd gladly eviscerate me."

She inhaled sharply in shock, "Jack! You shouldn't say such things. Father is many things, but he's not a murderer."

"Yes, he is, my dear," her mother corrected, walking through her door unannounced. "He is a Lycan of the First Order and he has killed many, many times in his long lifetime."

"Mother!" Nadia exclaimed. "There is a difference in killing to defend and murdering."

"Killing is killing, my love. You know that," Natashia purred as she stretched out on Nadia's bed. Jack couldn't help but notice that her mother still had a seductive look in her eye. "Your father, I believe, *enjoys* killing," she added absently. "Perhaps that's what makes him such an efficient Lycan?"

"You are horrible to say such a thing, mother." Nadia grabbed the last of her things and unceremoniously shoved them into her bag. "Father would be appalled."

"Not if it's true," Natashia said absently. "So, Jack, where are you and your people scampering off to while we traverse Europe?"

Jack gave Natashia a withering look and stiffened when she sucked on her lower lip in a most seductive manner. He gathered himself and informed her, "I believe that Viktor is heading to Vatican City, Colonel Mitchell is going to D.C. and my team is headed to Canada and then to Newfoundland—"

"Newfoundland? Good heavens! Whatever for?" she asked sarcastically.

"We need to have a talk with the wee folk," Jack said. "Find out if they'll assist us in our fight against the Sicarii. And, maybe they can help us reach the New World Elves."

"Oh, for the love of…" She trailed off. "You might as well ask them to just show up and kill themselves," she spat.

Now it was Jack's turn to be shocked. "Why would you say that, Natashia?"

"The wee folk? They're the peace people!" She laughed. "They'd no sooner fight than…well, anything!" She laughed again. Suddenly she sobered. "But the elves. Now that's a good idea. They are mean wee beasties. And if you can get the New World Greater Elves into the fight?" She shook her head. "Bloodthirsty savages…they are worse than gnomes because they are crafty…and very *large*."

Jack gave her a sideways stare. "Sounds like you've got a bit of experience dealing with them."

"More than a bit, my dear boy," she answered him, coming to her feet. "Much more than just a bit." She turned her attention to Nadia. "Are you ready, my dear?"

Nadia shouldered her bag and nodded. "I am. Just…give me a moment to say goodbye to Jack."

"Don't take too long. We have a grandpappy werewolf to find," she practically sang as she slipped out the door.

"She seems so flippant about this," Jack said. "I don't like it."

"She will be fine," Nadia assured him.

She pulled him close to her and inhaled his manly scent. She could smell his aftershave with its hint of sandalwood and pine. She had always loved the smell and had given some to Rufus for his birthday many years ago to help hide the scent of death on him, but on Jack, it took on a whole new life of its own. She loved the smell of him and wrapped her arms tightly around him. "I will watch her closely, I promise."

Jack held her tightly. "Who is going to watch out for you?"

"Mother, of course."

Jack laughed. "That's what I was afraid you'd say."

Dominic stood in awe with the silver slugs still biting into the flesh of his hands. The dark vampire sitting across from him on the pile of rubble was at least patient. Dom holstered his pistol and none of the minions tried to stop him. What would be the use? It held no more ammunition. It may as well have been a plastic hammer.

"So? Are you ready to discuss a few things, Mr. DeGiacomo?" the dark vampire asked softly.

Dom set his jaw, ready to spit out yet another smart assed reply, but the silver bullets biting into his hands reminded him that this was no ordinary vampire he was facing. "Maybe," he answered. "But cooperation is a two way street."

The dark vampire raised an eyebrow. "Ah. I see. You wish to gather information as well, yes?" he chuckled.

Dom noticed that the other vampires standing guard around them weren't laughing with him this time. They seemed to slowly drop back into the shadows of the night. He knew they were still there, watching the two of them, but they were giving the illusion that they were alone.

"Yeah, something like that," Dom said. "You want something from me, I want something from you."

"You want your freedom," the vampire stated.

"Fuck you," Dom shot back. "You don't get it, do you? I already wrote myself off as soon as that little traitorous turd from the cell pointed my own fucking gun to my temple. I don't give two shits about freedom."

"Yes you do. Your lies taste like acid in the back of my mouth," the vampire replied softly.

"Oh they do, do they? Well again, fuck you," Dom shot back. "If you plan to cut me loose to deliver your message, then I plan to milk as much information from you as I can."

"There! Now that is an honest answer," Sicarii said with a touch of glee. "But how can you know if the answers I give to your questions are as honest?"

"Because vampires as old as you have egos bigger than your... pride," Dom stated, careful not to say what he really thought. "You're too proud to lie and you think that no matter what you tell me, it won't change anything anyway. You could spill the entire fucking pot of beans and little old me couldn't do a damn thing about it."

The Sicarii thought about Dom's words a moment and then stood from the rubble. "You are absolutely correct," he said thoughtfully. "Not so much in your assumptions, but in the fact that no matter what I tell you, you and your people can do nothing to stop me."

"See?" Dom replied. "Your arrogance is so big I'm surprised you aren't tripping over it."

The Sicarii stopped and looked at Dom with his smug grin and simply shook his head. "Perhaps once I reveal to you what I need for you to do, you will realize…it is not ego, not arrogance. It is power. Pure power." The dark vampire turned toward the open window and the silver moon in the sky. "When this world is mine and the humans that are left realize that they are nothing more than breeding stock for food…then you can tell me again how big my ego is." He turned back to Dom. "Is that acceptable to you, Mr. DeGiacomo?"

Dom stared at the crazy vampire and shook his head. "Okay, fine," he snapped back. "And when my team tears your ass into itty-bitty pieces and hands it back to you on a plate, you can tell me again how your Bulldog mouth didn't over-bark your Pekingese ass, okay?"

The dark vampire smiled, then chuckled and finally broke into heavy laughter. When the laughter slowed, he approached Dominic. "I think I like you, Mr. DeGiacomo. You have *heart*!"

"It's called *balls*, bloodsucker," Dom muttered.

The dark vampire glanced at him sideways. "Yes. That too!" He placed a hand on Dom's shoulder and directed him out to the courtyard where the table and benches were. "This way, please. We shall sit and discuss the future."

"Oh, you mean how my team and I are going to stop you from doing whatever the hell it is you're doing and make you wish you had stayed in the shadows?" Dom said. "Sure, let's do that."

"Yes, let us do that." The dark vampire directed Dom to the bench and waited while he gingerly sat. It was obvious that he was in great pain. "Would you like something to drink? A meal, perhaps? Some pain killers?" he offered. "Before we begin?"

"Naw, I'm fine. Let's get this show on the road," Dom said, trying hard to sound tough, but wishing like hell he had at least a bottle of water.

The dark vampire looked to the side, into the darkened shadows and snapped his fingers. Dom didn't turn his head to watch, but someone brought him a bottle of water and a can of soda along with a

17

bowl of fruit. "In case you change your mind," the dark vampire explained. "Now, before we begin in earnest, I have a few questions for you, Mr. DeGiacomo."

"And I have a few for you." He opened the bottle of water.

"My pilot tells me that you have people working on a weapon. A weapon that targets *only* vampires?"

Dom stared at the dark vampire blankly, putting on his best poker face. "I have no idea what you're talking about."

"Oh, Mr. DeGiacomo, your lies leave such an acidic taste in the back of my mouth. It is most unsavory," Sicarii winced.

"Sorry, bub. No idea what you're chattering about." Dom shrugged.

"My pilot claims that you were most *talkative* on the plane before you were knocked unconscious..." he trailed off.

Dom continued to stare at the vampire and finally sighed. "Fuck, Momma always said I talked too much when I was nervous."

"I'm sure she did." The vampire nodded. Dom lowered his head and stared at the table. "So, tell me more about this weapon."

Dom shrugged his shoulders. "Who knows?" He looked up and met the vampire's gaze. "Seriously. I have no clue what it is or how it works. I just heard Doc talking about it. Said it targets natural born vampires." He watched the dark vampire studying him in the silvery light, assessing his truthfulness. "It was just an offhand comment he made and before he could go into any detail, the boss told him to drop it."

The dark vampire nodded. "What other weaponry do your teams employ against our kind?"

"You mean besides silver bullets?" Dom asked. "That don't work anymore," he added. He took a deep breath and thought about it for a moment. "Well, let's see. We have UV phosphorus grenades. Those are lots of fun. Turns a vampire to ash and gives us a real nice tan all at the same time." He shot a toothy grin at the vampire for effect.

"What else?"

"What difference does it make?" Dom asked. "Who the fuck *are* you, anyway? And why do you care what armaments we have? Aren't you the asshole that was testing us? You should know what shit we use anyway."

"What else?" the vampire asked calmly.

Dom stared at him a moment longer. "Who are you?"

"I already told you, I am the Sicarii," he said calmly. "What else?"

"What the fuck is the Sicarii? That tells me nothing!" Dom shouted. "Give me something of substance!" He pounded the concrete table with such force that his own teeth rattled and his head ached. He could feel his kidney throb where he had been punched.

The dark vampire stood slowly and reached across the narrow table, grasping Dominic by the face and pulling him slowly toward him. Dom tried to pull back but it was like a fly trying to pull itself from a spider's web. He had nothing to grasp but the table's edge and he was already leaning too far forward to get any real leverage. The dark vampire pulled him close and stared into his eyes and in what seemed only a moment, images flashed through his mind, a lifetime's worth of memories that weren't his. He saw life and death, he saw murders and entire families butchered. He saw happiness for such a short period and then pain and suffering…so much suffering.

When the dark vampire released him, Dom found himself sprawled across the cold stone floor, gasping for air. Slowly he reached up and held his aching head and tried to unsee what had been seen but he knew he couldn't. The vampire had implanted so many memories into his head…but now he knew. He knew *exactly* who he was. He knew *what* he was. He knew what he was capable of as a man, and he knew what he was capable of as a monster. He felt his stomach curdle on him and bile bit the back of his throat before he retched.

Slowly, Dominic gained his composure and rolled to his knees. He sat up and stared up at the starry sky and he knew. He gulped the cold night air and shivered. He pulled himself up to his full height and did his best to square his shoulders when all he really wanted to do was curl up in a ball and hide. He turned and looked around the courtyard and found the dark vampire sitting atop the same pile of rubble, absently picking at his fingernails.

"I wondered how long it would take you to recover. I must admit, you are much stronger than I would have suspected. I honestly thought you were full of false bravado, but you truly are a strong soul," he said softly.

Dom staggered toward the vampire and gathered himself as he approached him. "You're mad," he stated. "You showed me all of it...and you are one sick, twisted bastard."

"Perhaps. But they *will* pay," he replied.

"Oh, well that just makes all the sense in the world, now doesn't it?" Dom shot back. "God pisses you off so you make the rest of the world pay the price? What about the innocent people?"

"Aren't they all innocent?" he asked. "And yet, He arranged that they would be my food. Tell me that isn't ironic."

"You're shit-house rat crazy," Dom wheezed. "You still haven't thought this through."

"How so?"

"Once you've destroyed the world and killed everybody, who will be left to feed you and your vampire horde?" he asked sarcastically.

The vampire laughed. "We'll raise humans much like farmers raise cattle." He stated matter-of-factly. "There is plenty of beef in the world, is there not? And yet, the cattle do not rise up and destroy the farmers."

Dom sighed. "You won't succeed."

"And who will stop me?"

"We will," he said softly. "We'll find a way."

"You have already seen it," the vampire stated. "You cannot stop me. And you know it."

21

2

Robert Mueller knocked on Colonel Mitchell's door and waited to hear him bark before he entered. Mueller stepped inside and stood at attention and waited to be acknowledged. Mitchell looked up from his paperwork long enough to realize that Mueller wasn't going to speak until spoken to and said, "At ease, son. Spill it."

Mueller stood at ease and cleared his throat. "Permission to speak freely, Colonel?"

"Of course, Mueller. What's wrong, boy?"

Mueller's eyes darted about the room as if he wasn't sure how to start. "Just spit it out, son. We'll figure it out once it's on the floor, okay?"

Mueller nodded. "Yes, sir. Um…I'd like to go home for a short bit, sir."

Matt gave the operator a sideways stare. "To what purpose, soldier?"

"To say good bye, sir." Matt saw his eyes start to mist and he fought it. "To my ex-wife, sir. We were talking about trying to get back together…and now we can't. Ever. I need to at least let her know that it won't happen."

Mitchell's eyes started to widen, when Mueller added, "I won't mention what's really going on here, sir. I just need to see my son and…" He glanced away for a moment, then faced his CO again. "I need closure, sir."

Mitchell sat back in his chair and studied the young operator standing in front of him. He nodded slightly then asked, "Have you discussed this with Apollo?"

"Before I came here, sir. He gave me the green light. Said that now that the full moon is over, things are usually quiet for a while."

Matt nodded again. "He's right about that." Mitchell glanced at the calendar. "You can have a few days. I can't spare any more than that though. There's just too much going on and the clock is ticking."

Mueller lit up with a grin. "More than I need, sir."

"That includes travel as well. I've got First Squad going to Labrador and Northern Canada, I'm going to be in D.C. and...well, hell, we're all going to be scattered. With you out, Second Squad will be a man short...sorry, son. I don't mean to discount Dominic."

"I understand what you mean, sir. Gus is filling in for him. I just need to do this. And Third Squad will be here, just in case."

Mitchell nodded. "Haul ass, soldier. You're burning leave time."

Mueller saluted Mitchell, "Thank you, sir!" all but running from his office.

23

Rufus Thorn stayed in the shadows while his friend and Second, Viktor repacked for Vatican City. He held an uneasy feeling about this mission and was hesitant about sending him. "I am uncertain of this, *mon ami*. I think we should rethink this decision."

Viktor continued to pack and spoke softly. He knew that Rufus could hear him if he whispered. "We both know what is at stake here. We also know where Tasha and Nadia are going and the odds of them succeeding." He finally stood straight and squared his broad shoulders, stretching his neck. When he turned, Rufus saw only sorrow in his eyes. "I like it no better than you, but we both know that this would be far easier if I do it alone."

"If I were to go with you, I think we could convince this Secretariat of State what exactly is at stake," Thorn stated. "And I could make good my threat to turn him if he didn't cooperate." He grinned slyly.

Viktor sighed and placed his bag on the edge of the bed. "The man won't be swayed by threats, Rufus," he informed him softly. "Even threats that you would surely carry out. I don't intend to relieve them of all of their artifacts, but if I can get *some* of them..." He explained, "One of the pieces of silver, one of the cross pieces, one of the bloody rags, or...any combination." He averted his eyes, not wanting to disappoint his friend and master.

Rufus placed a hand on Viktor's shoulder and squeezed gently. "I trust you will do your best, *mon ami*. You have never let me down before," he said. "I just wish that I could be there for you as you have been there for me."

24

Viktor nodded, still feeling that he had failed Rufus. He had searched for years for a cure to the vampirism that Thorn had been infected with to no avail. He had spent untold millions of Thorn's money gaining access to the most secretive of vaults where information had been hidden away for centuries, spent years digging through archives all to come up empty.

He feared what Thorn feared: the only 'cure' was the true death.

Theologians who were in the know on vampirism had argued for centuries that there could be no cure for the condition. Those who were afflicted had to die to become the undead, and once they did, their soul left the body. If the body were one day 'cured' of the disease of vampirism, the soul was long gone, and the body would still be dead, therefore, only true death could be the result. Yet Viktor had vowed that as long as he were able, he would continue to search for a way to free Rufus of the curse that afflicted him. "I do have a plan. I will be making a stop before going to Vatican City," Viktor announced. "It should not take me very long and will aid in our efforts."

Rufus only nodded. He knew better than to question Viktor. If he felt that Rufus needed to know all of the intricacies of his plan, he would have laid them out for him. "Travel well, *mon ami*." He embraced the large man and patted his back. "May God bless your endeavors," he whispered.

Viktor pulled back and stared at Rufus. "You must be worried to invoke His holy name."

"I know what is at risk," Rufus simply stated. "And I know that we will not be fruitful if it is not His will."

"I never thought of you as a religious man."

"Can one truly be religious if his soul has been ripped from him?" Rufus asked. "It does not mean that one cannot still try to serve, *non*?"

Viktor averted his eyes and simply nodded. "I don't like thinking about it, Master."

Rufus' features screwed up and he tsk'd away Viktor's words. "Enough with the 'master' and titles. We have been friends for far too long, *non*?" Rufus captured his gaze again. "You and your people have served me well many long years. And I would have released you from your service if I could. You know this. You are as free as either of us can make you."

"I know this," Viktor replied softly, the subject still a sore matter.

"I still would release you completely if I could. But it is not up to me," Thorn stated. "If it were entirely up to me…"

"I understand. We both know the circumstances and you know that I appreciate all that you have done." Viktor hung his head and slowly shook it. "One day we will be released from our bonds and our honor restored." Viktor stood erect again and squared his shoulders. "And when that day comes, I will leave our island home and have my revenge against the evil she-bitch that dishonored my family name." A slow growl growing in the back of his throat.

"I still do not understand why you simply did not challenge her and take back your position—"

"I could not," Viktor interrupted. "Not while she held her position within the pack-formal. It would be akin to treason."

"Surely Maxwell could have cleared everything…"

"My father has nothing to do with me anymore, Rufus. You know this." Viktor turned, his vision turning red at the mere mention of his father. "He disowned me centuries ago."

"But he doesn't even know about Nadia. Surely he would like to know his granddaughter," Thorn offered.

"He's a pacifist now." Viktor bit back the bile in the back of his throat. "The very man who laid down the rules for the Lycans, the wolf who laid out the requirements for becoming a warrior to defend the pack, disowns his own son for clinging to the very laws that he, himself created!" Viktor cried. "Do you really think he would give a tinker's damn about my offspring?"

"But she's his own flesh and blood…"

"Flesh and blood means nothing to him anymore." Viktor whispered. "I wish you weren't sending Tasha and Nadia to him."

"He's our best hope to finding this Roman guard Claudius Veranus," Rufus explained.

Viktor's eyes glazed over. "He is long since dead, my lord. Long since dead…"

Natashia and Nadia settled into the jet for the long trip across the Atlantic. Nadia had asked for and received a soda and some crackers to settle her stomach as the large plane's acceleration had made her feel a bit nauseous. Natashia watched her daughter with a cautious eye and without warning pulled her arm close to her face and smelled deeply of her skin.

"Mother?! What are you doing?" Nadia asked, pulling her arm free.

Natashia smiled at her daughter and placed a hand to her cheek. The twinkle in her eye told Nadia that she knew something, but Nadia was afraid to ask. "Have you told Jack, yet?"

"Told Jack what, mother?" Nadia asked, suddenly worried. "Do not speak to me in riddles."

"That you are with child, my love," Natashia purred, a contented smile painted across her face.

Nadia could feel the blood drain from her face as her eyes widened. "What did you say?" she asked, unsure that she had heard correctly.

"You are with child, my dear. Surely you knew?" Worry suddenly crossing her features.

"How can you assume that I am with—"

"Darling," Natashia cried out, "You are upset at the stomach without eating, your temperature is high without sickness and your scent has changed." She stated matter-of-factly, "You *are* with child."

Nadia panicked for just a moment. She knew without a doubt that if her mother told her that she was pregnant, then she *was* most certainly pregnant. Her mother's nose was more sensitive than any test, and she had been feeling queasy lately. She thought it was from all the excitement and the fear of the upcoming battle. She placed the back of her hand to her forehead and felt slightly warm. She placed her hand to her lower stomach, as if she might feel a presence…something that would indicate the life that grew within. She felt nothing there.

Natashia laughed softly beside her. "Do not panic little one. Wolves have whelped pups for many centuries before you became pregnant, I assure you."

Nadia turned to her mother, a smile slowly creeping across her face, her eyes misting, "Mother, I'm pregnant!"

"Yes, you are!" Natashia laughed, holding her hand and kissing it. "Imagine that!"

"Yes! Imagine that," Nadia laughed. "But…how?"

"Well, my dear, when a mommy wolf and a daddy wolf love each other very much, the mommy wolf backs up and lifts her tail…"

"Mother!" Nadia screeched, swatting at her mother's hand.

"Oh, darling, how do you think? It had to be while you two were at the island. When you mated."

Nadia reflected back to when she and Jack had spent their time at the island. It seemed almost a lifetime ago, but it had only been a matter of weeks. She remembered every moment and she could almost smell his scent upon her again.

She sighed softly to herself and heard her mother huff next to her. "Oh, stop it. We're on a plane, Nadia." Nadia snapped out of her reverie and glanced at her mother again, blushing as she did so. Natashia leaned in close to her and whispered, "Just be happy that twins don't run in our family."

Nadia's eyes bugged at the thought. "Twins?"

Matt entered the outer offices of Dr. Tom Coburn, United States Senator and the newest member of the Monster Squad's Oversight Committee. Dr. Coburn had been chosen to replace Senator Franklin on the committee when Senator Franklin had taken his own life. The other committee members felt that, since Dr. Coburn was from Oklahoma and the squad was based out of Tinker Air Force Base in Oklahoma City, he was a perfect choice. He often returned home and it would be much easier for him to 'drop in' from time to time and check in on their little black budget operation. Mitchell checked out Dr. Coburn and felt the man might not be so hard to work with. At least not nearly as difficult as Franklin had been. Franklin was certifiably insane, yet somehow he continued to get reelected each year.

The secretary checked Mitchell's ID and escorted him into the inner office where Dr. Coburn greeted him warmly. "It's nice to finally meet you, Colonel." He extended his hand. "I was hoping to get a trip home next month and stop by to see things firsthand."

"The pleasure is all mine, Senator," Matt returned the greeting. "Our doors are always open to you, sir." The Senator offered Matt a chair and pulled the squad's file from a locked drawer.

"I went over the briefing with the other committee members and I have to admit, I was a bit shocked when they first clued me in. It was bad enough to learn that we had active duty military operating on U.S. soil, but that they were actively hunting..." he paused, searching for the politically correct word.

"Monsters, Senator. We refer to them as monsters," Matt said straight-faced.

"Yes. Monsters." He shook his head, still disbelieving. "It's all so surreal."

"I can understand, sir. But I'm sure that they filled you in to the reality of the situation?"

"Oh, yes. Quite so." He sat back in his chair and eyed Matt. "Might I inquire as to your visit? I doubt you came all the way here just to welcome the new guy to your Oversight Committee?"

"Hardly, Senator," Matt said, sitting up straighter in his chair. "I came here to see if I could convince you and the rest of the OC to pull your political strings for me, sir." He cleared his throat. "I need a military base."

31

Dr. Coburn's eyes widened slightly. "You need an *entire* base, Colonel? What are we supposed to do with the rest of Tinker?" he asked.

"No, sir. Not Tinker." Matt averted his eyes. "This base will be much tougher to get."

Senator Coburn didn't like the sounds of this, but he was willing to listen. "Shall I try to get the rest of the Oversight Committee in here?"

"They're unavailable, sir." Matt slipped him a cheesy grin. "I already checked. You may be the newest member, but you're the only one who's actually at work today."

Dr. Coburn actually chuckled at that one and nodded at him. "Carry on then, soldier. Hit me with it. What do you need? I can't guarantee anything, but I can promise to do my best."

Matt laid out the situation to the good Doctor, explaining the threat from the Sicarii, the intelligence gathered and the proposed fighting force. He explained the plan to try to concentrate their forces in the desert in hopes that it would draw the Sicarii and his forces there as well, rather than try to coordinate numerous battles all across the globe, all in an effort to lower civilian casualties. The key was getting access to and control of the Groom Lake base.

To his credit, Senator Coburn listened intently and didn't interrupt. He didn't question the method to the madness, and in the end, he understood the gist of it all. "You do realize that the odds of us being able to get you that base is next to zero, right?" Dr. Coburn insisted. "To start with, that base doesn't officially exist. I mean, you and I both know that it's out there and they do all sorts of top secret projects there, but the kind of horsepower that it will take to get that base commander to simply hand over the keys?" He paused and let his question sink in. "Would you?"

Matt shook his head. "Not willingly, sir. That's why I came here. Whoever that base commander is, he'll have to be forced. But again, it doesn't have to be a complete takeover, Senator. We just need to borrow his base——"

"To wage a *war*, Colonel!" The Senator interrupted. "With *vampires*, no less!" He lowered his voice, but still stressed the unbelievable enemy they faced.

"Senator, we have a few aces up our sleeve."

"You'd better have a deck full of aces from what you've told me," he quipped. "Look, Colonel...I'll take your proposal to the Oversight Committee and run it up the flagpole and see who salutes it. If there is anybody on there that has that kind of pull with the Pentagon and can get it done, then it WILL be done." He sat back and pulled his glasses off, "But, Colonel, I wouldn't hold my breath if I were you. I'd be looking for a 'Plan B' and trying to figure out another strategy."

Matt exhaled slowly and shook his head. "Senator, this all we have. We either bait these bloodsuckers out to the desert and toast their leader, or we *all* die as a Vampire Lunchable. There is no 'Plan B'."

Dr. Coburn studied Matt and realized that he, at least, believed every word that he was reporting. "There are no other options?"

"Senator, this Sicarii is the *first* vampire. He is so old that Mr. Thorn says even silver won't kill him. A stake through the heart won't slow him down. Hell, chopping his head off would probably just give him a slight headache. The *only* way to kill him will be with sunlight, and he isn't stupid enough to come at us in the daylight. We have to bait him out in the open and toast him with the satellite."

"What's to prevent this guy from just sending his army? He could stay wherever he is and watch from afar?"

"He fancies himself a leader. Leaders lead, they don't sit back and watch from a distance," Matt responded. "No, sir. He'll be at the head of the pack."

Dr. Coburn nodded and stood up. "I'll do whatever I can, Colonel. Again, I can't promise you anything, but I'll spur the Oversight Committee to twist whatever arms at the Pentagon to make it happen."

"You have no idea how much I appreciate it, Senator." Matt said standing and shaking his hand.

"I believe I have an idea, son."

First Squad touched down on the north end of Quebec near the Newfoundland border and dispersed into the woods surrounding Mount Caubvick. As the team worked their way into the foothills of the mountain, they looked for signs of the Elven People. The signs were hard to spot, and even to experienced hunters are often mistaken for animal markings. When Ing Jacobs reported a clearing near a brook, Jack ordered the team to make camp and prepare to wait until dark.

Tufo set up a perimeter with infrared cameras and motion detectors and Lamb broke out the black light gear. The Elven People would often mark their areas with a special dye made of lichen that would glow under black light and was invisible to humans. Somehow, it was always visible to the elves. The squad had reports that the Greater Elven People had taken up residence at the base of this mountain and he hoped to find them and recruit them to their cause. If he couldn't find the Greater Elves, then maybe he could find a lesser elf that could point him in the right direction.

As night slowly crept upon them the team began to notice sounds that didn't normally occur in the woods. Gunnery Sergeant Tufo fired up the infrared monitors and checked for movement. Other than a few small animals, the perimeter was clear. He glanced up at Chief Thompson and slowly shook his head. Jack stepped to the outer edge of the campsite where the glow of the campfire was lowest and stood on an outcropping of rock. He allowed his vision to grow accustom to the low level of light and peered out into the edge of the woods. He thought he saw eyes staring back at him.

Chief Thompson fished in his shirt pocket and withdrew a small wooden whistle that resembled a reed flute. Most humans couldn't hear the high pitch that the whistle resonated at when blown, but the augmentation that the Monster Squad underwent allowed them to hear the high shrill as it cut through the thin, cold mountain air. Jack noted many more eyes appeared along the edge of the tree line at differing heights within the underbrush. He stood a moment longer on the top of the rock and stared out along the perimeter.

"They won't come to you, human," a rough, gravelly voice said from below the rock.

Jack was startled as he hadn't heard the visitor approach. He looked down in the decreasing light and saw a rock gnome sitting below him packing a small carved pipe. His clothes appeared tattered but intact and his heavy boots were covered in many layers of dried dirt and mud. Although it appeared as though the gnome had just dug his way from underground, his hair and skin appeared to be clean. His beard was trimmed short and almost white with grey whiskers.

"Do they fear us?" Jack asked calmly.

"They fear the scent of your wolf," the gnome replied. "Lesser Elves be these and the moon is nigh. They fear being munched as a late night snack." He grinned up at Jack, his blue eyes twinkling in the twilight. He pulled a wooden match across the seat of his pants and puffed at his long-stemmed pipe.

Jack stepped off of the rock and landed deftly next to the small gnome. He knew that gnomes weren't known for being forthcoming by nature and wondered why this one was willing to clue him in. "I'm Jack Thompson. My men and I are looking for the Greater Elves." He settled in next to the gnome. Jack was trying to find a seat that would put him more at eye level with the little gnome.

The gnome took his time puffing at his pipe, getting the bowl to glow cherry red before he pulled hard and inhaled. The breeze shifted and Jack smelled the sweet aroma of cherry, apple blossoms and tobacco. The little gnome sat next to Jack and scratched at his beard, as if in deep thought. "I'm not exactly sure where the Greats went," he said after a moment. The gnome kept staring out at the tree line and the growing number of eyes peering back at them. "But I'd bet they'd know." He pointed at the Lesser Elves in the scrub brush.

"But they won't speak with me because they can smell the wolf on us."

"Ah yup."

Jack sat there with the gnome for a long while, silently watching as more and more sets of eyes reflected the campfire light. After some time Jack's earpiece crackled and Tufo's voice whispered into it, "Chief, we have *way* too much small animal activity on the perimeter for it to be small game. I think we have Lesser Elves out there."

"That's affirmative, Gunny," Jack whispered into his lip mic.

The little gnome looked up at him questioningly. "One of yours?"

"Yes, sir." Then Jack's eyes lit up. "And he's not a wolf...do you think they would speak with him?"

The little gnome sat quietly for a very long time. So long, in fact that Jack wondered if perhaps he had forgotten the question or might not have heard him.

Finally, the little gnome pointed to the tree line with his pipe and poked toward the numerous sets of eyes. "It wouldn't hurt to try."

Jack sat up and keyed his mic. "Gunny, converge on my location. Solo."

"Copy that," came the reply.

Within a few moments Tufo was standing over Jack and the small gnome on the outcropping of rocks above. "Down here, Mark," Jack called.

Tufo looked down and saw the gnome next to Jack and acknowledged him with a, "Sir."

The little gnome waved his pipe in return, "Hunter."

Jack stood and waved Mark down to the ground with him. Tufo jumped down and they stepped away a moment. "I need you to go to the tree line and see if you can make contact with the Lesser Elves. See if they can tell you where the Greater Elves are."

"Me? You're the Team Leader. I thought that—"

"Mark," Jack interrupted, "they won't allow me or any of the other team members over there. You have to do it."

Tufo gave the chief a confused look and shrugged. "Okay…"

"Look, go find out what you can about the Greater Elves. See if they'll disclose their location. If they need to know why…I guess tell them the truth. We have nothing to hide. Hopefully they'll understand. But I need you to do this. Act as our ambassador." Jack could tell that Tufo was totally confused. "When you get back, I'll explain everything. I promise."

Tufo acknowledged and took off across the clearing toward the tree line. Jack watched as some of the eyes withdrew into the scrub, but most stayed put. Tufo stopped part way and turned back toward Jack for a moment. He slung his rifle back over his shoulder and showed his hands empty to the eyes in the trees and advanced more slowly. Jack noticed that the remaining eyes didn't leave as Tufo continued forward. Jack strained his hearing as he listened for any sounds.

He heard Mark ask as he approached, "Who's in charge over here?" He stopped a few feet short of the tree line and waited. "We just have some questions that we really need answered." He waited a little longer, then added, "Please? We mean no harm."

Jack watched with the gnome still standing by his side and he felt a slight tug on his pant leg. "This may take a while," the gnome said. Jack looked down at the gnome and nodded.

Jack keyed his mic and informed Tufo, "Be patient, Gunny. Our friend here said it may take a while for them to open up." Tufo simply keyed the mic in return. Jack turned to the gnome and asked, "Are you hungry? We don't have a very big selection, but the MREs aren't that bad."

"Any mutton?" he asked hopefully.

Jack chuckled. "I doubt there's any mutton, but I bet we can find something you like." He led the little fellow back to the campfire and a hot meal.

"And perhaps while we enjoy your fine fare, we might imbibe in some grog or mead?" he asked hopefully.

"Sorry, friend, but we didn't bring anything like that with us." Jack smiled.

"Ah, well. Probably for the best as I tend to break into song when I allow myself the joys of spirits," the gnome admitted. "However, I am curious in your interest in the Greaters?"

"I'll tell you all about it as we eat," Jack said as he escorted him to the edge of the campsite.

3

Dominic felt drained as he sat at the foot of the altar in the abandoned cathedral. The dark vampire appeared to hover above him in the second story window staring out at the city of Rome, waiting for the first lick of sunlight to appear over the horizon. Dom sifted through the rubble and found the arm to an ancient marble statue. The fingers were broken from the hand, but the musculature and veining in the sculpture still felt smooth and lifelike. He hefted the broken piece in his hand and enjoyed the feel of it, a makeshift weapon, but at least it was something. He turned again to check on the dark vampire and was startled to find him standing directly behind him. Had the vampire needed to breathe, his breath would have tickled the back of his neck.

"Tsk-tsk, Mr. DeGiacomo," the vampire muttered, his eyebrows rising as he eyed the marble arm in his hands. "If silver bullets won't stop me, do you really think that will do me harm?"

Dom considered taking a swing anyway, but then considered otherwise. His head and kidney were still throbbing and he really didn't relish the idea of having any other parts of his body damaged. His jaw ticked as he reluctantly dropped the arm back into the rubble. "Can't blame a guy for thinking it, can you?"

"No, I cannot." The dark vampire wrapped an arm around Dom's shoulder and led him away from the cathedral and into the passageways leading to the labyrinth of rooms above and below them. "We still have much to discuss before I send you back to your people, Mr. DeGiacomo."

"Oh, please. Call me Dominic," Dom said with a sneer, feeling his skin crawl at the vampire's touch. "I feel we've grown so *close* lately," he added sarcastically.

The dark vampire nodded. "We have, haven't we?" He slipped his arm away from Dom's shoulders. "Perhaps I shouldn't have unleashed so many memories upon you so quickly, but you demanded answers. Without context, none of the memories I gave you would mean much, wouldn't you agree?"

Dom rubbed at his temples, his head still throbbing. "If you say so, man, but my head hurt like you wouldn't believe before you did that. You can't imagine what it feels like now."

"Ah, yes. The pilot did strike you quite soundly." The vampire stopped and turned Dom to face him. "Here, allow me to ease your pain." Before Dom could protest, he placed a hand on either side of Dom's face and peered deeply into his eyes. At first, Dom felt as though an ice pick was piercing him between his eyes; he inhaled deeply to scream when suddenly…the pain stopped. He panted a moment, trying to catch his breath as the sudden easing of pain caught him short.

"What did you do?" he gasped.

"I healed your concussion."

"You can't do that," Dom stated. "Maybe you can make me think I don't feel it, but you can't heal it."

The vampire stared at him blankly. "Why can't I?"

Dom was dumbfounded. "I…well…uh…*because.*"

"That was certainly a scientific answer." The vampire turned and slowly started down the hallway again. Dom fell into step behind him. "Just because I am vampire, does not mean that I cannot do good, Dominic."

Dom was startled at him using his first name, but then remembered him telling him to do it. "Yeah, well, for someone intent on burning the world and eating everybody in it, let's just say that I wouldn't expect an act of kindness."

The vampire at his side smiled softly in the darkness. "You know my past, yes? You saw the memories. You know who I am."

"I saw it, but I'm not sure I understand it all," he answered honestly.

"For a very short time, I understood that there is more power in kindness than in torment," the vampire informed him. "One good act to a person in need can be multiplied a hundred fold. One kindness to someone who doesn't *need* a kindness can be multiplied ten thousand times."

"So why not kill the world with kindness?" Dom asked, knowing the answer before he asked it.

The dark vampire shook his head. "Because I was forsaken and turned to the darkness. This is forever my lot in life."

"You said yourself that there is more power in kindness. You could still——"

"No!" the vampire shouted. "I cannot." He growled deep in his throat. "You have no idea what it is like. You *cannot* know what it is like. To have loved someone so dearly, to give them your life, to turn away from everything that you were and dedicate your life to protecting them from everything…and then be turned out as a traitor to the Word!" He ground his teeth together and Dom could hear them, his own teeth hurting from the sound. "I was his protection from any who would do him harm. I was his bodyguard. I was his right hand. His most trusted. He knew my sins, my faults, my deepest secrets and he forgave me. He loved me anyway." Dom saw his eyes begin to tear up and the vampire turned away from him. Dom tried a new tactic and reached out to him. He gently placed a hand on his shoulder and squeezed.

He pulled up close to the vampire's ear and whispered. "Is this what he would want you to do?" The vampire stiffened next to him. "Ask yourself that as you scream at his father, 'what would Jesus do?'" Dom whispered, instantly feeling corny.

The vampire turned to him with a sneer, "You did not know Yeshua!" he growled. "Do not pretend to know him. You are not worthy to——"

"Hey! Whoa! Easy there, big guy." Dom backed up, his hands held up in surrender. "You were the one telling me all the warm and fuzzy stuff, remember?" The dark vampire's eyes literally flashed in the darkness and Dom assumed a defensive stance preparing for an imminent attack. "If he taught you that kindness was truly where the power was, and he loved you unconditionally, then how could you turn from his teachings like this?" Dom asked softly. He watched the dark vampire's chest heave as if he were breathing hard, and he realized he was sobbing, yet his face was stone. "I get it, man. He loved you and you would have done anything for him. Hell! You *did* everything for him." Dom moved in closer, cautiously closing the space between them. "You did what none of the others could, because it had to be done. I get it."

The dark vampire stared at the space where Dom had been standing as Dom moved closer and placed a hand back on his shoulder. "You showed me, remember? You showed me your memories and I know how badly it hurt you to do what needed to be done." He stood directly in front of the vampire, but he wouldn't meet Dom's gaze. "You did what *he* asked you to do…maybe it wasn't his father's will…I don't know. Neither of us ever will know the mind of God."

"We know," the vampire replied softly, finally lifting his eyes to meet Dom's. "We know because he damned me for eternity." He stepped back and stood to his full height, his shoulders squared, his jaw set, his eyes determined. "And that is exactly why I must do what I must."

Dom groaned and lowered his eyes, his head shaking back and forth. "He would be so disappointed in what you're about to do," he muttered under his breath.

"Do not assume—" the vampire began with a growl.

"I don't have to assume!" Dom shouted back forcefully. "You showed me exactly what he was like." Dom pointed a finger in the vampire's face. "You tell me not to assume, not to pretend that I knew him, not to act as though I *know*, but *you* gave me those memories, *remember*? You shot my brain full of somebody else's memories, sights, sounds and feelings, and then you have the balls to tell me that I don't have the right to use them?" The dark vampire actually took a step back at Dom's forcefulness. "Well, fuck you! You don't have the right to say that!"

The two stood in the dark silence of the hallway for many moments the only sound between them was Dom's heavy breathing. After what seemed an uncommonly long and awkward silence, the dark vampire gave Dom a slight bow. "You are correct," he said softly. "You may make assumptions based on the memories I gave to you, but you are wrong in your conclusions that he would not approve."

"How can you possibly say that?" Dom asked. "He taught to turn the other cheek."

"He also said, 'Beat your plowshares into swords, and your pruning hooks into spears: let the weak say, I am strong.' For every Yin, there is a Yang."

Dom looked at him sideways a moment. "I'm no Bible scholar, but…that sure sounds Old Testament to me, bro. I ain't buying the bullshit you're selling."

The dark vampire smiled slowly at him. "A man not easily fooled. I like that."

"So you were bullshitting me."

"No. He did say it. He was repeating what was written in the older books from some of the minor prophets," the vampire stated with a dismissive wave of his hand. "I'm not saying he entirely agreed with them, but the words did escape his mouth."

"So you used them out of context," Dom argued.

"Pish-posh, your arguments will not change my mind." The vampire turned and continued down the hallway again.

Dom followed him but continued his argument. "Well, it's nice to see that all of that time you spent with him was a total waste. He taught you what was right and you totally disregard his teachings." Dom fished again.

The vampire would not rise to the bait this time. "You are correct. When his father damned me, it took me a very long time, but I finally accepted my fate."

"Oh really? And what is that?"

The vampire opened the door to a room so dark that Dom could not make out anything inside. He motioned his arm to usher Dom inside but Dom stood outside and waited a moment. "What is your fate? I'm curious."

"It is quite simple. I am the Harbinger of Death."

Mueller pulled his Jeep up to the house that he once shared with his wife and son and parked across the street. He had driven straight through, stopping only for gas and a quick bite to eat, then hitting the road again. Now he was finally here and found himself afraid to get out of the CJ.

He sat in the seat a moment and stared at the little house. This was his dream, the house that he would raise his family in. The picket fence was real, he knew because he built it just a month after they closed on the property. The jungle gym with the raised fort in the backyard was solid, he knew because he built it with a few of his best friends from the Rangers when Bobby was only three. They spent the weekend figuring out how the kit went together and Barbara catered to their every need, including running to the hardware store to get more bolts and washers and nuts that the boys swore wasn't included, only to find them when they cleaned up the boxes and debris. Robert had missed the plastic bag that held it all. Barbara teased him that had it been a snake, he would have been bit. He teased her back that had it been a snake, it would have moved and revealed its hidden location and then been soundly hacked to death with the hammer he had in his hand all weekend!

He stepped from the Jeep and crossed the road, slowly approaching the house. He didn't know why he felt such apprehension, but he did. He always did when it came to her. He would much rather face a truck load of Taliban than her. The Taliban could only torture and maybe kill him, but she could rip his heart out. And now, here he was, to face her and do the task for her. The news he bore tugging at his heart like a weight.

As he approached the entryway of the house, the door slowly opened and Barbara leaned against the door jam. She looked so damned hot in her white tank top and cut off denim jeans. She had a sly smile on her face and even without makeup and standing there barefoot she looked heart-wrenchingly beautiful to him. He froze in mid-stride and stared at her.

"You made it back alive," she said, a brow slowly arching and a devilish smile crossing her pink lips.

"Yes, ma'am," he replied, a smirk crossing his face. "You know me…always got to follow orders. Too stupid not to."

She ran from the doorway and jumped into his arms, wrapping her legs around his waist and her arms around his neck. The kiss she laid on him took his breath away. At five foot two inches, and ninety-eight pounds, she almost looked like a child wrapped around him, but her figure more than indicated she was any-thing *but* a child. Her short dark hair had grown out a little while he was gone, but still exposed her shoulders, which drove him wild. He held her, one hand under her bottom, the other hand slid up her back, his thick, meaty fingers slithering through her hair to hold the back of her head while her mouth probed his.

She finally pulled away from him and breathed a husky, "I missed you…" into his ear.

Robert felt an all too familiar pain in his groin and he groaned as he shifted her weight. He pulled her back slightly and stared into her eyes. He studied every nuance of her features as if he would never see her again. He felt his eyes start to tear up and Barbara felt his chest shudder slightly just before he pulled her to him in a crushing hug. Robert held her tightly and Barbara at first felt concern that something was wrong then felt panic because she couldn't breathe. She tapped him soundly about the shoulders. "C-can't breathe. Bob! Let up!"

With a start, Robert let her loose and almost spilled her on the front sidewalk of their home. "I'm sorry, baby," he told her. "I'm so sorry. I forgot..."

"Holy cow, you got strong," she gasped, staring up at him.

"Yeah." He smiled at her sheepishly. He glanced about the neighborhood and then carried her into the house quickly. He kicked the door shut with his foot and took her to the bedroom, where he quickly turned on the stereo and cranked it up a little too loud for her tastes.

"Whoa, a little quick there, cowboy." She eyed him suspiciously. "We are still technically divorced, you know." She gave him that devilish look again.

Robert sat her on the bed and shut the door, then closed the blinds and shut the drapes. Barbara watched him suspiciously then stood and put her hands on her hips, more than just a bit annoyed. "Bob, what the hell are you doing?"

"Is Bobby still at school?" he asked.

"Until three, yes. I have to pick him up in four hours." She was quickly becoming aggravated.

"Good." He turned to her, his eyes desperate. "That's just enough time."

She hiked her brows at him again. "Maybe for you, caveman, but I'd like a little foreplay, if you don't mind." She turned her back on him and pulled the covers back on the bed. "Is it too much to ask for flowers, maybe take me to dinner? Hell, I'd settle for something other than a 'hello' kiss..."

Robert spun her around, pulling her from her mutterings. "Not this!" he whispered. She opened her mouth to give him a double barrel of what-for when he put his finger to his mouth to silence her. "We need to talk!"

Before Barbara exploded on him, she stopped and realized this behavior was SO unlike him. His eyes indicated that he was scared and Robert Mueller *never* got scared. She sat down on the bed and he pulled her close to him and began his tale. He told her everything. For the first time in Robert's professional life, he broke every rule and as his story came out, so did the emotions. Tears flowed freely, but he didn't let it show in his voice. She had to turn her ear to his mouth in order to hear him over the stereo and she didn't have the opportunity to see his tears until his story was done.

At the end of Robert's outpouring, she had questions and he answered them as best he could. He waited for her to scream at him, to yell, to ball her fists and strike him, to hate him. He could have taken that. He would have preferred that. But she didn't. Instead, she did something far, far worse. She cried with him. She laid her head against his chest and they held each other while each took turns mourning the loss of something that they had both looked forward to exploring again.

Somehow in the emotional turmoil that had been the formal end of their marriage, they ended up in the floor, their bedspread pulled over them. Barbara called her mother and asked her to pick Bobby up from school and she arranged to pick him up a little later that evening. She told her mom that Robert was back in town and that they wanted to surprise Bobby; which was true, but neither of them was ready to face their son at the moment.

Robert explained that one of the team members had been abducted, and if they could steal away with an operator, then they could also come after a family member. Barbara practically shook with fear at the idea. Bob slipped out to his Jeep and came back with a small duffel bag. In a side pocket he had stashed a stack of magazines with silver bullets. "I took these from work. I would have gotten a gun for you, too, but they keep a pretty close eye on those." He handed her the magazines.

Barbara looked at him as if he were stupid. "What am I supposed to do with these, Bob? Throw them at a vampire if they show up?" she whispered.

He smiled at her and dug to the bottom of the duffel bag. He pulled out a small, flat black plastic case. It had a large FN embossed on the top. "Lucky for us, they happen to sell the same pistol to civilians. I picked one up as soon as I hit town." He opened the case and proceeded to show her how to break down the weapon and he cleaned the factory goo from the inside of it. "I'm going to take you to the farm and show you how to use this. I got you some practice ammo just for that so we can save the silver for when it counts. This thing is a lot easier to use then that 9MM you're used to."

She checked out the weapon and smiled at him. "I like this. It's light and just feels good in my hands."

"Wait 'til you shoot her."

She narrowed her gaze at him. "Why do guys always call guns a 'she'?"

He grinned, knowing he was about to step in it. "Because they're fun to play with, guys get off on squeezing them, some will go off half-cocked, they always have a loud retort, and if you're not careful, they'll kick you good and hard."

She punched him in the arm and he laughed at her, pulling her into his embrace. "Hey, you asked, remember?!"

Viktor left the Geneve-Cointrin International Airport and grabbed the first available taxi for downtown Geneva. He had an appointment to keep and another flight to catch. He kept glancing at his watch and asking the driver to increase his speed. The taxi driver would drive a little faster, weaving about in traffic as best he could, but slowed down again at regular intervals, aggravating Viktor and causing him to check his watch and utter curses under his breath. When he finally pulled to their destination, Viktor jumped out of the taxi and handed the man a crisp hundred Euro note and told him to wait for his return. The taxi driver's displeasure with the fare suddenly faded as he took the note and placed the taxi in Park.

Viktor went to the front of the curio shop and the bell rang above the door as he entered. He glanced around the shop, looking for the curator. He found him, sitting behind the counter, an espresso in his withered hand, his round spectacles at the end of his nose and a copy of the *Tribune de Geneve* spread out before him. "Ah, Viktor, I was beginning to worry about you."

"Alfonse, I would have called, but the plane would not allow cell phone use," Viktor replied. He approached the man and carefully embraced the aged man, a slight kiss to each cheek. The old man looked much worse than last Viktor had seen him, the wrinkles in his face more pronounced, the hair a duller shade of white, his eyes less of a gleam. Viktor knew that his years were catching up to him.

"I swear, Viktor, I don't know how you do it." Alfonse held him at arm's length and eyed him head to toe. "You look exactly as you did back in the war."

"You are too kind, my friend," Viktor lied. He was sure that Alfonse suspected his supernatural secret, but he never dared ask. "I hate to rush you, but do you have it?"

The old man patted his shoulder reassuringly. "Never have I let you down, have I?" He motioned Viktor to the back of the shop where he kept his safes. "This was a bit of a rush job, you know, but I think you will be pleased with the quality." He opened the larger of his safes and pulled out a small lock box. "I'm sure you'll appreciate how difficult it is to replicate such things from drawings, no?"

"I understand, my friend, and I do appreciate the rush." Viktor opened the lock box and with a jewelers loupe he inspected each piece. "These are exquisite."

"But, of course." The old man laughed. "You expected less? Viktor, you know me better than that."

"Alfonse, I'm at a loss. You had merely a few days' time and to work only from drawings...I am truly impressed." Viktor was at a loss for words at the quality and craftsmanship that he was holding in his hands. "You have truly outdone yourself."

"Anything for a friend," Alfonse stated proudly. Viktor stood erect and closed the lock box. He reached into his coat pocket and pulled out an envelope.

He pressed it tightly into Alfonse's hand. "Our agreed upon amount."

Alfonse felt the thickness of the envelope in his hand. "Unless I am losing my mind, there is a considerable amount *more* in here." He eyed Viktor cautiously. "Unless you have begun paying an old man in single Euros?"

"No, my friend." Viktor smiled sadly at him. He caressed his cheek and felt his own eyes begin to mist. "I fear that I may never see you again. I wanted to ensure that your remaining years were comfortable. That is all."

Alfonse nodded. "I do not know what you are up to these days, but I do hope you will be careful, Viktor. You and I have been friends for far too long for you to be taking wild chances." Alfonse pulled his glasses down and looked at him over the rims. "And just because you *look* the same as you did during the war, does not mean that you are the same young man. It is a young man's world out there. We are old men and we need to leave the dangerous things to the younger men."

Viktor nodded, "I plan to, Alfonse. I just fear that I may not be able to travel much more and…"

"Do not try to kid me, Viktor," he said emphatically. "We've been through too much together. Just promise me that whatever you have planned, you will be careful."

Viktor stared at the old man before him and nodded. "I will. I give you my word."

The two embraced one last time and Viktor headed back out into the brisk air and his waiting taxi. He knew as soon as he closed the door and heard the familiar chime of the bell above the door that he would never see Alfonse again. One way or the other, their history together had just come to an end.

4

Rufus and Dr. Peters worked in the near darkness of Evan's laboratory. Evan had given Thorn a walk-through and had shown all of the different projects that he had completed and the ones that he was in the middle of. Then he showed Thorn the ones that had him stymied. His biggest project was the one he had hoped would bring the upcoming war to a quick end…but he kept hitting dead ends. His idea was to design a weapon that only targeted natural born vampires. But the enzyme that the weapon was based on was too unstable and tended to also target living creatures as well. Evan had hoped to perfect the weapon prior to the battle's start and once deployed, it could devastate a huge portion of the Sicarii's forces, but with the setbacks and dead ends he kept hitting, the project was about to be shelved.

"This enzyme that you base your weapon on, it is only found in natural born vampires, *oui*?" Thorn asked Evan as he read through his notes.

"Well, yes and no." Dr. Peters set down the slides he had been working with and pulled another notebook from his shelf. "If you look here," Evan flipped to a page in the other book, "the same enzyme is also present in natural born werewolves. For the life of me, I can't figure out how."

Thorn looked up at him with a wry smile. "For the life of you? This is funny, *non*?" he chuckled.

Evan gave Thorn an odd look of misunderstanding until he realized the joke that Rufus had made. "Ah. Yes. I get it now." Evan flustered. "Sorry, it's just a phrase that…"

"*Non*, non it is quite alright. I tend to poke fun at such things simply because I, too, say such things and…" Thorn glanced away embarrassed, "I wish it were still true."

Evan sat quietly with Thorn for a time and shared a moment of regret. A camaraderie between two beings who both wished their fates had been different. Finally, Thorn looked up and broke the silence. "Perhaps there is something to this enzyme, *oui*? Something that binds all supernatural beings together?"

"That's exactly what I was thinking when I stumbled upon it," Evan explained, almost excitedly. He pulled two more notebooks and flipped through them. "If you'll look here, I found the same enzyme in the blood workups on trolls. And here, I found it in some of the woodland Lesser Elves. But…here, see? Nothing in the Greater Elves. And here, there's nothing in ogres or gargoyles."

Thorn read through Evan's notes and considered his findings. "Do you know if the Lesser Elves were all natural born?"

Evan turned a puzzled look toward Rufus. "I don't understand. All elves would have to be natural born, wouldn't they? I mean, an elf isn't going to bite a human and transmit a virus…"

"*Non*, you misunderstand me." Rufus was shaking his head. He searched for the right words in English. "In lore and history, many elves and humans have...inter-bred, *oui*? They have...hybrid children. Some would still have the characteristics of the Elven peoples, and would be required to be raised as elves."

Evan sat down slowly, digesting this bit of news. "I wasn't aware of this."

"*Oui*, it has happened many times. And if the human genes are passed on to their offspring, it could disrupt this enzyme, *non*?"

Evan considered this idea and nodded his head. "I suppose it could. But it still leaves me with the problem of separating the enzyme base so that it only affects vampires and not the elves. Or to affect only the werewolf and not the vampire. Or to only affect an elf and not..."

"Why?" Thorn asked.

Evan was shocked at Thorn's question. How could he ask why? Their goal at the moment was only to stop this rogue vampire from trying to force all of the world's vampires into his army and burning the world to the ground. "What do you mean, 'why'?"

"Why are you worried about speciation of the enzyme? We are trying to stop the Vampire Armageddon, *non*? You should be worried about making the weapon work," Thorn stated coldly.

"What? No. No, no, no, you don't understand." Evan felt the need to explain, surely Thorn was simply misguided. "If we weaponize this enzyme, then *all* creatures that carry this enzyme, including a handful of humans, will be killed."

"*Oui*," Thorn said, his face stony. "Acceptable losses."

"Acceptable...what are you saying?" Evan asked, stepping away from Thorn. "Kill everything that isn't human to save *one* race of intelligent beings on this planet?"

Thorn shook his head. "You do not understand, Doctor." Rufus stated quietly. "If the colonel's plan fails and Viktor fails to retrieve the artifacts from the Vatican...we have *nothing* else to fall back on. We will be defenseless against the single most powerful vampire in the world. A vampire who may well be able to conscript me and my entire army out from under me. A vampire who will be able to command his people from around the world by calling to their very blood." Thorn stood and stared into Evan's eyes with a steely glare. "Even *you*, Doctor. Whether you like it, or not."

Evan swallowed and sat down hard in his chair. He found that his hands were trembling and his mouth had gone dry. "I-I don't care. I won't be a party to this kind of warfare. It's akin to genocide."

"Doctor. Do you have *any idea* the kind of power I am talking about?"

"N-no, I don't," Evan stammered out.

Thorn unleashed his own power in a pulse that flowed out of him like a crashing wave that knocked Evan out of his chair and to his knees. Even though Dr. Peters was not a member of Rufus' *familia*, he felt the overwhelming urge to call him 'master' and bow to him. Evan instantly knew just how old and powerful Thorn was, and the increase in the number of his people had only made him stronger.

"Please…stop." Evan whimpered from the floor.

Rufus knelt to the floor and picked Evan up and placed him back in his chair while the effects wore off. "I apologize to you, Doctor. This is just a taste, a mere fraction of the power that the Sicarii has. While my years are measured in centuries, his years are measured in millennia. He is the father of *all* vampiri and his power is unequaled. Unless we can find a way to stop him, mankind will forever be lost."

Evan nodded. He understood now exactly what Thorn was trying to prove and it worked. But in his dead heart, he still could not bring himself to be a part of the genocide of countless other races. He sat in his chair, his limbs feeling as if he had been electrocuted, his hands still shaking and his mouth as dry as cotton. His head was still feeling loopy and he tried to focus on his workbench to keep the room from spinning out of control. His gaze fell to one of his earlier notebooks and he couldn't take his eyes from it. He didn't know why but his hands reached for it automatically. He clutched it for dear life.

"What is this, Doctor?"

"I'm not sure. But it's important," he gasped. "Give me a minute to gather myself." When his eyes began to focus again, he thumbed through his notebook and his hands stopped on one of his earlier prototype weapons. "Maybe it was this?" he said to nobody in particular.

"What is this?" Rufus asked.

"A weapon I designed years ago, but never finished. I couldn't find a power source for it that was portable enough for a man to carry. The thing was too

61

heavy," he said half-heartedly as he scanned over the diagrams again. "But that was a while back...things have changed a lot since then. I mean, just look at computers. They fit in your pocket now. I could almost cut this thing down by half in size. It wouldn't need to fit on a vehicle anymore."

"You are not making sense, Doctor."

Evan looked up from his notes. "Hmm? Oh. Um, well. This weapon here," he pointed into his notebook, "is a focused pulse microwave particle destabilizer. I designed this years ago, and the only way it would work was to mount it to a vehicle. It was simply too large to be carried. And the power source...oh my, the power source was simply too large as well. The military wasn't interested because of the size...I couldn't make it rifle sized. Even when the operators here became augmented, this thing was too big and too heavy to be carried, even with a backpack for the power source." He turned back to his notebook. "But...with modern electronics, and with modern lithium ion batteries...if I had enough of them...I mean, the batteries would probably still have to be in a backpack, but the weapon itself could be made so much smaller that..." He looked up at Thorn and smiled. "You said that the only thing that will kill this guy is the sun?"

"*Oui*. I believe that is true."

"This thing?" Evan said, stabbing his finger at his notebook, "Is basically a miniature sun gone super-nova in an area the size of a basketball." Evan was smiling now. "You want a Plan C? *This* is a Plan C."

Natashia and Nadia made their connecting flight and landed in Paris via the Concorde and Air France. Natashia wasted no time in renting them a car and heading south toward Avallon. Nadia still wasn't sure exactly how this meeting was to go, and Natashia had kept mum about Maxwell and his part in all of this. All she knew was that he was Viktor's father and he was the first step in their quest.

Natashia complained that the only car available to rent was a Citroen when she truly wanted a BMW or Mercedes. Nadia didn't care what the car was as long as it got them there in one piece and didn't break down along the way. Natashia hiked a skeptical brow at her daughter and told her not to count her chickens before they hatched. She had never had good luck with the Citroens and she doubted she would now.

As her mother navigated their way through narrow roads and toward the broader highways, Nadia reflected back to just how little she truly knew of her mother and father's pasts. Apparently her mother knew her way around France, how to drive in and around the narrow streets, and where to find her grandfather, yet, nobody had ever spoken of such things in Nadia's presence. She leaned her head against the window and took in the scenery of France and absently rubbed at her tummy and thought of the life that grew within her now. She hoped that her child would never sit across from her and wonder what sort of life her mother had lived and not have the heart to ask.

Natashia drove south and worked her way to the outskirts of Avallon, slowing only to look for road signs and familiar buildings. "Amazing how little things change in a century," she mumbled more to herself than to Nadia.

"The more things change, the more they stay the same?" Nadia asked.

Natashia shot her a puzzled look. "Not quite, my dear, but close."

"What are we looking for?"

"The Vickers house."

"Maxwell is a priest?" Nadia asked, somewhat shocked.

Natashia snorted. "Not hardly," she replied, still studying the signs and shop buildings. "At one time he played with the idea of being something of a holy man, but now...I don't really know what you might call him." She turned the car down an alleyway, still studying the landmarks. "He has more money than sense and he bought an old church. It looked more like a castle than a church if you ask me, but, the dreary thing came with a Vicker's cottage. He restored it and has been living in it ever since."

She pulled the car onto a cobblestone road and the car felt as though it was going to shake apart. Natashia gripped the steering wheel and Nadia tried not to smile as her mother sneered and threatened the French made piece of scrap metal to stay together or she'd melt it down into a Peugeot. Nadia giggled at that and her mother tried not to laugh at her own remark. Finally, she pulled the car to a stop and shut off the engine. Nadia stepped out of the car and caught her breath as she stared at the old church. Her mother was right, it did look more like a castle than a church, with its tall spires and grandiose doorways.

"This way, darling," Natashia called as she walked across to the cottage beside the outer wall of the church.

Nadia hurried to catch up with her and met her at the door just as Natashia beat on the front door with the ball of her fist. "Maxwell! Open the door! I've traveled too far in a piece of shit Citroen on this damned cobblestone and I have to pee!" Natashia yelled. Nadia shook her head and stifled a grin at her mother's brazenness.

The door flew open and Nadia saw her grandfather for the first time, standing in an artist's smock, paint smeared all over him. He was easily as tall and broad shouldered as her father with the same wide chin and solid brow. He had the same mischievous glimmer in his eye, and same nose, but rather than dark brown hair, his was reddish brown in color with a peppering of grey. His hands were large and calloused and he wore open toed sandals as he stood in the door, his mouth opened in shock at the two women standing there to see him.

Natashia pushed her way through without being invited, "I'm about to wet myself. Which way to the toilet?" she asked as she threw her bag on the nearest couch.

65

He turned and pointed to the hallway. "Second door on the left." His deep baritone voice echoed off the terra cotta floor, but Natashia was gone before the echo had died away. Nadia stood outside, unsure if she should enter or not. Maxwell turned and looked at her. "You look nothing like your mother." He eyed her from head to toe. "But you might as well come in."

"I'm Nadia." She extended her hand to him. "I'm very pleased to finally meet you," the nervousness in her voice making it crack slightly.

Maxwell looked at her hand and then wiped his hand against his smock, smearing paint across it. He grabbed it lightly and shook it. "I suppose it's nice to meet you. I figured they'd have a child eventually." He hiked a brow curiously. "Though I have to admit, I'm surprised it's taken them this long."

Nadia stood just inside the door, nervously looking around, unsure what to do next. Maxwell stood beside her and stared. After a moment he grunted and motioned toward the interior of his home.

"This way." He stepped in a bit and set his artist's palette down next to his easel. Nadia noticed that from where it was set, he could see out the window to the church and it appeared he was in the middle of painting the castle-like building during its heyday. He picked a few things up off of the couch and tossed them to the corner of the room and swept a few crumbs from the couch. "Sit."

Nadia took a seat, careful to keep her hands to herself. She looked around the spartan room with just the bare necessities and decided that even though he may have more money than sense, he didn't live a lavish lifestyle. After a few moments, her mother came from the restroom looking as ravishing as ever.

"Maxwell! So good to see you again," she purred as she approached the man and embraced him.

"I would say the same thing, Tasha, but I doubt this is a social call," Maxwell said, his voice deep and low, his face cautiously watching her every move.

"Why, darling, would you say that?" she asked as she practically floated about the room, trying to find *something* to compliment him on.

"Because I've known you for far too long," Maxwell admitted. "Why are you here?"

"Can't a girl visit her dear father-in-law once in a while?" she asked, batting her eyelashes.

"No," he deadpanned.

"But why not? Surely you have no animosity towards me…do you, Maxwell?" she purred again. She had searched every inch of the common areas of his domicile and realized, the man lived as a monk. There wasn't a single thing in his home worthy of comment.

"I'll ask you one more time, Tasha. What do you want?" He crossed his massive arms across his chest and stared her down.

"Wouldn't you at least like to meet your granddaughter?" she asked, using her hands to present Nadia who beamed up at him.

"Nice to meet you," he said. "There's the door." He turned to open it when Nadia stood.

"Mother! This isn't working," she whispered through clenched teeth.

"What isn't working?" Maxwell barked.

"Whatever it is that she's trying to do," Nadia tried to explain. "And I don't understand her behavior. This isn't like her." Nadia gave her mother a sideways look then turned back to Maxwell. "Grandfather, we've come—"

"Maxwell," he all but growled.

Nadia instinctively took a half step back. "Excuse me?" She didn't understand why he snapped at her.

"I've only just met you. You never bounced on my knee. I didn't watch you grow up. I never changed a diaper or had you spit up on my shirt," he explained. "I didn't even know that you existed until you walked in my door." Nadia stood open-mouthed and blinked at him, unable to grasp his animosity. "As far as you're concerned, I'm just Maxwell."

She inhaled a stuttering breath and steadied herself. It became obvious to her that *family* meant little to this man. Appealing to that side of him would do her no good. She turned and looked at her mother who had tears forming in her eyes and she turned away from the both of them, unable to look her daughter in the face.

"Very well then, Maxwell…we came here to seek your aid," she began. "We are on a quest most dire in circumstance and…"

"Who the hell talks this way?" he interrupted her.

Once again Nadia was shocked silent. "I am sorry?"

"Seriously? Who speaks this way? Is this some kind of joke?" he asked Natashia.

Nadia looked at her mother and she saw a tear escape her mother's eye and run down her cheek.

Natashia quickly wiped it away. "It was her father's idea to have her trained classically, thank you," Natashia answered without looking at him, her voice trying desperately to reflect some semblance of dignity.

Maxwell nodded, a sneer across his face. He snorted. "I should have known."

"What is that supposed to mean?" Nadia asked.

"Your father," Maxwell stated, "if there's a decision to be made, he'll choose the wrong path."

Nadia's anger flared and she stood to her full height and squared her shoulders. She barely met him mid chest, and she wouldn't weigh a third of what her grandfather weighed, but *nobody* would speak that way about her father in her presence!

"You will hold your tongue when you speak of my father or I'll remove it, sir!" she huffed. Her breathing and heart rate had increased and she felt her wolf starting to stir. "I'll have you know that my father is a Lycan of the First Order and both an honorable man and a warrior wolf. I will *not* stand idly by and listen to any man speak ill of him, not whilst breath still flows through me nor my heart still beats!"

Natashia jumped up from the couch and grabbed Nadia by the shoulders to pull her back away from Maxwell. "Nadia! Please! Remember, darling, you are with child!"

"So?!" she cried out, struggling against her mother's hands.

"If you allow yourself to change this early, you could lose the baby. There are things we must do before the shift to preserve the pregnancy."

Nadia trembled with anger as she stared up into her grandfather's eyes. She knew that her eyes had already shifted to amber and she fought the urge to shift and tear him limb from limb, but she forced herself to calm down and slowly got herself under control. Maxwell stood his ground the entire time, staring at her impassively.

Once she was calm again, he looked to Natashia. "Spunky little pup, isn't she?"

Nadia turned again and swung at him, but Maxwell caught her hand in his own, easily encompassing her entire fist and holding her. "Calm yourself, pup." Something in his voice acted as a balm to her anger and Nadia found herself almost instantly calming. He directed her back toward the couch and maneuvered her into taking a seat.

"Let's try this again." He turned to Natashia. "No candy-coating or bullshitting this time. Why are you here?"

"As Nadia said, we need your help." She still wouldn't meet his gaze.

"With what?" he asked. "You know I won't have anything to do with pack business anymore."

"Oh, we are *well aware* of that," Natashia spat.

Maxwell gave her a hard look, but she wouldn't look at him. "What is that supposed to mean?"

"Nothing. This is not pack business," Natashia muttered softly.

"What's going on, Tasha? Is Victoria okay?" he asked, suddenly sounding a little concerned.

"She lives," Natashia sneered.

Maxwell crossed his arms again and glared at her. Natashia cautioned a glance at him and wished she hadn't. His face was one of concern and anger. "What happened?"

"Which time?" she asked. "In the past, or why are we here now?" She felt like a child being scolded by a parent.

Max pushed away from the wall and took a seat opposite of Natashia so that she could no longer avoid his face. He saw the tears that she had been fighting back and he knew that whatever it was that was eating at her must be bad. Tasha never got teary. She was too strong of a wolf for that. He leaned forward on the couch and forced her to look at him.

"Tell me everything."

Colonel Mitchell was just about to board his military hop back to Tinker when his cell phone sounded. He answered the call and was ordered to report to the Pentagon. He hated going to the Pentagon but it was one of those necessary evils when you served in today's military. The big boys that worked there worried more about whether your uniform was absolutely correct and your shoes spit-shined to a mirror finish and Matt had more important worries. But orders were orders, and he was not about to disobey one now.

71

When he arrived Mitchell logged in and an escort took him to General McAfee's office. He sat and waited twenty minutes before he was allowed into the inner office to meet with the general. This gave Mitchell twenty minutes to race through every possible scenario as to why a general he'd never heard of wanted to speak to him. Usually that meant that somebody was about to get their ass chewed, and while there were any number of things that Mitchell could think of that probably warranted an ass chewing, he couldn't think of why this McAfee would be the one doing it.

When the general's secretary let him in, he wasn't the slightest bit surprised at the size and luxury of the office. Walnut paneling with numerous awards and commendations adorned the wall, flags in each corner, plush carpet and a desk that reminded him immediately of the one seen in pictures of the oval office in the White House. The general himself was a small man in stature, but large in personality. Matt's first impression was a smaller version of John Wayne. The man even resembled the Duke in the face and had a slow Texas drawl in his voice that made Matt warm to him immediately. The general invited him in and even apologized for making him wait, which Matt was not expecting.

"Sorry to keep you waiting out there, Colonel. Had a last minute phone call that I couldn't get out of and I didn't think it right to make you sit through it." He offered a hand.

Matt took the hand, "That's quite alright, General. No trouble at all."

The General offered Matt a seat and then went back behind his desk and settled in. "I know that this meeting must seem a bit unorthodox to you, Colonel, but I wanted to meet you face to face."

"Sir?" Matt questioned.

The general's eyes twinkled as he measured Mitchell. "I heard you were still in town and I hoped to catch you before you left. I guess I was lucky I did."

"I'm afraid I'm not following you, sir," Matt replied honestly.

"Any man that can blow into town and ask for one of my most highly guarded top-secret bases, *and get it*?" the general said, a slight bit of astonishment and a taste of anger in his voice, "Had to have balls the size of Volkswagens." He leaned back in his chair. "To be honest, I wanted to see how the hell you walked, Colonel."

Matt's eyes widened with realization. "I think I understand now, General."

"I wished to hell that I did," McAfee said. He leaned across his desk and opened a humidor. He pulled out a cigar and offered one to Mitchell. "We're not supposed to smoke here in the Pentagon anymore. I told them to kiss my ass. I *earned* these stars and it's my damned office. I'll smoke a stogie in here if I want to." He shot Matt a wink.

Mitchell stifled a smirk. "Thank you, sir. Don't mind if I do." After both men lit up, McAfee sat back and blew a blue-grey smoke ring that hung lazily in the air.

"So, Colonel...from what I've been told, and please, feel free to kick me in the backside if I'm a dipshit for listening to the bigger dipshits that told me this…but you want my base in Nevada to wage World War Three?" he asked cautiously.

Matt rolled the cigar in his mouth and enjoyed the flavor of the cigar. He debated how much information to share with McAfee. "Exactly what *were* you told General?"

McAfee stared at Mitchell through the hazy smoke accumulating in his office. "Are you going to make me say it out loud, Mitchell?"

Matt smiled weakly. "I'm afraid so, sir."

McAfee sighed audibly. "You're a son of a bitch then…vampires!" he stated firmly. "There!? You happy now? They told me it was to fight off vampires."

Mitchell nodded. "You were told correctly, sir."

"Poppycock!" McAfee yelled. "There's no such thing as vampires, Mitchell. And you must think I'm a blamed idiot if I'm going to give up my base at Groom Lake for some hair brained—"

"General," Matt interrupted.

"What!"

"I can prove it," Matt said, studying the cherry at the end of his cigar.

"Bullcookies, Mitchell. You're trying to sell me a bill of goods here and I won't stand for it."

Mitchell pulled on his cigar again and let the nutty flavor of the cigar coat his mouth. "Feel like taking a little trip, General?"

McAfee stared at Mitchell through the growing haze of cigar smoke, not sure what he was up to. "You're serious?"

74

"As a heart attack." Matt's eyes dared him to accept. "Come with me back to Tinker. I happen to have a vampire on staff out there," he offered. "And I have another vampire that is the leader of…well…let's just say, 'the good guys' and he's visiting for a little bit." Mitchell pulled on his cigar again. "You come out there, take a tour, meet the boys, say hello to the bloodsuckers, and if you aren't convinced…fine. The Vampire Armageddon happens and the world goes up in flames and we all die and you can die believing that vampires aren't real and nobody will have ever touched your precious Groom Lake base." Matt sat the cigar in the ashtray on McAfee's desk. "But when you come out and see that the vampires are real, you don't argue, you tell Groom Lake's base commander to secure operations, lock up any sensitive materials, get all non-essential personnel off the base, secure all classified materials and anybody who can't fire a weapon gets the hell out of there. Then he hands over *temporary* control to me. No questions asked."

McAfee stared at him for a long moment, rolling the cigar in his mouth. Finally he pulled the cigar away and said, "Book us a flight, Mitchell. I fly first class."

"We both fly military hops, General. You'll be lucky if your old wrinkled ass won't get bruised on a wooden plank in the rear of a C-130 cargo plane."

McAfee shook his head and chuckled. "Yup. Balls as big as Volkswagens."

5

While Jack and the remaining members of First Squad sat around the campfire with their new friend, Benburr the Gnome, Gunnery Sergeant Tufo had waited patiently along the edge of the tree line trying to make contact with the Lesser Elves. Jack had introduced Benburr to every flavor of MRE that the squad had opened that night and so far, Benburr's favorite was the chicken and rice casserole. He gave an honest opinion of each one that he tried, but his most constant comment was that it 'needed mutton'.

Benburr had asked why the humans were out here looking for the Greater Elves and Jack explained to him about the looming vampire threat. Benburr nodded and as he lit his pipe he mentioned that this would explain the unease of the elders of late. Jack inquired why the elders may be uneasy and Benburr took his time answering again. Jack began to realize that answers to questions took a backseat when one is lighting a pipe after a meal. Or enjoying a pipe. Or if one isn't sure of the correct answer and just wants to appear wiser than his years would reflect.

Benburr informed him that many of the Gnome elders had the gift of sight. Some more clearly than others, but of those who did have the gift, they had seen visions of something very dark looming on the horizon and it frightened them. In fact, it frightened them so badly that many Gnomes dared not reveal themselves any more, and some had gone so far as to move underground, risking the wrath of the Ogres and Orcs.

Jack and the squad members listened to Benburr, who they now affectionately called Bennie, tell of the Gnomes who had been lost horribly due to the fears of the elders. Jack was about to offer some measure of solace when Tufo returned to camp.

Mark trudged into the camp appearing completely worn out. "I do not *ever* want to have to do that again."

"Bad night at the office, dear?" Lamb asked with a chuckle.

"Bite me," Tufo proffered. Lamb laughed at the offer.

"So what did you find out?" Jack asked.

"That those little bastards are scared to death of you guys, for one," Tufo said.

"And, two?" Jack asked.

"The Greater Elves are on the next ridge. Over there." Tufo pointed to the next ridge which appeared to be about five clicks away. "If we take off at first light, we can be there by breakfast."

"Sweet. Good job, Gunny." Jack gave the man a solid slap on the back.

"Thank you, thank you, throw money, not jabs." He smiled. "Now...spill it."

Jack gave him an innocent look. "What?"

"You know what. Spill it. You promised me the real deal once I was done." Tufo glanced down at the

77

Gnome smoking his pipe and poking the fire with a stick. "Don't take my word for it, ask Travelocity here. He heard you, I'm sure."

Bennie looked up at the two of them arguing and shook his head. "No idea what he's talking about. Unless you have some grog? Maybe a little mead?" he said smiling, a twinkle in his eye. "That always seems to loosen my tongue."

Jack chuckled and told Tufo to grab some chow. He'd fill him in while he ate. Mark stepped around Jack to pull an MRE out of his pack when Jack noticed something on his shoulder. "Tufo, What's this?" Jack reached for his shoulder when the strange object took flight and flitted around the front of Mark and landed on his other shoulder.

"Aw, shit. I thought she stayed in the woods," Tufo groaned.

"What is it? I can barely see it in this light," Jack said. Jacobs and Lamb got up and tried to get closer to look as well, but Donovan sat back on his log and began to snicker. "He's got himself a Sprite, Chief!" Donnie said as he crunched on a granola bar. "From the looks of her, I'd say she's probably a woodland nymph."

"Oh, hell, she's cute as a button," Lamb said.

"She looks like Tinkerbelle…" Jacobs said in awe.

"She's annoying as hell." Tufo swatted at the little sprite. She flitted around his head and landed on his other shoulder.

"Hey! Don't do that. You might hit her," Lamb said. He stuck his finger up toward her hoping she might land on his finger so that he could get a better look.

"I wouldn't do that, buddy," Donovan said.

Lamb turned and looked at him. "Why do you say that? She looks totally harmless...OOOWW! Holy shit!" he yelled and jerked his finger back with a snarl. He saw a dark fluid dripping from the side of his finger and knew it was blood.

"'Cuz they *bite*," Donnie said quietly and laughed to himself. "If they get attached to you, you can't beat them away with a stick. They'll even defend you with their own lives. But don't let somebody else get too close." Donnie looked at Tufo and wiggled his eyebrows. "That includes *wives*, buddy. Those little bitches get JEALOUS."

"Oh, for Pete's sake," Tufo muttered and threw his pack down. He kicked a chunk of log into the fire and watched as sparks flew into the air. "How the hell do I make her go home?" he asked Donnie.

"There's a couple of ways." Donovan finished his granola bar and threw the wrapper into the fire. "You can do something to *really* hurt her feelings."

"Like tell her that her little ass is fat?" Tufo asked.

"Naw, she wouldn't care about that," Donnie said. "But maybe if you caught her and chunked her cute little butt into the fire...*that* might piss her off enough to leave."

Jacobs jumped up. "Dude, don't you dare torch Tink!"

"I'm not going to torch Tink!" Tufo yelled back at him. "Christ, do you think I'm a monster?" He looked back at Donovan. "What's the other way to get rid of them?"

He grinned at him like the cat that ate the canary. "Knock her up."

Everybody but Bennie and Jack stared at him open mouthed. Finally, Tufo flipped Donovan the bird. "Up yours, Donovan. She's barely three inches tall. I'd split her like a banana peel if I even tried to...well, if I...just...*never mind!*"

"Dude, you don't understand, just because she's tiny doesn't mean that you can't still..."

"I don't want to hear it, Donovan," Tufo barked.

Donnie chuckled. "Okay, man, but I'm telling ya, that's the only way you're going to get rid of her."

Lamb crawled over close to Donovan and whispered to him, "How do you know so much about these things?"

"Got stuck with one once," Donnie said sadly.

"No shit?" Lamb asked.

Donnie nodded. "Three years ago." He looked down into the fire and kicked a loose log with his boot. "You're right. They do look like Tinkerbelle."

"Okay, so I gotta ask. How did you get rid of yours?"

Donovan looked him in the eye and without smiling said, "I didn't throw her in the fire."

Tufo sat next to Jack, the Sprite sitting on his shoulder playing with his hair. "Okay, Chief. Clue me in."

Jack sighed and poked the fire with a stick. "I guess I might as well. You're probably going to find out anyway."

"Find out what?"

"That we're werewolves," Jacobs said straight faced.

Tufo snorted and almost choked on his beans with bacon. "Yeah, right. We fight those things, remember?" He was grinning at the team and turned back to Jack. "So what's the real deal?"

Jack nodded, "Yeah, that sort of *is* the real deal, Mark." He looked at Mark and saw that he wasn't really buying it. "Remember when Mitchell first let you go? You were so pissed about it?"

"Of course. I'm still pissed." He shoveled another spoonful into his mouth.

"Well, it was a little before that time that the CIA had sent some spook scientists down to do some research and they came up with the first 'augmentation' plan. Ring any bells?" Jack asked.

"Yeah. Vaguely." Tufo set his MRE to the side and started paying a little more attention here. "Why?"

"The 'augmentation' that they came up with was really just the werewolf virus. They figured out that if they give subjects a combination of wolfsbane and some other stuff, it would prevent them from actually shifting. So you still have the strength, the speed and the stamina, but you don't shift on the full moon. You still get better hearing, a more sensitive nose and way faster reflexes—"

"But we don't hike on the furniture," Jacobs interrupted, smiling.

"Or shed on the couch," Lamb added.

"Or chase the mailman," Donnie put in.

81

"Okay, okay, knock it off," Jack said.

"Wait, you're really serious here, aren't you?" Tufo asked.

Jack nodded. "And the reason Mitchell let you go was because you had a family. He knew that if he allowed you to be infected with the virus, you could pass it on to your wife by accident. Or if you two had any kids after the infection, then the child would be a carrier, too." Jack told him. "Mitchell told me himself that you were the closest thing to a true friend that he had and there was no way in hell that he would let that happen to you. He cared about you too much."

Suddenly Mark felt like a total tool. All of these years he had been directing all of his anger and animosity toward Mitchell, when the man had simply been trying to protect him. "He still should have told me," he said softly as he reflected on the days when he and Matt were still friends. He suddenly wasn't feeling very hungry as his stomach knotted up on him.

"He couldn't, Mark. He was under direct orders. He didn't even tell us until just recently. He's made a lot of 'changes' lately and broken a lot of rules."

"So, now that I've forced my way back, will I have to go through the augmentation?" Tufo asked.

"No. This is only temporary. Just until we get Dom back," Jack said.

Tufo sat silently for a while before he turned to Jack again. "What if I wanted the augmentation?"

"It wouldn't happen," Jack said. "You're married. You have a family, Gunny."

"Yeah," Tufo agreed, staring into the fire. "Yeah. You're right."

Dom stepped tentatively into the dark room and allowed his eyes to adjust, but he simply couldn't see anything. He felt his vampire host pass by him and he could hear him moving about in the room. Dom heard the scratch of a match and smelled the sulfur of its burn before the room glowed from an oil lamp in the middle near its center. When the vampire placed the glass globe over the open flame, the entire room lit up and he could see the many tapestries on the wall, most from the Middle East. He saw a small desk in the corner and a mattress along a wall. Pillows were scattered about and it appeared to him to be somebody's place, but long abandoned.

The vampire turned to Dom and gestured to the room. "This shall be your room during your stay with us." He pointed to a door across from the one they entered. "Your private restroom and shower. You will find a change of clothing in there as well. I shall see to having the clothes you are in laundered before you depart here."

Dom shot him a less than trusting look. "You still expect me to believe that you're going to allow me to leave here?"

"As I have explained to you, Dominic, you are worth much more to me alive."

"Really?" Dom kicked a pillow out of the way and fell onto the lumpy mattress. He propped another pillow up behind his shoulders and eyed the vampire. "How do you figure that?"

"You have information that I require. You will give it to me and then you shall leave."

"What about this 'message' of yours that you want me to take back to my people?" he asked sarcastically.

The dark vampire bowed in the glow of the lamp's flame and Dom realized how dead his eyes truly were. "You already have my message, Dominic. I gave it to you when I gave you the vision of my life and the future that awaits you."

Dom shivered involuntarily when he spoke of the memories that flashed through his mind. "So I'm supposed to go back and tell my boss that a vampire with delusions of grandeur intends to destroy the world, enslave mankind, eat everybody we ever knew and make breeders out of a select few, all because he thinks God is mad at him?" Dom eyed the vampire, hoping he was getting under his skin. "Yeah, that ought to go over like a fart in church," Dom shot at him. "Look, Drac…I'd much rather go back to my boss and tell him that this was all one big misunderstanding. That…maybe you skipped a few meds and that now you're all better, okay? Maybe you're not crazy? Maybe you just have a mineral deficiency? Maybe you're just a little low in high velocity lead? I'm sure we could hook you right up."

The vampire stared at him stonily. "Are you quite through?"

"Naw, I could go on all night if you let me." Dom grinned at him. "I'm full of insults for shitbags like you."

The vampire turned his back to Dom and stared at the floor, the oil lamp casting an eerie shadow against the wall and making him appear much larger than he truly was. "Mr. DeGiacomo, you have insulted me. You have tried to appeal to my humanity. You have tried to reach me through spiritual ways. You have tried to reason with me. And now you are back to insulting me." He turned back to face Dominic. "When are you simply going to accept that my path has been laid out and I can no more change the fates than you can? Your attempts to reach me are futile."

"Bullshit," Dom said. "You know that what you're wanting to do is…well, it's just plain *wrong*."

"And?"

"And?! And *what*? There is no and!" he yelled. "It's just wrong!"

"You act as if I may care, Mr. DeGiacomo. I do not. No more than you would care if you stepped upon an ant."

Dom got to his feet again and shook a finger in his face, "That is a lie! I *know* that is a lie!" he shouted. "You can't deny that you were once human. You had a human family and human feelings. You cared about things. You *felt* things! You can't stand there and tell me that you don't care…you aren't that good of a liar." The veins in his forehead were bulging as he yelled.

The vampire remained stoic and stared at him through his tirade impassively. "I do not." He sighed. "Not any longer."

Dom gave a frustrated laugh. "You are so full of crap...and what's worse is that you're buying it yourself," he muttered. "I saw your life, remember? You might can convince yourself, but you can't convince me." He fell back on to the mattress and stared off into a corner. "Go ahead. Ask me whatever you want. Apparently you've got yourself convinced that this is your only avenue." He turned and looked at the vampire again. "But personally, if I were as damned and miserable as you *pretend* to be? I'd find somebody willing to take me out of the game rather than threaten to destroy the world."

The dark vampire stared at Dominic for a very long time and said nothing. Dominic finally turned his gaze back to the vampire and studied him, a realization striking him like a hammer. "That's it, isn't it? You *want* somebody to stop you, don't you? You've finally gotten so tired of suffering that you're hoping we can stop you..."

The vampire jerked his attention back to Dominic, his eyes wild with anger. "You could not stop me if you tried!" he hissed.

Dom felt a smile sliding across his face and he was nodding at the vampire, "No, I'm right and we both know it. You may not have realized it until I said it, but that's exactly what you're hoping for. You want us to stop you, no matter what it takes."

The vampire's eyes narrowed at Dominic and a low guttural growl escaped him as Dom began to chuckle. "It cannot happen. It *will* not happen. I am unstoppable," he hissed as he turned and placed the oil lamp on Dom's table and made his way to the door. Dom began to chuckle at the idea that the vampire desired death and the chuckle turned into laughter which fueled the vampire's rage even more. He stormed to the door and threw it open. "When you have yourself under control again, we shall continue this conversation."

He slammed the door on Dominic as he lay across his mattress, laughing to himself at the idea that this vampire with ultimate power was truly nothing but a coward hoping to commit suicide by Monster Squad.

Bob Mueller had spent the day with his wife and son. After taking Babs to the farm and teaching her the nuances of the FiveseveN, she was shooting the handgun like an old pro in no time. It was such an easy weapon to master and having experience with other handguns made her an easy student. After running the weapon through its paces, they picked up Bobby from her mother's house and went for pizza. He spent the evening playing ball with his son in the backyard and Bobby talked non-stop about school and his coach-pitch baseball team and how he wanted to play football but mom wouldn't let him and could he *please* talk to mom about letting him play pee-wee football 'cuz the other kids get to and he thinks he could be really good at it 'cuz he can run really fast and he can tackle and catch a football...

The words ran into each other as Robert listened intently to his son.

Barbara watched from the window as father and son played catch in the dwindling sunlight. Her heart swelled and she felt a pang of loss as she realized once more that this might be the last time they see him for a very long time. She felt her eyes begin to tear and she turned away from the window and wiped at her face. She sniffled and blew her nose quickly, trying to hide the evidence of her emotions.

After a few more minutes, the two Mueller boys came in and set their ball gloves on the table. Little Bobby hugged his mom and Robert picked him up for a quick tickle session and hug. "I've got to get back to the base, buddy, but I'll come back and see you as often as I can. I'm sorry they stuck me in Oklahoma, but it probably won't be forever."

Bobby nodded and hugged his dad tight around the neck. "I love you, Dad."

"I love you, too, buddy." Robert misted. "So very, very much." He looked at Barbara who had to turn away from them. Robert lowered his voice to a whisper. "And I'll talk to mom about football, okay?"

"Thanks, Dad," Bobby whispered back.

"Okay, champ, upstairs and in the bath, okay?" Robert set him down and play swatted his bottom.

Bobby ran upstairs, leaving a trail of clothes behind him. Robert turned to Barbara and pulled her close to him. She tucked her head under his chin and held him close.

"He told you about football?" she asked.

Robert chuckled. "Yeah. He really wants to play. Made me promise I'd ask you about it." He said nothing else as he held her closely.

Barbara inhaled deeply, smelling his cologne. "I'm so afraid he'll get hurt."

Robert nodded. "I know."

She was silent for a little longer. "You think I should let him, don't you."

"I'm not going to try to coerce you." Robert held her, enjoying the feel of her tiny, warm body next to his.

"Oh, no you don't. You're not going to be passive aggressive with me, mister." She poked him in the ribs and made him jump. "What do you *think?*"

Robert heaved a sighed and shook his head. "I think they pad those kids up so much that the only way he could get hurt is to get hit by a truck. But I also think that you're the mom and what you say *goes*," he added to protect himself.

"That's not fair, Robert. It makes me the bad guy." She stared up at him.

"No, honey…I'm not trying to make you the bad guy," he explained. "You're here with him all the time. You have to be mom *and* dad because I can't be here. You have a tough job and even though I wish I could be here…" He looked away to regain his composure. "Look, all I'm saying is, I'm going to support whatever decision you make and I'll stand behind it." He held her face and stared into her softening eyes. "I love you,

Babs. And Bobby will get over it. If you say no, then I say no and he'll understand when he gets older."

She nodded and held him closer. "So I guess he starts football Monday." She shook her head, a silly grin crossing her face.

Robert laughed. "Boy, you're a pushover."

"I can't tell my boys no when they tell me they love me." She smiled into his chest.

Robert held her and kept inhaling her scent. He wanted to memorize everything about her. He knew he needed to leave, but he didn't want to. "I wish I could take you both with me," he whispered.

She looked up at him with her dewy eyes. "Why can't we just run away? So what if you accidentally…" He quickly put a finger over lips to shush her. She lowered her voice to a whisper. "So what? We could move to the mountains and…I don't know…chase deer on the full moon or something."

Robert smiled at her. "What about Bobby? What if we had another child? Would that be fair to the kid?"

She shook her head and buried her face in his shirt. "No," she muttered into the flannel. "None of this is fair, Robert."

He pulled her into a smoldering kiss and walked with her toward the door. "I have to go, baby." He gave her a longing look. "Be safe."

She blew him a kiss as he stepped out into the twilight and softly shut the door behind him. Barbara Mueller sat down at the table and did her best to keep herself together as she listened to Bobby sing 'Rubber Ducky' at the top of his lungs upstairs off-key.

"Guess who is playing football, Monday?" she yelled up the stairwell.

"Way to go, Dad!" Bobby yelled, and Barbara heard splashing in celebration. It brought a small ray of sunshine to her evening.

6

Viktor sat across the ornate table from Cardinal Angelo Sardelli and nervously explained the reason for his visit in hushed whispers. Although the two were locked behind the doors of the Holy See's private office, the cardinal knew that no place in Vatican City was truly free from prying eyes or curious ears.

Cardinal Sardelli was one of a few within the Vatican who were aware of the existence of vampires and other supernatural creatures, but the news that Viktor brought was more than unsettling, it was earth shaking. The cardinal, as Viktor feared, was not one for allowing the Vatican's Holy relics to escape their hard-earned grasp. Not for love nor money, nor even the salvation of mankind would they be allowed to leave the safety of the Vatican's vaults. Sardelli kept his voice low, but firm as he explained to Viktor that if this mad vampire were to destroy the earth with fire, it must then be God's will, and the souls of the vampire's victims would be delivered unto Him for judgment.

Viktor sat quietly and maintained a quiet and calm demeanor while the cardinal extrapolated all of the reasons why the Vatican could not allow the Holy relics, nor any artifacts in their possession to leave the walls of Vatican City. Finally, Viktor stared the good cardinal in the eye and explained to him, "Your

Grace, do you have any idea what this madman intends to do with Holy men?" The cardinal reacted only with a raised brow. "Regardless of faith or denomination, he intends to convert all men of the cloth to soulless undead and unleash them upon the masses. Those of you who dedicated your lives to the salvation of mankind will now become the instruments of its undoing." He allowed a moment for the cardinal to envision this apocalyptic hell. "All of the good works of His church will be twisted into an abomination, an evil bent on nothing more than the destruction of God's own creation.

"Holy water will not harm this creature. Silver will not harm him. A stake through the heart will not harm him...alas, we are not even sure if sunlight will do much more than temporarily burn him." Viktor leaned in and whispered desperately at him, "Only these Holy relics stand a chance at killing him for he is the Sicarii, Judas himself, cursed by God to walk the earth for the traitorous acts that he committed against the Son of the Most High!" The cardinal sat back, his eyes wide and mouth slightly agape as realization sunk in. "The very silver that he received, that you now hold in your vault? That may be our only hope to stop him!"

The cardinal's hand was shaking as he stood and began pacing in his office. "Even if I were to allow this...this *thing* that you ask of me, Viktor...we have only three pieces." The cardinal's mind was racing at the possibilities that lie in store for mankind, for the church...for *him*. "They would surely be missed!"

"I have taken care of that possibility."

The cardinal turned and eyed Viktor cautiously. "And of the other…items that you request?"

"They are taken care of as well."

The cardinal approached Viktor and leaned over his desk, whispering in his ear. "We could both be imprisoned…or worse if we are caught."

"We won't be." Viktor whispered back. He withdrew a velvet cloth and unfolded it inside his coat pocket. The cardinal's eyes grew wide.

"How did you get those?" he whispered excitedly. "They were locked in the inner vaults, they are inventoried regularly, they are…"

"They are replicas," he whispered back. "We replace the originals with these. And note, I only have one coin and one piece of the cross." His eyes displayed so many emotions, sorrow for having to do such a thing, fear for his friend if they were discovered, sadness for what would become of them after he removed them…Cardinal Sardelli knew that it was not something Viktor wanted to do, but rather something he felt he had to do.

The cardinal inhaled deeply and tried to calm himself as he exhaled. He patted Viktor's shoulder. "Then let us do this before I lose my resolve." Viktor nodded and placed the objects back inside his jacket.

The two men worked their way through Vatican City and deep into the bowels of the main bunker under the Sistine Chapel. As they approached the hermetically sealed doors, Viktor allowed the cardinal to take the lead and sign them in to the ledger. The Swiss Guard who maintained the security of the bunker and the secret vault stood at either side at attention.

Both the cardinal and Viktor did their best to act re-laxed and carry on light conversation as they waited for the antechamber to pressurize and the doors to open.

The cardinal walked Viktor through the many shelves and pointed out the different areas of the vault, which Viktor already knew, having spent months re-searching the numerous documents in the vault, but he knew that it was more for show than an education. Viktor also knew where all of the cameras were mounted and that the Swiss Guards manning the mon-itors would be switching from camera to camera to keep both men in view at all times. No matter how mundane the task, one was always under surveillance when in the vault.

Viktor had thought through the next steps thor-oughly. He had brought his notebooks with him and would use them as a diversion to make the switch. When the two got to the area where the relics were, Viktor pulled out his notebook and showed the cardi-nal his sketches. The cardinal nodded and pointed to the shelves where the relics were stored. Viktor knew that the Swiss Guard had eyes on them, but couldn't hear them, and he counted on them reading their body language.

The two men retrieved the relics and positioned themselves so that the cardinal's back blocked the cam-era to his rear and Viktor's back blocked the camera to his rear. He placed the notebook on the counter at the base of the shelves and reached into his jacket, sup-posedly to pull out his reading glasses, and allowed the velvet cloth to drop between the two men onto the notebook.

As the two men went through the motions of smiling and nodding and pointing at the notebook, Viktor made the switch with the piece of wood and carefully wrapped the original back in the velvet. The hard part would be getting it back into his jacket. He placed the silver coin in his notebook and laid the replica on the edge of the counter. He gave the cardinal a signal with his eyes and they allowed the coin to be knocked to the floor. The cardinal made an animated attempt to grab it and then dropped to the floor to retrieve it as Viktor stooped to get it at the same time and slid the velvet cloth back into his jacket. His hopes were that the guard's eyes would be on the dropped coin rather than Viktor.

As Viktor and the cardinal stood, the cardinal held the coin up triumphantly to show Viktor who placed a hand over his heart and exhaled deeply. The men then placed both the replica coin and the replacement chunk of wood in the airtight containers and on to the shelves. Viktor picked up his notebook and allowed the real coin to slide from the pages and into his hand where he deftly slid it into his pocket and allowed it to mix with his spare change and his keys. The two men then walked further into the vault and the cardinal finished the 'tour', pointing out other artifacts and relics and important documents, some of which he took great pains to show Viktor and the two were quite animated as they discussed them, the entire time growing more and more relieved that the Swiss Guard didn't show up to arrest them.

Once the two men felt that they had spent enough time acting in front of the cameras, they slowly made their way back to the doors, lowering their voices and discussing the possible future. "Do you really think that this is the only way to stop the monster?" Cardinal Sardelli asked, his voice low.

"I would not have come had I thought there any other way," Viktor admitted. "And I give you my word that, should we find another way to stop him, I will see the relics returned to their rightful place."

The cardinal shook his head. "The risk is too great, Viktor. Do not attempt to return them. There are others," he said sadly. "Besides, it's not so much the reality of the relics now, but more the perception of them that gives them their power. At least…to the people here."

"Like the shroud of Turin?"

The Cardinal shrugged. "The jury is still out on that one, eh?"

Viktor patted his shoulder and for the first time since he left Thorn, felt that perhaps their side stood a fighting chance. "For what it's worth, I believe it is real."

"I do not care if it is real. I see what it does for the people. It strengthens their faith," Sardelli said as the doors finally opened. "Anything that can strengthen the faith of the people cannot be bad, can it?"

Viktor thought about that for a moment. "As long as one doesn't try to profit from it, then no."

The Cardinal nodded. "I agree." The two men walked back through the doors and the Cardinal signed them out of the vault log. Viktor never made eye contact with the Swiss Guard and the two men walked back to Cardinal Sardelli's office. "This is where I say goodbye, my friend."

"Thank you, Angelo." Viktor reached for his hand, "I know this hasn't been easy for you."

Sardelli pulled him into a hug and kissed his cheeks. "It was good seeing you again."

"And you," Viktor replied emotionally.

"Next time, let's just do lunch, okay? My heart cannot take such excitement."

Viktor chuckled as he headed back to his rental car.

Maxwell had tried to remain calm while Natashia recited the events that had taken place during his absence from the pack. He fought the urge to scream more than once and he noticed that Nadia seemed to be in a form of stupor as she lay back on the couch, drifting in and out of near sleep. Natashia tried to be brief, but he urged details from her about how his wife, Victoria had banished their son and his family, including his entire entourage from their pack and had given them over to serve as indentured servants to a *vampire*!

Maxwell had given up his desire to be a warrior and decided instead to follow a meeker path, a path of righteousness…a path that drove a wedge between his son and himself, but that did not mean that his son deserved to become a slave to a bloodsucker. He wanted to rush back to the pack and confront Victoria, but when he left, he put her in charge as she was his second, but only until she felt that Viktor was strong enough to lead. That time should have come a long time ago. All this time he thought that his son was leading the pack, only to find out this…

Then Natashia told him the reason for them coming to him now. The threat of the Sicarii, the need to find this Roman guard, the first father of the werewolves, this Claudius Veranus. Maxwell's eyes widened as she went on about how the vampire that her family served only fed on livestock and had entered into an agreement with these humans that hunt monsters to protect the world from supernatural creatures that would harm them. How the hunters just found out that the secret to their own strength came from a virus in the werewolves and that his own granddaughter was now mated to one of them.

Maxwell's head was spinning as she went on and on, and he had to fight to keep up. Finally, he held up his hand to stop her. "So you're here to find an ancient Roman guard? Claudius…somebody?"

"Yes," she said, still averting her eyes from him. She didn't feel worthy of speaking with him. He was still technically the grand master of the pack and they had been excommunicated. "Monsieur Thorn feels that he may well be the key to our victory."

Maxwell sighed. "Then you're probably screwed."

"How so?" she asked.

Maxwell shook his head. "He's been dead for...centuries," he said matter-of-factly.

Natashia gasped. "No! This cannot be!" She choked back a sob.

"I'm afraid so."

"But, he is the father of all wolves. If he died, then all wolves would die with him."

Maxwell shook his head. "No, that's a misconception. If he had been *killed*, then...perhaps. Maybe. But he died of natural causes," he explained. "Old age. I mean, come on...the geezer would have been over two thousand years old!"

"But...we do not age hardly at all over centuries and surely..."

"Hey, sweetheart, we're not immortal. You're thinking of vampires. The reason they don't age is because they're *dead*. Dead flesh can't age. But us? Hell, we still live. We age. We just age at a much slower rate," he explained. "We are most definitely NOT immortal."

Her eyes darted about as she considered his reasoning. Her breath came in short gulps as she realized that their best shot at stopping the monster was lost. Her eyes began to tear and she wiped at them as best as she could, but her vision continued to grow fuzzy.

Nadia awoke and sat up, shaking her head slowly. "What happened to me?"

"I think you got light-headed. Probably from the pregnancy," Maxwell offered. "Would you like a drink of water or something?"

She looked at him and it took a moment for her to remember who he was. "You're my grandfather."

100

"Maxwell," he corrected.

Then she remembered. "Oh yes. That's right. The asshole." She glared at him.

Maxwell glared back at her. "Excuse me?"

"I may have been trained classically, but I'm mated to a military man. I do know how to curse, thank you." She looked at her mother and saw the state she was in. "Mother?"

"I'm okay, darling. But I think we need to be leaving now. Our journey has come to an end," Natashia said softly.

"I do not think so." Nadia turned to Maxwell, "Where is the Roman guard?"

"Dead."

"Show me his body," she demanded.

Maxwell shook his head. "What?"

"You heard me, old man. Show me where he is buried," she demanded, her hands planted firmly on her hips.

"Nadia! You do not speak to him in such a manner," Natashia hissed.

"I will speak to him however I wish, Mother," she shot back. "He is a coward. He hides here in the shadows of his church while *true* wolves prepare to defend their packs. Lycans, true of heart, ready to die if need be, prepare to do battle against a foe so powerful that most would rather hide than stand against him. And he only has the courage to hide in France and paint? Perhaps growl at a few stray women?" she spat.

"Forgive her, Maxwell!" Natashia pleaded. "She has no idea!"

Maxwell stared at Nadia for a moment then looked down at Natashia. He shook his head and chuckled. "She is so much like her father, isn't she?"

"They are both like you used to be," Natashia replied.

"That was a long time ago," he said softly, reminiscing.

"Mother, what are you saying? I thought he was a holy man?" Nadia asked.

"Nadia...your grandfather...he is the *founder* of the Lycans. He is the one who laid the groundwork, made the rules...he is the one who set the standards."

Nadia turned to him, open agape. "You were a Lycan?" she whispered.

"Were?" Maxwell repeated. "Once a Lycan, always a Lycan, little pup."

"No four wolves could defeat your grandfather in his day," Natashia said with honest awe. "He was a most fearsome fighter."

"Only four? How the mighty have fallen over time." Maxwell laughed. "Usually over time, one's heroics are heralded and their triumphs grow larger!"

Natashia gave a nervous laugh. "Fine then, no *five* wolves could defeat you. Perhaps six even!"

"Why not make it eight!" Maxwell shouted.

Nadia stood with her hands on her hips and eyed him. True, he was large and imposing; and yes, his strength was fierce, but was he truly as great as her mother let on? She acted as though he could best her father and Nadia just couldn't imagine *any* wolf capable of that. "Was he as good as father?" she asked.

"As good?" Maxwell asked. "Who do you think taught him?"

"I'm sure he's learned much more since then," Nadia stated.

Maxwell nodded. "I'm sure he has."

"Too bad you gave it all up to become...a painters" she spat.

Maxwell stiffened. "Careful there, pup. You're treading in places where you ought not to go."

"Or what? I, myself am a Lycan of the Third Order. My father taught me," she said. "I don't see him running away from his family to...paint."

Maxwell squared off and crossed his arms again. He eyed his brazen young granddaughter. "No, he just runs from his bitch-mother rather than challenge her authority, and becomes a slave to a *vampire!*" he shot back at her.

Nadia seemed unfazed by his insult. "Rufus has been very kind to us."

"She has known nothing but the island, Maxwell," Natashia explained.

He grunted his disapproval. "And yet you come here looking for my help."

"Only to find the Roman," she shot back. "A man of *honor*."

"Honor! What would you know of honor?" he spat. "You know nothing of this Roman! You know only of rumor and fairy tales!"

"I know that he was a warrior. And warriors rise to the occasion!" she yelled back at him. "We need a true warrior now to help lead our people to victory."

Maxwell stared at her, his eyes piercing her, but she never backed down. Her chest heaved and her arms flexed and her heart pounded in her chest as she fought the urge to scream, but she never flinched. He admired her tenacity and her bravery, even if he felt her actions were foolhardy. "And what would you say to this Roman if you were to find him?"

"I would ask him to rise up and lead his people. I would ask him to take his rightful place as the leader of the wolves. I would ask him to lift his shield and his spear one more time in the name of all that is right and honorable and defend those who are weaker against an enemy who is bent on destroying everything in his path!" she yelled. "I would ask him to do the right thing! For mankind. For wolves throughout the world. For glory! For God!" she screamed so loud her voice was growing hoarse. "I would beg him to unite our people and lead them through the darkness and back into the light! I would beg him to shake off the yoke of centuries of dust from hiding in the shadows of history and step forth and make himself known and take his rightful place as the Lycan of all Lycans!" Tears were running down her face now as she shook her fists at him, her voice cracking with emotion.

Drained and broken, she wept. "I'd beg him to save the world so that I might raise my child in a place free of oppression from a force of darkness so frightful that I haven't slept in…" she lifted her red eyes to him and the sadness nearly broke his heart, "I can't re-member how long. The visions are so horrible…" She broke down and sobbed.

104

Maxwell stepped forward and embraced her. He looked to Natashia who was wiping away her own tears. "She's missing her true place, you know. She should be a politician or an orator," he said with a slight smile.

Nadia pulled away from him, "For the love of my child, do not mock me

"I'm not mocking you, pup," Maxwell soothed. "That was a helluva speech. Gave me goose bumps and everything."

Nadia shook her head and buried her face in her hands. Maxwell rubbed at her back. "There now. Calm yourself," he said. "You did good, pup." He felt her relax slightly in his arms. "You've got your Roman."

It took Nadia a moment to register what he said. She lifted her head and looked to him. "You'll take us to him?"

Maxwell shook his head. "No, I won't." Nadia's face twisted in confusion. "I'm right here. *I* am Claudius Maximus Veranus."

Mitchell escorted General McAfee through the hangar and pointed out the various stations and personnel, describing their duties and the work going on at each one. The general didn't seem too impressed at

the moment. Mitchell worked his way to the elevators and, rather than take him down level by level, went straight for Dr. Peter's laboratory.

Matt had the foresight to contact Laura and inform her of their visitor and she made arrangements for the general's visit. Evan was waiting and ready for the general as well. He had a little trick up his sleeve should the general refuse to accept the truth.

Thorn had retired for the day, but Evan was still working on his retired weapon project for the upcoming battle and had electronics and schematics scattered throughout his lab when Mitchell and General McAfee showed up. "Dr. Peters, I'd like you to meet someone," Matt said as they entered his workspace.

"One moment, Colonel…" Evan was digging through his workbench looking for something and was growing agitated that he couldn't find it. Finally he emerged from under a pile of electronics with a silicon chip clamped in his fingers. "Got it!" He placed it gingerly on the green board he had been working on, then turned and addressed the pair. "General McAfee, I presume?" He stuck his hand out in greeting.

The general grasped it, then withdrew quickly. "Good heavens. Your skin is ice cold."

Evan looked at his hand a moment then answered awkwardly, "Um, yes, General, it's because my flesh is technically dead." Then he quickly corrected himself, "Or, *undead* depending on how you look at things." He smiled sheepishly at the man.

The general leaned in and looked at Evan's smile. "I don't see fangs, Colonel."

106

"They only extend as a defensive move or when feeding, sir," Mitchell informed him.

The general nodded. "May I see them?" he asked.

Evan seemed a bit embarrassed and would have blushed had he been capable. "I suppose so. Give me a moment, sir." He seemed to concentrate a bit and tried to extend his fangs, but they failed to do so on command.

"Bit of a problem there, son?" the general asked, a bit annoyed.

Evan tried to act as though it was a common occurrence for the fangs to not extend on command, but he hated having 'performance issues'. "I apologize, General. It's not like I practice extending my fangs on a regular basis. I so rarely use them."

The general nodded. "Defensive use?" he asked. Mitchell nodded. The general turned to leave then suddenly picked up a screwdriver from the workbench and brought it up in a striking position and screamed at Evan as if he were about to attack.

Evan threw an arm up and crouched, his fangs extending automatically and his eyes bled out their color to a pale white in a reflexive move. The general slowly withdrew and lowered the screwdriver. Evan slowly stood, touching his tongue to the tips of the fangs. He never really cared for the pointy things, but...there they were. He stood slowly and opened his mouth for the general to get a better look.

General McAfee closed in and peered carefully in Evan's mouth. "A lot bigger than I would have thought. Pointy as hell, too. Looks like it would really tear your mouth up when those things drop down," he mumbled. He finally looked at Evan and truly addressed him. "Does it hurt when that happens?"

"No, sir. I don't really feel it at all. It just feels like I have something stuck in my upper lip a bit and—"

"Okay, Mitchell, show me more," McAfee said, cutting Evan off.

As the two walked away, Matt shot Evan an apologetic look and Evan felt, for just a moment, worse than a second class citizen. The realization of his situation set in on him again and he heaved a sigh. He felt his fangs recede back into their pocket and his vision restored to normal as he contemplated his fate. It was one thing to live it daily. Laura and Matt did their best to accommodate his needs, and he appreciated what they did for him. He did his best to adjust and he worked tirelessly to develop weapons to help them in their fight against all kinds of monsters. All the while, he worked to find a cure to the virus that robbed him of his humanity. But when someone like this general comes in and talks to him like this, like he was a lab animal, a test monkey…it just brought home the pain and loneliness that he felt all the time and refused to deal with. He realized that it stripped him of the one thing that he had been clinging to…hope. Hope for a cure, hope for a way back to being human. Hope to be normal. Hope to be able to walk in the sun again. Hope to love and be loved. Just…hope.

He turned and saw Mitchell and McAfee work their way across and over to the training area. For the briefest of moments, he wondered if Mitchell would tell the man about the augmentation and the fact that the squad members were genetically altered to be werewolves, but then, he already knew the answer to that one. Why would he? They could pass for human. He felt forlorn and wanted to give in when Laura walked by and gave him a wink. He smiled at her and she smiled back and that small little gesture, that single act of kindness, borne not of necessity, but out of love brought him back from his edge of despair and reminded him why he was doing everything he was doing. It didn't matter if there were people like McAfee out there. He had people like Mitchell and Thompson and Apollo and Donovan and…well, all of the team members who treated him like a person. And then there was Laura who genuinely cared about him. Despite his awkwardness with women, she loved him for who he was.

His condition didn't have to be a handicap, it could be a strength; and he would use his strength to better the squads and make for a more efficient team. With renewed vigor he set himself back to task and refocused on the project at hand, a smile crossing his face and a song in his heart…his cold, dead, shriveled heart that no longer pumped blood except after he fed.

As the first rays of sunlight broke across the mountains, Lamb woke Jack and Jacobs. They were afraid to wake Tufo because his woodland Sprite was sleeping on his shoulder and nobody wanted to get bit.

109

Bennie had slipped off during the night, presumably to go back to his own people, so they couldn't talk him into shaking Tufo awake. The man snored like a chainsaw and they didn't know how the little Sprite could sleep through all the noise.

Finally, Jack found a stick and poked Tufo awake with it. The Sprite on his shoulder wasn't very happy about it, but nobody got bit and all of the members were up and about. Donovan trudged back down the ridge and reported that the way to the Greater Elves was littered with rock and would be a rough trek. The team packed their gear and set out along the crest of the ridge, trying to keep the area in view so as not to lose sight of it to the woods surrounding them.

Tufo occasionally swatted at the Sprite as she buzzed around his head or flittered too close to his ear. "Damn, I wish she'd go away."

"I think she has a crush on you, Gunny," Jacobs teased.

"Oh, she has more than a crush," Donnie agreed.

"What's that supposed to mean?" Mark shot at him, annoyance more than evident in his voice.

"She thinks you belong to her now," Donnie informed him. "Or, vice versa, I'm not exactly sure how that works."

"Great," Tufo muttered as they marched along. "I'm a pet to Tinkerbelle."

As Lamb passed the Gunnery Sergeant he quietly said, "Maybe if you're nice to her and learn a few tricks, she'll give you a treat." Mark shot him a hateful glare. "Maybe she'll even rub your tummy," he added with a snicker.

110

"Alright, knock it off," Thompson barked. "We only have about five clicks to go, let's try to do it a little quieter. We don't want to scare the Greater Elves any more than we have to."

"Oh, you'll not scare us," a voice to his left said.

Jack nearly jumped out of his skin. He neither smelled nor heard the elf as they approached his position and the man had been standing against a tree, nearly perfectly camouflaged. They all had to do a double take to notice him and he didn't truly come into focus until he pushed away from the tree and his body lines separated from the foliage surrounding him. It was almost a chameleon effect as he moved and his skin changed color to something closer to human.

"You're far too noisy to sneak up on us, that's for sure."

Each of the team members assessed the elf as he stepped toward them. At first glance, he appeared like a Native American with a loin cloth and long hair pulled back into a loose pony tail, except his hair was nearly snow white, his eyes a crystal blue and his skin almost glowed a golden color when he wasn't camouflaged. He was nearly the height of a human at almost six feet tall and he carried a handmade spear and a bow with a quiver of arrows across his back. "I am Horith of the Greater Elves of the North," he said, holding his right hand high and empty. He pointed behind the team with his spear, "That is my brother, Kalen." Jack quickly turned and saw the mirror image of Horith standing on his other side against another large tree, appearing bored. The elf peered up from a knife he was sharpening and simply nodded. "We were

111

about to start a ritual hunt when we heard you out here scaring away the game, so we thought we'd come and find out why you were stomping about in our woods."

Before Jack could answer, Kalen stepped from his tree and stated his mind, his voice slightly deeper than Horith's, but it was still clear that they were related, "You're obviously not hunters, and it doesn't appear that you're here to camp." He pointed to the automatic weapons they carried. "I don't believe those are actually legal in this country, are they?"

Jack smiled at the two elves. "We're military. And these?" He held up the carbine and showed it to them. "Are approved by the Canadian government for us to use. We're actually Americans, but we have an agreement with this country." Jack shook his head. "Look, fellas, we're actually here to find your people."

"I gathered as much." Horith eyed Jack cautiously. "But I'm not so sure I want to be bringing you to my people. I hear stories of people like you. Tromping through the woods hoping for nothing better than to kill one of us."

"And there's not many of us left," his brother added.

"We're not here to kill anybody," Jack tried to argue.

"Uh, Chief," Tufo interrupted.

"Not now, Gunny," Jack shot back through the side of his mouth.

"No, Chief." Lamb said, nudging him. "We're surrounded. And they don't look happy."

Jack turned and peered over his shoulder. All through the woods, around trees, up in branches, behind rocks, arrows were pointed at them, eyes peered from between leaves, spears jutted out of brush, and yet none of them had heard or smelled a thing.

"Look... Horith, was it? We came here to speak to your tribal chief or village elder or...hell, whoever it is that is in charge."

"I imagine you did," he said, looking slightly put off for having to waste his time with the human.

Tufo stepped up and stuck his hand out. "Mark Tufo, ex-Marine Gunnery Sergeant." He stood there with his hand extended, waiting for the elf to take it. The elf looked at him with a puzzled look. Mark raised an eyebrow. "You extend *your* hand the same way, like this." Mark waited and Jack watched until the elf finally extended a hand tentatively. Mark slowly grasped it and shook it. "This is how we make a 'formal introduction' when we haven't met somebody before and mean them no harm," Mark said.

"Now, I know this may look a little... 'off' to you. A bunch of military men marching through your hunting ground carrying guns and when we find you, we just say, 'take us to your leader', but the truth of the matter is, there is a huge shit-storm coming. Like *end of the world* HUGE, and we are trying to reach out to all the different...people that we know of to see if they can offer any kind of help in dealing with this thing." Mark never broke eye contact with the light-haired elf. Finally, he turned and, with a sweep of his arm, he indicated all of the other elves. "The evil that is coming will affect ALL of you!" he shouted. He turned back to Horith. "Now, if you guys aren't up to helping us defend against this thing...fine. We'll turn around and go home. But if you are? Then we could really use your help. And all of this posturing isn't going to get either of us what we need any faster." He studied the elf's face and couldn't read a thing.

Jack leaned forward and whispered, "You were doing pretty good there until the very end. I think you may have blown it, buddy."

"Thanks for the critique," Mark whispered back.

Horith nodded to the elves in the woods and they stepped out, lowering their weapons. "Come, let us speak of this great evil." He turned and began walking in the direction the team was originally headed. "Many of our elders have had visions of a darkness falling on all the lands. I believe maybe this is the evil you speak of."

Jack fell into step alongside Horith, with Kalen behind him. "I would bet money on it." Jack said. "I've spoken to a few people with the gift of sight and they all have been seeing something like what you're telling me about."

"Do you know what this darkness is?" Horith asked.

"A vampire. A very powerful vampire with an army behind him large enough to destroy anything that gets in his way," Jack said.

Horith paused and stared at him. "You *do* realize that vampires crave Elven blood, yes?"

"Yes. Elf and faerie blood does pretty weird things to vampires from what I understand."

Horith continued along a path that only he could truly see, but he agreed, "Vampires are evil creatures."

"For the most part, yeah, they are." Jack couldn't help but think of Thorn and Dr. Peters. Although they were technically vampires, he couldn't bring himself to actually think of them as 'evil'. "But there are a few that aren't so bad," he muttered.

Horith shot him a strange look that he couldn't quite read. "There is no such thing. ALL vampires are bad," Horith stated. "If I had the power to remove them all from creation, I would."

Jack simply nodded. Better not to piss off the elf. At least not until they were truly allies.

7

Dominic actually slept a bit, but his sleep was fitful. The images that the dark vampire injected into his mind kept coming back to haunt him and he'd wake from his slumber in a cold sweat on the verge of a scream. He'd jerk awake and realize that the images weren't real, weren't his own, fight to recognize where he was, then relax again and fight to calm himself. He'd eventually fall back asleep and start the cycle all over again. The room was completely dark save for the small oil lamp that had been lit and turned very low, acting as little more than a nightlight. At one time, he went into the lavatory and washed his face, relieved himself, drank from the tap and then crawled back to the mattress to try to sleep again.

When the door opened again, Dom barely registered who entered, but they brought food and drink into the room and set it on the table next to the lamp. Later, long after it had cooled and he had tired of trying to sleep, he picked through it and ate what he could then laid back on the mattress and simply thought of how best to deal with his situation.

When left alone with nothing but your thoughts and the countless horrifying images of a madman, time drags its feet. He didn't know if he had been in the room for days or hours. But when the door opened again and the dark vampire entered, he almost welcomed the company.

Almost.

"Are you feeling rested, Dominic?" he asked as he entered and shut the door behind him.

"As rested as I can be with the crap you shoved in my head." Dom held his arm over his eyes, as if he could prevent the images from drilling back into his mind.

"Good. I had hoped that you would be more cooperative after a meal and a good day's sleep."

"How long have I been in here?"

"Oh, I am not sure an exact time. Perhaps, nine or ten hours," the vampire replied.

Dom moaned. It had felt like days. He grunted as he sat up. "If this is some new form of torture, I think it's working," he moaned, his body still aching from the beating.

"Torture? I think not. Food and rest are not torture."

"Shoving those images into anybody's head and then locking them up alone to deal with them over and over and over again, yeah, that's torture." Dom finally forced himself to look at the vampire.

"You are a big boy. I believe you can handle it." He replied. "Besides, it is nothing compared to what is about to happen to the rest of the world. And you, my dear Dominic, will have a front row seat for the event."

"Joy," Dom deadpanned.

"You are ready to cooperate now, yes?"

"I've already told you everything I know."

"Somehow I doubt this," the vampire replied. "I need to know details."

"About?"

"Everything."

"Okay. Well, my mom's name was Ethel. My dad's name was Charlie," Dom began. "I grew up on this street in Jersey where everybody knew everybody, ya know? Mr. Angelo used to let us play baseball in his backyard and Mrs. Angelo used to make the *best* apple pie every fall. Oh, my God, you should have tasted—"

"ENOUGH!" the vampire growled. "You know what I am speaking of, Mr. DeGiacomo, and toying with me can only bring you more pain."

Dom eyed the vampire and debated messing with him further. "Dude, you're going to need to be more specific. You told me 'everything' so that's what I was doing." Dom gave him a defeated look.

The dark vampire opened a door and motioned in two of his underlings. They brought in two wooden chairs and set them near the small table then left without saying a word. The dark vampire sat at the table and motioned for Dom to join him. Dom made a slow move to get up and dragged himself to the chair. When he sat down he hung his head. "Okay, dude. You ask, I answer," he groaned. "What do you want to know?"

"Let us begin with the squad itself. I want names and weaknesses."

"Weaknesses?" Dom asked, not truly understanding.

"Yes. Weaknesses. Do any of them have a love interest? Family? Very good friends?"

"What the fuck does that matter?" Dom sat up straighter and glared at the vampire. It was one thing to threaten the entire world, but to attempt to target an operator's family? That was just dirty play.

"Just answer the question."

"Then, no. None of them have family, love interests or—"

"You forget that I can taste your lies, Mr. DeGiacomo," the vampire hissed at him. "Let us try again." He stared at Dom whose jaw was clenched so tight that he feared his teeth might actually break. "Do any of them have family?"

Dom was so angry that he was shaking, but he could feel the vampire *pulling* the answer from him. "Y-yes."

The vampire nodded. "Very good." The bastard actually smiled at him. "Do any of them have a 'love interest'?"

Dom's entire body shook and he could feel his muscles cramping as he fought not to tell him, but the answer spilled out of him against his will yet again, "Y-yes."

"Excellent." The vampire clapped his hands together. "Isn't this fun?!" he exclaimed.

"Go fuck yourself you crazy son of a bitch!" Dom spat, realizing that he couldn't even move his hands now.

"Oh, Mr. DeGiacomo, we have many more questions to go. It will be much easier on you if you do not struggle."

"And I liked you better when you were suicidal," Dom moaned.

119

Laura Youngblood scrambled with the daily reports then checked in with the duty officers, she signed off on the call logs then double checked for any initial reports. The daily grind was starting to wear on her and she was really wishing that Mitchell would hurry up and dump the visiting General and pick up some of the slack. She was stopping to slam her fourth cup of coffee when she saw Mitchell and McAfee drop into the training area. She stood above the area on the catwalk outside their offices and observed as Mitchell escorted the man through the different training areas. She was about to turn and leave when she felt a presence behind her. She glanced behind her and saw Rufus Thorn standing slightly behind her, observing the two men as she had been.

"Who is this?" he inquired.

"That is General McAfee. He's in charge of the base we need. From what Matt tells me, he needed convincing that vampires are real and that the threat is valid enough before he'll sign off on letting us have Groom Lake."

Thorn watched the two men stoically. After a few moments he turned to Laura and excused himself. "I have things to prepare before Viktor returns. If you will excuse me." He silently slipped past her and disappeared down the hallway. She only watched for a moment more before slipping away herself and sneaking to Evan's lab. Her duties could wait for a few more moments while she recharged her emotional batteries.

She found Evan diligently working on one of his projects and his attention focused solely on the tasks at hand as she snuck up the steps to his work station. She picked up an electronic component and eyed it curiously. "Looks like this square peg needs to fit in that round hole," she commented, not really knowing what she was talking about.

She watched him jump slightly, obviously startled out of his deep thoughts. "You scared me," he said sheepishly.

"Boo, you big bad vampire," she teased.

He set the soldering iron down that he was holding and took off his goggles. "Well, I probably would have smelled you coming if it weren't for the smoke from the solder."

She feigned shock at his comment. "I'll have you know that I shower quite regularly!" as she fake punched him in the arm.

Evan almost panicked. "No! I meant, I would smell your *perfume*!" he backtracked. "I mean, I could probably also smell your scent, if I tried hard enough, but..." he stopped himself and then glanced away. "I'm just burying myself deeper, aren't I?"

She stifled a grin. "Oh, yes you are. Much deeper," she teased again.

Evan plopped into his chair and threw his arms up in surrender. "Leave it to me. If there's a way to stick my foot in my mouth, I'll find it," he said. "And with fangs like these, once that foot is in there, it's a bitch to get it back out." He gave her an impish smile.

Laura sidled up to him and wrapped her arms around his neck. "I think I can find it *deep down inside* to forgive you," she purred.

"You can?" he asked hopefully. "And you won't have to use me for my body to do it?"

"Oh, a gentleman never reminds a lady of such events," she whispered in his ear causing a tremor to rock him through his chest. If Evan didn't know better, he'd think that his heart was trying to beat so that it could SKIP a beat.

"My apologies, miss," he whispered back. "I guess I'm a bit rusty on the ways of treating a lady."

Laura lowered herself so that her mouth hovered right above his and her lips barely brushed his own as she spoke. He could feel the heat of her breath against his cold flesh as her words slipped from her. "I think we can take the time to refresh your memory, young man."

He swallowed hard and leaned ever so slightly forward, allowing his lips to slightly brush hers. "It might take a while...I'm *very rusty.*"

She fought the urge to smile at their playful teasing. "I'm sure we can get you...UN-rusted." Her lips brushed his and her tongue slipped out and tasted his lips for a brief moment. He inhaled sharply and she felt his arms wrap around her middle, slowly pulling her to his lap. She lowered herself so that she was sitting in his lap facing him. "Why, Dr. Peters, are you about to take advantage of me?" she asked in her best little girl voice.

"I certainly hope so," Evan said softly.

Their mouths finally found each other and his fangs slowly descended as they kissed. It wasn't the first time this had happened, but rather than push her away and beg her forgiveness this time, he pulled her closer and she gently probed his mouth with her tongue. She slipped her tongue between his fangs, avoiding the sharp tips, excitement coursing through her veins knowing the added danger of what was in his kiss. She felt his excitement grow not just in his mouth and she wiggled her hips to add to both of their pleasure.

Evan brought his hands up her back and pulled the pencil she had used to hold her long dark hair up and allowed it to cascade down her back. Her ran his fingers through the silky strands and felt her heart race in her chest as her excitement grew. Finally she pulled back and sucked in a deep breath. "Oh, wow."

Her breaths came in deep pants and she stared intently at his mouth, his eyes, the angle of his jaw. "Tell me you love me," she whispered.

"I love you," he obliged as he pulled her back to him and kissed her again.

From the other side of the area Hank and Maria exited the gym, covered in sweat, practice swords in hand. They spotted Laura and Evan in their lover's embrace. Hank quickly grabbed Maria's arm and held a finger to his mouth to silence her.

He whispered to her, "Even the soulless need love." And they quietly exited back the way they came. They could go the long way around to the showers.

123

Nadia stared at her grandfather with teary eyes, confusion muddying her thoughts. "Why do you say such things, grandfather?" she finally managed. "Please, if you will not help us, then do not try to deter us."

Natashia sat upright on the couch and stared intently at Maxwell, studying his body language. She could not smell a lie upon him, and yet...

"Young pup, hear me," Maxwell's deep voice felt like smooth silk as it flowed from him. "I am Claudius Maximus Veranus." His eyes penetrated her as he spoke and Nadia felt the urge to drop to one knee before him, but she could not explain why.

"My liege," Natashia whispered as she fell from the couch to the floor.

Maxwell sighed at her, "Tasha, get up. I'm still your father-in-law." But she lay on the ground, quivering.

"I don't understand, grandfather. You said that he was dead," Nadia said. "But now you say that you are he...you speak in circles."

Maxwell led her to the couch across from where Natashia lay prostrate on the floor. He sat with Nadia and tried to explain. "Little pup, Claudius Veranus is a name long since dead," he began. "So, in essence, the man is as well. I gave up the name because the myth…or, the legend had grown so large over time that wolves the world over thought of me as a god or, rather, something larger than life." He looked her square in the eye. "Do I appear to be a god to you?"

Nadia pulled back and studied him. "No," she replied honestly. "A confused old man, perhaps, but not a god."

Maxwell was taken aback by her honesty, but he suddenly burst into laughter. "I like this pup, Tasha! She speaks her thoughts exactly as she thinks them!" He continued to laugh for a moment longer then grasped Nadia's hand. "Oh, little pup, you are a breath of fresh air. What I wouldn't have given to have had you around here all these years."

"Perhaps if you had made yourself available, I could have been," she said rather sharply.

"What?" Again, Maxwell was taken off guard. "Oh, yes. Well, you do have a point there." He nodded.

"Tell me more of why you are no longer Claudius Veranus," she urged.

Maxwell nodded. "As I said, many wolves saw me as…well, something I wasn't. And, to be honest, I was simply sick of all the politics and the backbiting and the fighting and…" He shook his head. "I needed a break from it all. I wanted *peace*. So I turned to what I knew was truth.

"Tell me something, pup." He stood and walked to his window, pointing out to the church beyond. "Do you know the difference between faith and knowledge?"

"Of course."

"Truly?"

"Faith is based on trust. Knowledge is based on truth."

Maxwell smiled. "The benefits of a classical education. Perhaps your father was not as foolish as I thought."

Her face hardened at his comment.

"Oh, don't get your knickers in a twist, pup. Your answer is correct," Maxwell said. "And I turned to what I knew was *truth*. I turned to Him." He pointed upward.

"You turned to the church?" she asked.

"No! Not the church, to God!" he said. "The church is run by men and men are corruptible. God is pure."

She appeared puzzled, still unsure of what he was getting at.

"Pup, I could sit here all day and discuss different theological dogmas, but that doesn't mean that any one of them are more correct than the other. Each man must interpret the word as it reveals itself to him."

"You gave up on your people and devoted yourself to studying the word of God?"

"Not just the word, but the works, the creation...everything!"

Nadia shook her head. "Your people needed you more at this time than any other and you turned your back on them," she whispered.

"Viktor was supposed to lead them. His mother was supposed to hand over leadership to him when he was ready."

"She sold him into slavery," Nadia said. "Because she didn't want to give up the power that you left to her. And because he would not rise up against his own mother, my father abided by her banishment order," she spat. "He lives in dishonor amongst the other pack members because his mother is a power hungry bitch."

"Easily remedied," he replied with a sly grin.

"And what of Claudius Veranus? Will he return with us to face the Sicarii? Or will Maxwell Verissimo continue to sit in his Vicker's house and study the works of God?" she asked bitterly.

Maxwell turned to her. "The Sicarii?" he turned and stared daggers at Natashia who was still laying prostrate on the floor. No wonder she was not acting herself. No...she couldn't have known their past history. Perhaps Nadia's pregnancy was affecting her mother? The hormones were somehow affecting Tasha? Perhaps Tasha had simply lost her mind?

"Yes, the vampire who is raising an army to destroy the world calls himself the Sicarii. Does that name have meaning to you?"

Maxwell nodded. "Oh, I am very well aware of who and what the Sicarii is." A deep grumbling growl escaped his throat. "I'm the one who cut him down from the tree."

"So you will return with us? As Claudius Veranus?" she asked hopefully.

Maxwell stood and took her hand, helping her to her feet. He walked through his house and to the far side of the structure. He pushed a large, heavy wooden bookshelf aside and slid a portion of the wall back, revealing a small hidden room behind it. Nadia peered inside and saw what lay hidden in the darkness. Her grandfather's breastplate, helmet, shield and spear...the Spear of Destiny.

He withdrew the items and placed them on his bed. They were covered with centuries of dust. "I haven't worn these in so long. I swore I never would again."

"Why?"

He looked at her wondering eyes. He knew that she was trained to lust for battle as all Lycans were. She was taught from a young age that to die in battle was a glorious thing, just as he had been when he was young. But he had once had his eyes opened, standing upon a hill over two thousand years ago when he pierced the side of a young Jewish carpenter who had been sentenced to death on the cross. Right after he pierced his side, the earth shook and the mountain itself split like an overripe melon. The clouds that darkened the sky and the winds that blew that day left no doubt in his mind that this Jewish carpenter was no ordinary man. People had spread rumors that He was the Son of God, and after that day, Claudius KNEW, those rumors were true.

It's a strange thing to not have faith, but knowledge. People around the world held their faith as a very dear and treasured thing, but Claudius never had that luxury. To him, he only had knowledge. Knowledge and the damnation of the Father who touched him for defiling the body of the Son with his Roman spear while He hung lifeless on the cross.

But after centuries of torment, Claudius turned to the very religions that he had despised. He studied them all and he learned something…you cannot have evil without a good to balance it. You must have a Yin for Yang. For Satan to exist there must be a Christ. In order for there to be a Hell, you must have a Heaven. There must be a polar opposite…there must be *balance*. Therefore, in order for there to be a Judas, there had to be a Claudius. The Sicarii needed a Sentinel. And Maxwell Verissimo chose his last name well, for it meant 'He who affirms the truth'.

So when Maxwell stared into the wondering eyes of his granddaughter who asked him why he swore to never wear the armor and shield of Rome again, he could not lie to her. "Because Rome was an evil empire that raped, plundered and pillaged its way across a continent…and I swore to never be a part of that again."

Nadia nodded and reached out to hold his hand. "You do not wear your armor and bear your shield in honor of Rome, grandfather. You do so in honor of yourself and Lycans throughout the world." She squeezed his hand and brought it to bear on his spear. "This is *your* weapon, not Rome's. It is he who wields the weapon, not they who forged it that shall be re-membered once the dust is settled on the battlefield."

Maxwell smiled at his granddaughter and it spread all the way to his eyes. "How is it that a pup as young as yourself could be so wise?"

"Father says I have an old soul," she replied quietly.

Maxwell pulled her into an embrace. "I think you simply have a very smart father." And Nadia felt a

129

warming run through her heart that she'd not felt in a very long time.

"Mitchell, I've seen everything I need to see. You run one hell of an operation," General McAfee said.

"So you plan to release Groom Lake to us?" Matt asked hopefully.

"I'll make the call when I get back to D.C."

Matt breathed a sigh of relief. "Thank you, General. Your actions may well be what saves mankind," he said somberly.

"Don't paint me as a saint, Mitchell. I said I'd do it. I didn't say I'd like it," McAfee told him. "The base commander out there is a Colonel Anderson. He's an up and comer. Academy man. Looking to get his star quick."

Matt nodded, understanding exactly what the general was telling him.

"Don't misunderstand me, Mitchell. Anderson's straight as an arrow, but he's still a good man. Try not to bruise his ego too much."

"As I said in D.C., General, I'm not looking to try to take over for good, I just need to borrow the area for a bit. If he can secure any kind of classified operations—"

"Classified operations?" the general interrupted. "Mitchell, the entire *base* is classified! They'll be lucky

130

if they can shove enough classified projects into secure hangars so that you and your people will have usable space!"

Mitchell nodded. "Well, sir, anything we can do to assist, we will most certainly do it."

McAfee nodded. "I'll have him call you. But, you might prepare yourself. I doubt seriously that he's going to be happy about any of this."

"I'm sure he won't."

Matt escorted the general to a waiting Humvee and had Spalding drive him to Will Rogers International Airport so that he could fly in comfort back to D.C. Matt grabbed his two-way radio and keyed it for Laura Youngblood. "XO, come in."

It took Laura a bit to answer her radio and she sounded a bit breathless when she responded. "Go ahead, Colonel."

Matt stared at the radio a second before he responded. "We're a 'go' for Groom Lake. We need to start making plans for packing up and bugging out. What's your twenty?"

"I'm uh...in my office. I'm going over a few weapons designs with Dr. Peters and...I can meet you somewhere?"

Matt smiled to himself then chuckled. "My office in twenty minutes." He thought about it a moment then came back on the radio. "Make it thirty minutes. Over."

"Your office. Thirty minutes. Copy, sir." *Your welcome, Ms. Youngblood,* Matt thought as he put his radio away.

First Squad walked with the Greater Elves through the massive forest with Horith and Kalen alternating being the lead. Jack had tried to drum up conversation a couple of times to no use with Kalen who seemed to be more interested in the Sprite flitting around Tufo. Finally Jack asked Horith, "Is he always so chatty?"

Horith shook his head. "Kalen doesn't use words much. He prefers the bow." Horith laughed, showing perfect teeth.

Jack simply nodded and trudged on. He felt they must be getting close to the ridge where the Greater Elves lived. He tried not to stare at their ears, the only real physical indicator that they weren't actually human. However, he did notice that a few of the others were still actively camouflaging themselves as they walked through the woods.

Jack nodded toward two smaller elves who were camouflaged and told Horith, "I'd love to be able to do that." Horith glanced at the two young hunters and nodded.

"They are practicing. They have only recently been allowed out to hunt with us and they practice the melding as often as they can."

"The melding?"

Horith thought a moment, trying to find the correct words. "When we hunt, we allow ourselves to become one with our surroundings. The forest then hides us from prying eyes." He pointed to the two younger elves. "They practice this often so that it becomes easier."

Jack nodded. "Do the animals you hunt not see you as well either?"

"Some. Others, not so much," Horith replied. "It depends on what is in the woods."

As they approached the ridge, Jack noticed a stand of even larger trees, the base of which was thick with brush and large rocks. As they approached the stand, rather than begin around the rocks, Horith and Kalen walked up to the largest of the rocks and swung the face open like a door and ushered the squad inside. Jack had to duck slightly to step in, but once he stepped through, it was as if he stepped into another dimension. Stepping out on the other side of the rock was like stepping into an enchanted garden. The sunlight felt thicker and more golden, the water in a nearby brook was more clear and tinted as blue as the sky. The green of the trees was vivid and alive. He could smell honeysuckle in the air and sweet dogwood and pine and other scents that made his senses wild with the desire to run and…frolic.

He heard children laughing and people talking and activities going on around him that wasn't there just a moment ago outside the rock. It was like stepping through a doorway into another place in time. His first thought was this couldn't be happening. His second thought was that it couldn't be real. But then he reminded himself that they hunted vampires, that he had been infected with a virus from a werewolf, and was being escorted by an elf. One of his teammates had a woodland sprite with a crush on him, so…why couldn't this be real?

"Follow me," Horith said as he stepped past Jack and led them down a path toward a stand of large trees with heavy rope ladders and pulley systems attached to them.

Jack looked up into the branches and saw that many of the trees had houses built into them and not the tree houses that kids have in their backyard, but actual *homes*, some with multiple levels with decks and windows. Elves of all ages were stepping out onto their decks to observe the visitors and some were waving at them. Jack waved back and smiled at a few of the smaller children who laughed and squealed with delight that someone new had come to their small village.

The squad and the hunting party eventually worked their way over an arching footbridge and to the base of the largest tree where a door was cut into the trunk. Horith stopped and knocked on the door and waited silently for the occupant to open it. Jack assumed this tree must belong to one of the village elders and was not prepared for the beautiful young woman who stepped out of the trunk's darkness. She was dressed in a flowing translucent white gossamer gown, her hair pulled back and braided into an intricate and ornate braid with beadwork throughout and her eyes were the deepest shade of blue that Jack had ever seen. When she stepped from the tree and into the golden sunlight, Jack caught himself staring at her and felt an instant twinge of shame for his attraction to her. He was mated to Nadia and shouldn't be looking at this woman with the thoughts that he held.

She looked out over the band of mixed Elven hunters and human-wolf hybrids and stated simply, "Welcome to our home. I am Loren, the Wyldwood, the elder of this village." She stepped forward and placed a hand on Horith's shoulder. "Who speaks for these hybrids?" she asked.

Jack turned and stole a glance at his team who displayed a mild shock at her calling them hybrids. Horith pointed to Jack. "The man called Thompson."

Jack stepped forward and raised an open hand, a greeting he was taught that meant 'I come in peace' and was also the equivalent of an Elven handshake. "I am Chief Jack Thompson of the human hunters. We come to seek council with the Greater Elves."

Loren observed his actions and nodded a slight bow to him. She raised her hand in mirror image and stated, "You are recognized, Chief Jack Thompson. You and your men are welcomed to Gristwood."

Jack bowed to Loren, the Wyldwood and she nodded her acknowledgement of his affirmation. With the formalities out of the way, she turned to Horith and Kalen once more, "Have the bakers and the cooks prepare for us a meal and bring the elderberry wine. We shall speak in council."

Horith bowed to her and replied, "As you wish, my lady."

Loren then turned to Jack and smiled. "You have paid me an honor by respecting our ways, Chief Jack Thompson."

"The honor is ours, ma'am," he replied. "And please, you can call me Jack. Or just Chief. It's more of a nickname than a title anymore."

She nodded. "Once we are in council, you may call me Loren if you wish. Council is very non-ceremonial. But out here, my people need for me to be more...proper."

"I understand, ma'am."

She turned and led them to a large round structure that looked very much like a beaver dam, but out of the water. It was made of thousands of individual sticks and branches in the shape of a dome, but with round windows surrounding the perimeter. An arched doorway led the way inside. The inner walls were plastered with a light brownish plaster that Jack assumed was an adobe earth mixture. Within its walls sound was deadened so that conversation didn't carry out of the building well, but the windows allowed a nice cool breeze to flow through.

"This place feels almost magical, ma'am," Jack noted. "It's almost like stepping into a dream."

She smiled at him and he felt a familiar tug in his chest. The same tug he felt when Nadia smiled at him. "Yes, it *is* magical. That is why nobody stumbles upon it from the outside world," she said. "The only way to this place is through our portal."

"That is amazing," he said softly. "So where exactly *is* this place then?"

She smiled as she looked about her. "That is a difficult concept to explain to someone who is not an elf." She struggled to find the right words. "It is here upon the world, but not exactly in the same time as the rest of the world. It is between the now and the *not* now."

Jack wasn't grasping her line if thought. "Moved through time then?"

She shook her head. "Not exactly." She paused and thought a moment. "It's as if you are in your chair, but you are not in your chair entirely. Someone else could come along and sit in the same chair at the same time and never know you were there. You wouldn't see that person, and that person would not see you, but you would both be in the same chair at the same time."

Jack smiled and shook his head. "Okay, but what if one of us moved the chair? Would the other feel it?"

She frowned. "Perhaps that was not the best way to put it."

"A different dimension?" Ronald Lamb asked her.

She gave him a puzzled look. "I'm not completely familiar with that term, but, that sounds close. If it means that we are here, but not here, and that others could be here and not know that we are here, then yes."

Lamb and Jacobs looked at each other and shrugged. "Sounds like different dimensions to me," Jacobs said.

"Alternate reality," Tufo stated without looking up.

"Say again?" Donovan asked.

"Don't any of you read Sci-Fi?" Tufo asked. They all shook their heads negatively. He sighed. "There are only so many dimensions you can work in. If this place was in a 'different' dimension, some part of it would be at least visible in the others. But an alternate reality? That works."

Jack gave him a puzzled look. "How does that work?"

"The theory holds that there are an infinite number of universes all occupying the same space, or near space, and that for every person and every choice that there is, each time you make a choice, an alternate reality pops into being where that choice is made. If that theory were true at all, then somehow they found a doorway to one of them and live in it." He looked at them and saw that they were all lost. He threw his hands in the air. "Let's just go with 'different dimension', okay?"

"Either way," Jack said, "its way cool in here. I love the whole atmosphere."

"Thank you, Chief Jack. So do we," Loren replied. "So, tell me why you seek our council."

Jack took a deep breath and began the story as close to the beginning as he could. He laid out the entire story of the Sicarii and the threat of annihilation, his desire for dominion over the earth, enslavement of any race that could be enslaved and the squad's plan for a coalition of forces with both the *Lamia Beastia*, the werewolves if they can be found and any other supernatural forces that they can find that will agree to aid in their struggle. He explained how they hoped to acquire the base in Nevada and lure the forces of darkness there and away from populated areas and he was sent there to see if the Greater Elves would be willing to assist in what might be the ultimate war of good versus evil.

To her credit, Loren remained still throughout his story and did not interrupt. Although her features belied her desire to have no part of it, her face also showed her fear at what would happen if they did nothing. By the end, her features were stone as she absorbed every word he said. She contemplated every possible outcome, weighing both the pros and cons. She knew that no matter how well hidden her village may be, a vampire as powerful and evil as the Sicarii would stop at nothing to find it and burn it as well.

Finally, she said, "While I cannot speak for all of the village elders, I will take your request to them."

Jack reached out and took her hand. "Thank you for this. I know that wasn't an easy decision to come to."

"On the contrary, Chief Jack. It was the only decision I could make."

8

Dominic's eyes fluttered open and he gulped in air as if he had been suffocating. His arms flailed against an unseen opponent and he scrambled about in the ramshackle room until he realized he was alone again. He lay still on the stone floor, panting in the near darkness, on hands and knees, still gulping at the cool air. He leaned forward and pressed his forehead to the cool stone floor.

After a few moments, he staggered to his feet and shambled into the washroom and splashed water onto his face. He ran his hand across his cheeks and felt the stubble of his beard, assuming he had been captive for at least a week now, he stared at the darkening circles under his eyes. The lack of sleep due to the nightmares and the constant drilling of questions and mind-fucking by this twisted, dark son-of-a-bitch had him ready to cut his own throat.

Dom sat on the toilet and rested his head in his hands. He wished that he wasn't so damned huge. He'd drown himself in the commode, but he knew that wouldn't happen. The werewolf virus would find a way to bring him back, he was sure. The way that cuts and bruises healed on him was ridiculously fast, he was sure that even drowning would probably just be an experiment in pain.

Dom sighed and got up again, staggering back into the main room and collapsing to the mattress once more. This existence of his was so bad that he was seriously thinking of trying to rush the next guard to open the door and pray for a bullet to the brainpan. He wasted most of his time trying to sleep because of the perpetual darkness. His body was mostly healed, but they practically starved him. He was used to eating four times what a normal person ate, and they fed him scraps once a day. Barely enough to keep a church mouse alive and his energy stores were drained.

Dom wondered how much longer he could keep resisting the vampire. He had been mind-raped so many times now that he couldn't remember what he had been forced to tell and what had been nightmares. He rolled over and faced the wall. The mental anguish and frustration tearing at his soul until he wanted to cry, he wanted to scream, he wanted to beat something. He lashed out and punched the wall in front of him and felt the bones in his hand crack, the pain shooting up his arm and into his shoulder. But he also felt something in the block wall give. Through the pain and electric shocks running through his arm and wrist, he forced himself to open his eyes and stare at the wall in the dim light. It wasn't his imagination…the stone had moved, the centuries old mortar having dried out and giving way under his blow.

Dom shifted his weight and slid closer to the wall, wishing now he hadn't punched the wall, but kicked it instead. He felt around the mortar line with his good hand and felt the mortar crumble away like dried mud between his fingers. Moving with renewed vigor he

141

rolled off the mattress and grabbed the oil lamp and set it where he could see the block. It had recessed into the wall nearly three fourths of an inch. He knew that the wall was at least ten inches thick. It would be no easy feat to knock blocks out, but he was about to try.

He rolled onto his back and aimed his feet at the block and pushed with all of his might. The block resisted and barely a hiss of grinding mortar came to his sensitive ears as it shifted ever so slightly. He moved closer and placed his feet again pushing harder this time, resulting only in sliding himself across the stone floor. Dom knew the only way he would be able to do this would be to make some noise. He knew the risk was much higher and that he would be attracting attention to his actions, but it was the only way.

He repositioned himself and aimed his feet once more. With teeth clenched, he drew his legs to his chest and pushed out with all he had and slammed his booted feet against the stone and felt a bone jarring shock drive up his legs and into his spine. He paused and caught his breath, listening intently for any running feet or noise outside of his room. When he didn't hear anybody, he felt around the block and was shocked to find it had moved at least another inch and a half. He moved closer, positioned himself and kicked the block again, this time hearing the block slide further and feeling his feet slide into a hole in the wall. Dom rolled over and inspected the block. It was more than half way, the mortar having crumbled away and allowing the block to move more freely.

Dom knew that this opening wouldn't be large enough for his huge frame to slip out. He'd have to remove the block next to it as well, so he positioned his feet against it as well and kicked with everything he had. The stone refused to budge. It was cemented in place. He moved to the other side of the loose block and tried it and found that the mortar was loose and crumbling, some of it damp from outside moisture. He positioned his body and aimed his feet against this block and with a quick prayer kicked with all he had and both blocks shot out into the daylight, bathing the room with bright sunshine. Dom's hand automatically flew up to shield his eyes and he forced himself not to shout with joy.

He allowed himself time to adjust to the brightness of the light before he placed the oil lamp back at the table and slipped over to the hole. Slipping his head out of the wall, he checked his location. Dom wanted to dance a jig as he realized that the wall he kicked out was an outer wall facing a hillside away from the facility. There were hedgerows below to help cushion his fall, but he still worried that in his emaciated condition, he might break something once he went out. He estimated the height at about twenty feet. Normally, not a problem, but in his weakened state, he worried if he would even be able to make the run to a populated area.

He checked one more time to ensure that nobody was on perimeter patrol and then slipped out feet first. As Dom's upper body wormed its way out the hole, he grabbed the mattress on the floor and pulled it to the hole and did his best to prop it up with his wounded hand. *Better to block the hole should anybody check on me.* He thought to himself. He held himself aloft with his one

143

good hand as he propped the mattress as best he was able, then using both hands, pushed away from the hole and landed deftly on his feet. *Just like old times.*

Dom glanced to the sky to try to get his bearings, but the sun was at high noon. He worked his way to his right, hoping that his internal compass was right and it would lead him back to the entryway where all the vehicles were parked when he was captured during his first escape attempt. Staying low and close to the hedges so he could dive in for cover, he circled the large building until he came around to the entryway. His internal compass hadn't failed him.

Dom slipped into the hedges and hugged the stone wall, working his way to what looked like a portcullis. He glanced inside and saw one lonely guard making slow, lazy rounds on the other side of the courtyard. Dom slipped lower in the hedges and waited until the guard went around a corner before he dared sneak another peek from around the hedge. He spied two vehicles. One was a Fiat and the other a Mercedes van.

Dom waited another few moments to see if the guard was going to come rushing back before he slipped over to the Fiat. There weren't any keys in it. He slipped over to the van and the keys were sitting in the cup holder. Dom grabbed the keys, slipped back to the Fiat and unscrewed the cap from the tire valve stem and using the keys, held down the center pin on the valve to allow the air out of the tire. His jaw clenched at the loud hiss of air escaping the tire, knowing that the guard would come running back at any moment, guns blazing, but the courtyard remained silent save the escaping air from the Fiat's tire.

When the tire rested firmly on the ground, Dom slipped back to the van and jumped behind the wheel. His mind jumped back to his first escape attempt and he expected a gun to be jabbed under his chin or pressed to his temple at any moment.

His hands shook as he fumbled with the keys and he nearly dropped them as he slipped the key into the ignition and started the van. As soon as the diesel engine erupted, he threw the van into gear and tore out of the courtyard and past the portcullis. He turned the van onto the nearest road and let loose a whoop of victory!

He had only gotten a few hundred yards down the road when the passenger side mirror exploded and he heard the thump-thump-thump of bullets hitting the back and sides of the van. He floored the accelerator and concentrated on keeping the van on the road. He kept checking his remaining mirrors for any other vehicles that might be following him, but he didn't see any.

At the first turn off, he pulled the van off the main road and began working his way away from the stone prison he was at in a zigzag pattern. He didn't want to make it easy for his captors to find him again, but he wanted to put as much distance as he could between them.

He checked the fuel gauge and he had a little over half a tank. Dom continued to check for pursuers and when he felt safe that there weren't any, he slowed the van and pulled over. He checked the van for anything that he could use. There was a pack of clove gum, some cigarettes, matches, a 9MM in the glove box...that could be useful. He tucked the weapon into his waistband and continued digging.

He went to the back of the van and saw a pine box that looked suspiciously like a coffin. Dom's lip curled into a snarl as he worked his way back to the front of the panel van and exited the vehicle. He went around back and opened the rear cargo door. He grabbed the long box and jerked it out of the van, ignoring the shooting pains in his hand. He grabbed the lid of the box and ripped it off, hoping that the sun's rays would instantly toast the box's occupant, only to find the box was filled with dirt.

Dom stood there panting alongside the road, dirt spilled out alongside it, feeling a mix of emotions that he couldn't quite explain. He wanted to scream, to rip something apart. He picked up the box of dirt and threw it with all of his might into the ditch alongside the road and screamed at the top of his lungs. Exhausted both physically and mentally, he fell to his knees and sat there, staring at the broken pine box, its contents scattered across the roadway and the ditch, feeling like he had been robbed of some small victory.

Finally, he pulled himself to his feet and continued his search of the van. He found various tools and maps. He found a change of clothes for someone half his size. He found bottles of water and a half eaten bag of pretzels. He wolfed down the pretzels and washed it down with a bottle of water, feeling every drop run through his veins as he took the wheel back and drove again looking for some semblance of civilization.

After twenty minutes of driving, he happened upon a gas station, a telephone kiosk on the outside wall. Dom pulled up alongside the station and stepped out to the kiosk. He picked up the receiver and dialed the prefix for an international operator.

As soon as she picked up, he nearly cried. "Operator, I need to make a collect international call."

"What number please?"

"It's to the United States. Area Code 405."

Dom gave the number for the command duty officer and his name. He waited breathlessly while she put the call through and he felt the phone shaking in his hands. He wasn't sure if it was his nerves or if it was from his lack of eating, but he couldn't ever remember being so happy as when Lieutenant Gregory came over the line after accepting the charges.

"Dominic? Is it really you?"

"Yes, sir, LT. It's me," he said, his voice breaking.

"Where the hell are you? Hold on, I got to tell somebody—"

"No! Don't go anywhere. They may be right on my ass," Dom said. "I don't even know where the hell I am. Can you trace this call? Can you send somebody for me?" he practically begged.

"I'm already on it, buddy," Gregory said. "I can have somebody from Team Two there before you know it," he replied excitedly. Dom could hear activity in the background and knew that the LT had him on speaker.

"Tell them to bring some food, will ya? I'm starving, man."

Gregory laughed, "When aren't you?" he said. "Maybe they can stop by and get you a dozen cheeseburgers at McDonald's or something."

"Oh, man, that sounds so fucking good right now. You don't even know."

"I've got your location, Dominic, and we're sending your coordinates to Team Two as we speak. They've been actively looking for you since you went missing," he said. "Man...have you been missed."

Dom sighed. "I hear ya, brother. I hear ya. Do me a favor and tell Apollo that I'm ready to come home."

"I'll definitely do that," Gregory said. "In fact, knowing him, he may insist on flying out there and escorting your butt home himself."

"I wouldn't mind that one bit," Dom laughed. "The way my luck has been running, I probably need him to."

"Dom, we just got word from Team Two. They're thirty minutes out from you. Can you hold that long?"

Dom looked down the street and had no idea what traffic was friendly and what wasn't. "Honestly, I have no idea. What direction will they be coming from? Maybe I can meet them. I have a van..."

"They'll be coming from your north. If this trace is correct, you're at a filling station near Benevento. They're coming at you at full speed and should be able to meet you at Isernia. Give me a description of your vehicle so I can forward it to them."

"It's a white Mercedes panel van. No markings," Dom said.

Gregory was silent a moment. "Yeah, like there aren't ten thousand of those in Italy."

"Yeah, I know. What other options do I have?" he asked. "I'm a sitting duck out here."

148

HEATH STALLCUP

Gregory laughed. "Think you can wait another five minutes?"

Dom paused, unsure what Gregory was getting at. "Why?"

"Team Two dispatched a chopper as soon as we told them where you were. Coming in hot from Aviano. Should be there in about five minutes."

"Five minutes? Must be one helluva fast Huey."

"They were already out on maneuvers and they gave a command override. You're getting a ride back in style," Gregory quipped. "Must be nice to be considered a high value asset."

"Must be," Dom muttered. "Yeah, five minutes is cool with me. Any idea where I'm going?"

"Back to Aviano, then probably to Groom Lake," Gregory said.

"Where?!" Dom yelled. "I don't think I heard you correctly, LT."

"We're bugging out of Tinker. Relocating to Nevada. We're going to bait the vamps to the desert to keep the collateral damage as low as we can." He said. "All the teams are converging there, so you'll probably ride in with Team Two."

Dom shook his head. "Hey...whatever, man. As long as they bring me a sandwich, I don't care if they take me to Disneyland."

"Oh, right. Yeah, I should probably cut the chatter. This line isn't secure."

"Copy that, LT." Dom could just pick up the blades of a chopper cutting through the air in the distance. "I think I hear it approaching, LT. I'm going to let you go."

"Good to have you back, S3."

"Good to be back, LT." Dom put the phone back on the receiver hook and looked off in the distance. He could just make out the outline of the chopper as it crept toward him over the horizon. He stepped away from the kiosk and out toward an open field. He took the 9MM and shifted it to the back of his waistband, just in case the chopper crew got nervous when they saw it. He waited until he thought the pilot could see him clearly then waved his arms and bent down to avoid the blades and downdraft as the bird settled in next to him. A crewman stepped off the helicopter and asked if he were Dominic DeGiacomo. Dom told him yes and gave a thumbs-up. The crewman ushered him aboard and helped him to buckle in. He donned a set of headphones and the pilot took off again, heading for the small Air Force Base.

Dom looked out the side window and finally heaved a sigh of relief. "There's no place like home…"

Viktor returned to Tinker Air Force Base with a heavy heart and a small package in his briefcase. He found Thorn in Evan's lab waiting for him to bring the artifacts in for analysis. Thorn and Dr. Peters were discussing something that Peters was constructing as Viktor arrived and set his briefcase to the side.

150

Thorn turned to him, relief and worry both crossing his features. "Viktor, I am pleased you have returned safely." He embraced the man. "Were your endeavors fruitful?"

Viktor lowered his head and nodded solemnly. "They were." Thorn was confused by his reaction.

"I would think you would be elated, *mon ami*," he replied softly. "We have another weapon that may be useful against the Sicarii."

Viktor raised his eyes to meet his master's gaze. "I am torn by many different emotions." He replied softly. He opened his briefcase and handed the relics to Thorn, wrapped in the velvet material. "These are holy relics, never to be replaced and we are about to destroy them to stop a mad man." His eyes bore into Rufus. "And should we be successful, then legends say that *you, too* shall be killed as well. I can find no solace in such endeavors."

Rufus nodded solemnly, suddenly realizing the lengths that he had pushed Viktor. He pulled the man into a hard embrace. "I have known you for far too long and asked of you many things." He patted his back. "I will ask no more."

Viktor nodded and pulled back, trying to maintain his composure. Thorn had grown to become more than just a friend, but almost a surrogate father to him over the many, many years they had been together. Aiding to find the relics that could well lead to his death was more than Viktor's heart could take.

Evan interrupted and requested the artifacts. He pulled on surgical gloves, then cotton covers over them and carefully unwrapped the velvet material. He

151

placed the coin under a lighted magnifying glass and studied both sides of the coin. "Remarkable," he breathed.

"It was verified numerous times before the Vatican accepted it into their care," Viktor stated, almost taking offense that the vampire wanted to analyze it.

"Of that, I have no doubt," Evan said without looking up. "I just want to test something really quick." He opened a drawer and pulled out a small plastic bottle of nitric acid. With a swab handy and a pipette, he placed a micro dot of acid along the coin's edge to see what color the acid changed to. It quickly changed black and he blotted the acid with the swab, a smile spreading across his face. "It's silver. Pure coin silver."

"What do you think would be the best delivery system, Doctor?" Thorn asked, almost assured he would say a bullet.

"The most effective spread would be to liquefy it and make a silver nitrate bomb," Evan answered, "but that would mean diluting it, and I have no idea how affective that would be to the Sicarii. If we melt it and cast a bullet, the bullet could fragment before it left the barrel. This isn't pure silver so the impurities could weaken the casting at any point.

"We could mix it with pure silver to strengthen the bullet and stretch it out, making MORE bullets, but again, we'd be diluting the mixture, and we have no idea the effect." Evan sighed and sat back in his chair. "In all honesty, the most effective application that I can think of is to somehow get this coin on or *in* the Sicarii himself."

Thorn stared at the other vampire dumbfounded. "How would you propose we do this?"

Evan scratched his chin as he studied the coin. "That is the question, isn't it?"

Viktor listened to the two discuss the coin and decided to bring the piece of the cross to their attention. "We also have the wood, as well. It is large enough to perhaps make two stakes."

Evan turned to it and placed it under a lower magnifying glass. He studied it for quite some time, nodding and moving closer to admire different aspects. "Are these different discolorations supposed to be blood?"

"They are, but they were not tested," Viktor stated.

Evan pulled a scalpel from his autopsy test kit and scraped lightly from the wood onto a sheet of paper. He funneled the paper and tapped the contents into a test tube. He began mixing his chemicals and liquefied the sample, then added the reagent and smiled when it changed color.

"It is blood. And it is human," he turned to the others and stated. "Of course it is impossible to determine exactly whose blood or get a DNA sample at this point. It's too old and degraded for that level of testing. At least, with the equipment that I have here…maybe with someone with more knowledge than I have and a lot better equipment, but I can't do it."

Thorn stepped closer. "I suppose we could do the battery test."

Evan looked away from the sample. "What is the battery test?"

153

"My dear Doctor, do you mean to tell me that as a child you never stuck your tongue to a 9-volt battery?" Thorn smiled at him deviously.

Evan gave him a blank look, obviously no clue what he was talking about.

Viktor grunted with disgust. "He means a vampire could lick the wood and if his mouth caught fire, then BINGO! It's the blood of Christ."

Evan gave a startled jump. "Why on earth would you do such a thing? I thought the Vatican was positive that this was real?! Isn't it verified?" he stammered.

Thorn laughed. "I am teasing with you, Doctor." He clasped the man's shoulder. "Relax." Thorn used the velvet and picked up the wood. "How do you propose we use this, hmm? Carve a couple of stakes from it?"

Evan tried to calm himself, but the idea of setting his mouth on fire had him unsettled. "I, um, well…I'm thinking since wood is simply wood that we could maybe mill a few crossbow bolts from it. It has become much denser with time. It appears to be a type of cedar wood and it looks like this part is from near the heart of the tree, so it was fairly hard to begin with. Now with time, it's just that much more so. If there is any way to preserve the sawdust and extract the blood, we can maybe spray it with an epoxy mixed with the blood to give it a one-two punch, don't you think?"

Thorn nodded. "I like this idea very much. Much more than I like the idea of making the Sicarii eat the coin. *Oui*?" he asked looking at Viktor who nodded his approval.

"Yeah. As much as I'd love to shove the coin up his…er, down his throat, I'd rather shoot him with an arrow."

"Doctor, perhaps you can find a nice silver chain to put the coin on for me? Something I can use to drape around the Sicarii? Meanwhile, a crossbow for my friend Viktor here. You will have your pulse…thing… backpack to use and the human hunters shall bring the sun. Perhaps together, we shall find a way to stop him."

Evan nodded in agreement. "Well, the pulse microwave particle disruptor isn't for me. I'm no warrior. But I should have the weapon prototype finished soon and ready for testing," he replied. "If we can't stop him, maybe we can at least change his mind."

"*Exactement.*" Thorn turned to Viktor and draped an arm over his shoulder. "Come, *mon ami*. Tell me of your travels while we prepare for the return of your family."

"You have heard from Tasha?" he asked.

"Only that they had spoken to Maxwell and should be returning shortly," Thorn replied, a knowing smirk across his face that Viktor could not see.

"Then I fear our task of finding Claudius Veranus has hit a dead end or they would be going there next," Viktor commented as they walked out of Evan's lab. Evan watched the two men walk away discussing the future and turned to go back to his work when a puzzled thought crossed his mind.

He went to a drawer and opened it. He fished through the junk in it and dug past wires and probes, spare parts for equipment and other bric-a-brac.

Finally he pulled out a small 9-volt battery and held it up to the light. He studied the small object a moment and glanced over each shoulder to see if anybody was watching him. He had the unnatural feeling that he was being watched and he couldn't shake it.

Tentatively he brought the small battery to his mouth and touched it to the tip of his tongue, feeling the electric buzz cross between the two connections and the shock across the super sensitive tissue of his tongue. He quite literally jumped and jerked the battery away and stared at it. "Good heavens. Why on earth would anybody do that on purpose?" he asked himself.

Evan startled again when his telephone rang right next him. He looked around and saw nobody, and cautiously picked it up. Before he could answer, Laura's voice said with girlish laughter in her voice, "Shocking experience, isn't it?" Evan looked up at the window in her office to see her peering at him through her blinds.

"I was just um...testing a theory."

She laughed at him. "Don't tell me that's the first time you've ever done that?"

"Well, actually..."

"Oh, my God..." she laughed harder and Evan felt his face try to flush. Had he fed lately he would have. "I have to go. Matt's waiting on me. Kisses." She hung up and left him standing there with the phone in one hand and the battery in the other.

It had taken 'Max' some time to pack his belongings. It's just nearly impossible to find a suitcase that will fit a Roman breastplate, helmet and spear. Commercial air flights simply won't allow you to carry any kind of weapons onboard, so Max did the next best thing…they took his private jet. Nadia was honestly surprised that he owned a jet because of the way he lived, but Max explained that he often needed to travel the world, sometimes at the drop of a hat in his search for ancient artifacts to rebuild the church. It was a centuries old labor of love and he wanted to do it correctly. Every aspect of the small castle turned church needed to be restored to its former glory.

As the three of them settled in for the long flight, Natashia seemed to grow worse in her 'falling apart' and Max was growing concerned. Nadia seemed to be more aloof and somewhat disconnected from her and somehow Max knew this was not right. He mixed Tasha a drink and made her drink it to calm her nerves and sat alone with Nadia.

"This is your first child, yes?"

"Yes." She stared out the window absently.

Max nodded. "How long have you and your mate been trying for a child?"

She turned and gave him a puzzled look. "We weren't trying. It just happened."

Max raised his brows and nodded. "Truly?" This seemed odd as most wolves spent years trying to conceive. "How many years have you two been together?"

Nadia tilted her head as she looked at him, her brows tightening. "Years? We've been together only a few weeks."

Max's mouth fell open as he stared at her. This is *most unusual* indeed. In fact, in his many centuries, he had never heard of such a thing. "Is he from one of the royal families?" he asked.

Once again she was puzzled. "No. He is human," She answered. "Or, rather, he *was*. He was created." She shook her head to correct herself. "He says that they genetically altered him so that he is *like* a natural born wolf, but he was actually created."

Max sat across from her completely dumbfounded. He didn't know what to say. The humans were not only aware of werewolves, but were now creating them at will? By choice? Why wasn't this scattered all over the news? Why hadn't he read this in the newspapers? What the hell was she talking about? "Little pup, you need to explain to me what you speak of."

Nadia sat back in her seat and began from the beginning. She explained how her Jack was a human hunter and Natashia had rescued him for Thorn, their Vampire master from an ambush. She explained how Jack had discovered that he and his fellow compatriots were infected with the werewolf virus and then later it was revealed that it was a genetic re-engineering that made them as if they were born with it. She told him how they took wolf's bane to prevent the shift and that they had incredible strength and speed and agility, yet didn't shift with the moon. She also told him how it was her Jack that theorized that a natural wolf who shifts prior to the full moon can keep control of their mind during the moon's pull.

Max sat and listened intently to Nadia's entire story, absorbing every detail. "He sounds like a very intelligent man."

Nadia nodded. "He is. With the heart of a wolf." She studied her grandfather. "You didn't sound surprised when I told you what Jack surmised."

"About shifting prior to the moon?" he asked her. "No. I learned that centuries ago."

A muscle in her jaw ticked and her fists clenched. "You might have thought to share that information. It could have saved many a wolf from being hunted for things they did without knowledge."

Max gave her a haunted smile. "Little pup, that is one of life's little secrets that every wolf needs to learn on their own," he told her quietly. "When one comes in tune with their wolf, that 'secret' is revealed to them on its own. It is not something that should be revealed." He caught her still glaring daggers at him. "It would be like having someone tell you how your life ends without ever getting to live it," he tried to explain.

"I disagree."

"You don't have to agree. You don't even have to understand. That is simply how things are," Max said. Nadia shook her head at him as she turned back to her window. "Tell me more of Tasha. How has she been until recently?"

Nadia seemed surprised by his question. "She has been fine. She has been as she always had."

"So, she's always been a quivering, cowering, spineless whelp?" he asked, reclining in his seat and crossing his legs.

Nadia leaped to her feet, "How dare you? You know that she is not!"

Max hiked a brow in question and slowly turned his head toward the simpering mess that Tasha had now become in the seats across from them. "She certainly seems that way now."

Nadia stared at her mother as if for the first time and concern slowly spread across her features. She went to her and knelt at her feet. "Mother, what has befallen you? Why are you this way?"

Max watched them a moment while Tasha stared forlornly out the window and Nadia hovered over her mother. He chewed at his inner cheek and sat up. He went over behind her seat and placed a hand on her shoulder. Nadia felt a mild electric shock travel through her fingers. "What are you doing?"

"Fixing your mother's mess."

"I don't understand..." she began to reply as a flood of emotions hit her. Nadia felt her knees growing weak and her eyes watering from emotions she didn't know she felt.

Tasha looked up at the two of them and croaked out, "No, please. She needs my strength."

"Not all of it," Max told her. He pulled back his hand and Nadia sat abruptly, catching her breath.

"What just happened?" she asked, her eyes darting between the two of them.

160

"You were overwhelmed and your mother loaned you her strength." Max knelt beside her. "She gave you too much and it...changed you." He stole a glance at Tasha trying to gather herself again. "Both of you. And not necessarily for the better."

Nadia took a few deep breaths and exhaled very deeply. "I didn't know we could do that."

"Few can." Max patted her knee reassuringly. "And it's not wise to do so. It's very easy to give too much of yourself and end up lost as Tasha did."

Tasha sat up and cleared her throat. She squared her shoulders and took a sip of the drink that Max had given her to wet her mouth. "I did what was necessary to aid my daughter with her first child." She stated. She turned and looked Max square in the eye. "And I would do it again if I felt it was needed," she added defiantly.

Max simply nodded and shot her a charming smile. "I'm sure you would, Tasha. A mother would do anything to protect her child."

"Exactly," she said, holding her head high and proper.

"Mother, I don't know what to say." Nadia's eyes were watering. "I didn't know that you were so worried about me."

"I only wanted to calm your nerves and give you strength." She stroked her daughter's hand.

"Thank you," Nadia said, laying her head in Tasha's lap, a tear sliding down her cheek. Tasha stroked her hair and soothed her.

"It was nothing you wouldn't have done had you known how, little one. Shh, think nothing of it. Just be still," Natashia whispered.

Max watched the two and a twinge of regret hit his chest. He saw Nadia as a child sitting at her mother's feet needing comfort and envied his son. He who molded the child in his own image, making her a warrior Lycan, educating her classically as he had been, following the same steps as Max and Victoria had when raising Viktor. Max remembered when Viktor was born and he chose the name. Victoria was so pleased that he had named their son after her, but in Max's warrior mind, he had named his son Viktor so that he would grow to become a victor in whatever battle he chose to fight. He wanted his son to rise to any occasion and be victorious. But he never told Victoria the truth in why he chose the name. He allowed the Fates to direct his son's path when he left the pack and the Fates planted the knife firmly in his back.

"We have quite a ride ahead of us. Why don't you two try to get some rest?" Max handed them both blankets from the storage locker and showed them how to recline their overstuffed leather seats. "They're actually quite comfortable."

He dimmed the lights in the cabin and stepped to the forward area and flipped on the overhead light. He pulled out an ancient leather bound log book that he had carried for years. He flipped it open and carefully turned the yellowed pages, trying not to allow them to crumble. He knew what he was looking for and soon found it. A drawing of a face, a face he had not laid eyes on in nearly two thousand years, but a face he

162

thought he would not forget. Still, he found the best artist of the time and had the face put into his book so that it would never be forgotten. The face of the Sicarii.

9

Laura had just stepped into Matt's office when he shoved a scotch into her hands. "You're going to need that." His face was solemn.

"What happened?" she asked, her mind racing at the possibilities.

"Drink up first," Matt insisted. Laura turned a cautious eye to him and sipped her drink then sat where he directed her. Mitchell leaned against his desk and watched her intently. "We got a call today."

Laura waited for him to expound on his statement. "Who from?"

Mitchell sighed then slowly smiled. "Dominic escaped. He's with Team Two at Aviano Air Base."

Laura jumped up, tossing her drink as she flung her arms around Matt. "That's wonderful!" she cried. "Oh, my God." She found herself at a loss for words. Then a flood of worries hit her and came rushing from her mouth, "Is he okay? Was he hurt? How did he escape? What did they do to him? Is he—"

"They're debriefing him now and we'll get the report soon," Matt interrupted her, trying to get her to calm down. "It looks like he may have broken his wrist during the escape, and he was a bit dehydrated, a little underfed, but they're taking care of him. The biggest thing was getting him back on the shift-blockers before it was too late."

Laura's eyes widened as she realized that she had never considered that Dominic hadn't had his wolfs-bane to take. "I'm so relieved that he's alright. I've worried myself sick over him these past days, it's just been constantly in the back of my mind." She felt the weight lift from her shoulders, but she feared actually believing it.

Matt's face hardened slightly. "I spoke to him briefly," he said softly. "He's a mess, Laura. They did…things to him. I don't know what exactly, but he's not the same."

"What are you saying?" she asked, fear creeping into her voice.

"I'm not sure," he admitted. "Either they found a way to break him, or…"

"Or what?"

"Or they found a way to turn him." He didn't want to say it, but he knew that anything he told Laura would remain safely between them. "Call it a sixth sense, but I have this nagging feeling that something is wrong. *Bad* wrong, and it comes from them getting their hooks into that boy."

Laura tried not to think too much into his words, but she felt compelled to defend Dominic. "Could it be that you're just relieved that he got away and now you're worried? Like when Phoenix returned?"

"This is more than that. I guess you would have had to hear his voice," Matt told her. He shook his head as he thought of the possibilities. "Physically, he'll

165

heal, but they got into his head somehow. I can just feel it."

Laura paused and tried to imagine anybody breaking Dom, and she couldn't bring herself to think of the way they did it. Her mind wouldn't allow it. "At least he's safe now."

"We have that. And as soon as his debriefing is over, we'll have hard copy on it as well."

"Who's doing it?"

"Team Two is bringing in a specialist. Someone they've worked with before. Supposed to be one of the best in Europe," Matt said. "Guy does a lot of work with operators who've been in the field too long. He's done a lot of work with our boys in the agency that were in deep cover work, too."

Laura nodded and wrapped her arms around herself. "I'm glad they've got a specialist to help. But, Matt, this job is starting to be too much." Mitchell studied her as she gripped herself tighter. She rocked slightly as she allowed herself to think too much about the events of the recent past. "I seriously don't know if I can take much more," she said more to herself than to him.

"You knew what you were signing on for, Laura," he said softly. "And I need you too much now to let you go." He rose and touched her shoulder in a friendly, supportive way. "Remember, we have the end of the world to stop?" He gave her a boyish grin.

She snorted. "Oh yeah, like I could forget that," she replied sarcastically. "If it isn't the end of the world, it's some kind of boogey man wanting to eat you, or some unknown monster wanting to destroy Tokyo or—"

"Yeah, well, technically Tokyo is outside of our jurisdiction," he jabbed.

She gave him a sideways look. "Fine, Detroit then."

"Pfft. Like anybody would notice if a monster tore up Detroit," Mitchell shot back. "You could nuke that city and it would be an improvement."

"Stop it, Matt. I'm trying to have a pity-party and you aren't helping."

"Sorry. I was just trying to lighten things up a little." He held his hands up in surrender. "You've just been acting all doom and gloomy lately and it's been a real buzz kill."

Laura put her hands on her hips and glared at him. "With our job it's very hard to be Little Miss Suzy Sunshine."

"I know," Matt said trying to be more understanding. "I just thought you'd be happier about Dom."

"It's kind of hard to when you're telling me that he's been compromised."

"We aren't sure that he has, it's just a feeling." Matt plopped down in his chair and rubbed at his head. "I wish that feeling weren't there, though."

"How soon until we get the report?" she asked.

"Probably not until we are set up at Groom Lake." Matt was actually glad to have a subject change. "Speaking of, how are things coming with the bug out?"

"Most departments are about ready to go. It would have helped a lot to know what assets we could have when we got there, though. If we didn't have to move all this radio equipment, it would save us a lot of room."

"I know they're set up for aircraft radio, but…I just don't know what they're going to lock up as 'classified' before we get there. Their base commander is supposed to call me any time now."

"Do you know him?"

"No, this guy runs in different circles. He's an academy man. Real up and comer, and although McAfee says he'll play ball, I'm not holding my breath." Mitchell's features soured. "He's going to see us as coming in to piss in his backyard, so he won't be happy."

"Ha! So besides the vampires we're hoping to bait there, we may also have to deal with the base CO? Great." She sighed. "Things just keep getting better."

Matt nodded. "Just have our people pack the absolute minimum that we need to operate. We'll make it work once we get there. But we have a lot to do and very little time to do it in."

"Any idea what kind of timeline we are talking about?"

Matt turned a serious eye to her and nodded. "This next full moon."

Laura's brows shot up on that one. "You're only talking a couple of weeks, max."

"Fifteen days."

"We have to move our entire operations, get set up, bait the beast—"

"Don't forget test the satellite."

"Oh my God. Matt…we're sunk."

"Don't count us out of the fight yet." He began counting off on his fingers, "The Duty Officer reported that Viktor returned today, so hopefully he has some good news for us. Evan has been working on a few surprises himself. Jack's wife and mother-in-law are on their way back so maybe they have some good news on the whole werewolf front. Not to mention we still have our Predator drones and the C-130 that can bring the rain. Even if we can't stop the Sicarii himself, we can decimate his forces."

"If we can't stop him, he'll be back. He won't stop. Thorn says that he's lost his mind or something and feels he's on a holy crusade."

"We will do whatever we have to," Matt said, staring her down. "Whatever we have to do," he reiterated, emphasizing each word.

Laura studied him a moment before asking the question that was nagging at the back of her mind. "Are you talking a nuclear response, Matt?"

He leaned back in his chair and repeated himself, "Whatever we have to do."

Fist Squad enjoyed a meal with the Greater Elves that was mostly vegetarian fare, though there was some roasted meat that the men thought may have been either a mountain goat or something similar. They had many different kind of breads ground from

169

different wild grains and honey, berries and a sweet paste for dipping foods into that was heavenly, but they were afraid to ask what it was made of.

For the meal, the hunting party and other young men, now dressed in tunics, joined the squad and the atmosphere was much lighter. Donovan and Tufo were approached by the twin brothers Horith and Kalen and asked about the upcoming battle against the vampire horde. "There are many rumors about their numbers. Do you know how many they are?" Horith asked.

Donnie sighed as he shook his head. "We can only estimate and even then, we could be off by a wide margin. The vampire who is helping us said that—"

"There are vampires *helping you*?" Kalen asked, surprise more than evident in his voice.

Donovan smiled and nodded. He washed down the last of his meal with some elderberry juice. "Oh yeah. Surprises are everywhere," he said. "We found out about this whole 'Vampire Armageddon' when we went to meet this one vampire to talk to him about..." he paused to try to figure out how to explain the circumstances, "well, it's complicated."

"Please, try," Horith said, the shock still showing on his face. "Our experience with vampires is limited, but we've yet to find any that are trustworthy."

Donovan nodded. "I agree with you there, buddy. But apparently, there are some." He took a deep breath and plunged in. "Apparently, there is a whole group of vampires that actually remember what it's like to be 'alive' and value life. *All* life," He began. "They are a quiet group that keeps to themselves and sustains themselves on the blood of animals. They don't kill the animals, they just bleed enough to sustain themselves. I guess…like milking a cow.

"Anyway, the other vampires who still feed on humans were setting them up as the patsies so that when the bad guys did something terrible and we would swoop in for the kill, we'd end up wiping out the quiet good guys." He shook his head. "They were fighting their own version of a civil war and the more vicious of the two were using US to fight their battles.

"So the vamps that feed on animals asked to have a sit-down meeting with our boss. And, it was during that meeting that all of us became aware of the upcoming Apocalypse." Donnie shook his head. "Talk about timing."

Horith looked to Kalen. "Would you trust a vampire? Ever?"

"Never. I don't care if they did feed on squirrels and rabbits. I could never trust one."

"Normally, I'd agree with you," Donovan said. "But, we've also had a vampire working for us for quite a few years now." Donnie watched their eyes grow wide with shock. "I'm sure you find it hard to believe, but he's the nicest guy you'd ever want to meet. He's as normal as you'd ever find."

"And he works beside you?" Horith asked, looking about the room.

"Not *right* beside us, like, in the field, but back at our base. He is a scientist. He actually designed a lot of our weaponry." Donovan pulled out one of their UV phosphorus grenades. "He designed this grenade. It still explodes like a normal grenade and sends shrapnel

171

pieces in all directions like a normal grenade, but it also has silver nitrate inside which is poisonous to a vampire. And, as a one-two punch, it emits a high dose of UV light somehow that is like throwing a vampire into a tanning bed and letting them get a big batch of sunlight in a flash." He reattached the grenade to his vest. "Pretty damned ingenious, and to be honest, they've saved my life more than once."

Horith looked to Kalen once more and shook his head. "I do not understand how a vampire could help in killing his own kind? It doesn't make sense."

"It does if you understand that he hates vampires more than he loves being alive," Donnie answered.

Mark had listened to their conversation with some interest, but he was more interested in trying to speak to the elder alone if possible. He saw Loren and Jack speaking and when Jack finally milled away, he excused himself and worked his way over to where Loren, the Wyldwood, stood.

"Excuse, me, Ma'am?" Loren turned to him and Mark was struck by her beauty just as he had been when she first emerged from the tree trunk. It took him a moment to realize she had addressed him and he nearly had to shake his head to think again. "I wondered if I might have a word with you, please?"

"Of course," she said. Her voice was soft and low.

Mark did a quick glance to either side and lowered his own voice. He wanted to be sure that nobody else overheard their conversation. "I have a 'little' problem that I'm hoping you might can assist me with?"

"Perhaps. What is it?" she asked.

Mark tilted his head and shot her a 'duh' look. "This little pixie-pest buzzing around my noggin…I'd really like to have her vamoose!" he whispered desperately.

Loren glanced at the small sprite at his shoulder playing with the hair by his ear as Mark twitched his head. "Ah, the wee spriggan. Well, you really only have three options, fine sir."

"Three? Three is good. Three is better than two. Let me have it!"

"You can kill her," Loren offered.

"What?! No. I couldn't kill an innocent little…well, okay she's a pest, but it's not like swatting a mosquito, okay?"

"Then you can offend her greatly, but that could result in great pain, and possible disfigurement," she informed him.

"I don't want to hurt her or disfigure her."

"For you, not her," she said stonily.

"Oh," Mark gulped. "Well…still…that probably isn't a great idea."

"Then the third, and easiest option, is to give her what she wants." Loren smiled sweetly.

Mark's eyes bugged. "What?!" he whispered excitedly. "I'm a married man."

Loren gave him a 'so-what' look and shook her head. "She wishes only to procreate, sir. She has chosen you. If you do not allow her to, if you reject her, then eventually she will fly off into the woods and die. She will choose no other."

Mark's jaw dropped. "But wouldn't…I mean…if I…even if we tried it would…kill her. Wouldn't it?"

173

Loren chuckled sweetly. "No, my friend, it will not. She is a spriggan. They are magikal." Loren leaned in to him and whispered lightly in his ear, "Give her what she wants. You might find that you enjoy it."

Mark flushed at the idea. "How am I supposed to…"

"I thought you said that you were married?" Loren said coyly. "Simply find a quiet spot and allow her to claim you." Loren patted his back as he stood there shocked. "Try not to scream when she does so." She smiled at him and walked away.

The dark vampire stood in his second-story window staring out upon his city. Oh, how he wanted to see it burn to the ground, to hear the citizenry scream in agony. He longed to hear them beg for his mercies. The irony, how he hated Rome for doing what he was about to do, but rather than hold the people as slaves to the aristocracy, he would grind them under his heel and keep only the healthiest for his own hedonistic pleasures.

His messenger stepped into the crumbling cathedral and called to him, "Sicarii. The prisoner has escaped."

"Good," the dark vampire said softly. He turned slowly to the messenger and allowed a slow smile. "It certainly took him long enough." He stepped from his

174

perch in the second story and appeared to float to the floor. "Tell me, Puppet, have I over-estimated these human hunters?"

"I cannot say, Master. You know that I am only your loyal servant," the little messenger groveled. "My mind is not one for making such assumptions."

The dark vampire patted his head. "Of course not. And you are too big to be a lap dog, so tell me, Puppet, what am I to do with you?"

The little messenger began to tremble, fearing his days were numbered. "I do not know, Master. Of course, my life is yours. Do with it what you wish." Inside he was begging for his life.

"Where is the hunter now?" the dark vampire asked. "On his way back to America, I would assume."

"No, Master, he is still at Aviano. The other hunters are there with him as well," the little messenger replied. "And..." he began, but thought better of it.

"Go ahead, Puppet. Spit it out."

"Well, Master, it is a curious thing," he began quietly. "We have reports from our spies who are watching the human hunters. They say that *all* of the hunters are up to something...peculiar."

"Peculiar, how? Do not speak in riddles, Puppet. Tell me what they report and I will make determinations," the dark vampire warned, allowing a small wave of his power to pulse out from him.

The messenger quaked and trembled, but stayed on his feet. "They report that the human hunters are *packing*, Master. As if they are all leaving," he began. "The human spies noted increased activity during the daylight hours and thought that perhaps their teams

175

had a mission, but they were simply...*packing*. Then when nightfall came, the vampire spies continued to see the very same activity. They are loading their belongings onto trucks and making their way to cargo planes."

"Which of the hunters are doing this?" the Sicarii asked.

"That's just it, sire...it is *all* of them," the messenger answered. "Well, except for the French. They still haven't replaced their team since we killed them all, but..."

"All of them?" the dark one asked again, to be sure.

"Yes, Master. All of them," the messenger stated. "What could this mean?"

The dark vampire paced a moment, thoughts running through his mind. "I need to know where each of them goes. If we cannot get a human spy on a plane, place a tracking device of some kind. No matter the cost. We must know where they go."

"Master?" the messenger questioned. "What difference does it make where the humans go? Your army will destroy them no matter where they end up. Even if they came here, they are no match for you..."

"*Track them!*" the dark vampire growled another wave of power so strong that the messenger fell to his knees, pebbles and debris biting into his kneecaps, tearing flesh.

"And Puppet..." the dark one continued.

"Your will be done, Master, whatever it is!" he quickly shouted.

176

"If the humans are on the move, then surely their loved ones must know where they are going as well. Move up our timetable. Send our people for the families."

"Master, we only know of the one family. The others were dead or...lovers between hunters, and..."

"Then get the one family, Puppet. Find out what they know about the hunter's movements and then kill them."

"Y-yes, Master," he stammered. "As you will, so mote it be." He crawled from his master's presence to send out the order as quickly as possible, knowing that failure would mean his untimely death.

The dark vampire stepped back up to his second-story window and stared out across the horizon. Surely the humans couldn't have delved into the brain of the escaped prisoner and found a weakness already. They didn't have the resources to do such a thing...no, the prisoner had only escaped that morning and the human spies were watching the hunters begin packing that morning, so the two acts happened at the same time. Still, he didn't like coincidences. Somehow, the humans were aware of his plans. Not that it would really matter.

He wanted his domination of the world to be announced to the human hunters by the escaped prisoner, and yet somehow he felt that they already knew he was coming. Or they felt that *something* was coming. Perhaps they had a clairvoyant in their midst. Regardless, they might know something, but they could never truly prepare for *him*, an unstoppable vampire hell-bent on death and destruction.

177

He knew his purpose and he truly was the Harbinger of Death.

"Are you certain?" Viktor asked again, hoping he hadn't heard correctly.

"*Oui*, Maxwell is returning with Natashia and Nadia," Rufus stated, hoping that Viktor would be pleased to see his father again after so many centuries.

Viktor paced in the break room, nervous tension evident as his hands clasped and unclasped. "Why would he return with them rather than direct them to the Roman Centurion?" he growled. "It makes no sense!"

"She did not say," Rufus offered. "But Natashia did not sound herself, *mon ami*."

Viktor spun on him. "What do you mean?"

Rufus shook his head and shrugged. "She sounded...weepy."

"Weepy?" Viktor asked. "Tasha?!" Viktor was astonished. "Tasha does not become 'weepy', she makes others curl into a ball and cry." He growled again and resumed his pacing. "Something is not right."

"We shall find out soon enough." Rufus tried to calm him. "They shall be here before we know it. In fact, the hunter Spalding has already left to retrieve them from the civilian airport." Rufus hoped that knowing they would be here soon would calm Viktor, but he seemed to grow more agitated with each passing second.

"Why didn't she call me?" he growled.

"You were in the air, *mon ami*. She called me here," Rufus explained. "They are coming on Maxwell's private jet and will not have to go through—"

"Private jet?" Viktor interrupted. "Since when does Max own a private jet?"

Thorn shook his head. "I do not know. This is what she said when she called me."

Viktor pulled his phone out and dialed her number, but it went straight to voicemail. "Her phone is either off or the battery is dead." He swore through gritted teeth.

"Or she could still be on the plane," Rufus offered. "You need to calm yourself."

Viktor inhaled deeply and released it slowly. "My father is with them, Rufus. Do you understand what this means?" Rufus simply stared at the floor, allowing his friend to vent his frustrations. "It means that he knows of my dishonor. It means that she has told him of our banishment." He turned to Rufus and through clenched teeth he growled, "I'm positive that he cut their quest short in order to bring himself to face me." He practically trembled with rage.

"You do not know this for certain," Thorn interjected. "We know nothing of the circumstances behind their return, and until we do, you worry yourself for naught."

Viktor rolled his head and the crack of his neck worried Rufus. "Do not become so distraught that you act before knowing the reason for their early return! Viktor, I must insist…as your friend…"

"You mean, 'as my master', don't you?" Viktor growled at him. Thorn's eyes rounded with shock at his verbal attack.

"*Mon ami*, I will forgive your outburst, for you are obviously upset. But I must insist that you contain yourself." Thorn squared his shoulders and faced Viktor, his jaw set and a touch of anger in his voice. "I have *never* commanded a position over you or your family. I have always treated you as a friend and your family as my own." He closed the distance and lowered his voice to a whisper, "But if dealing with your father is the only way we can find the Roman Centurion, so be it." Rufus turned and started to leave the room. "If you are not up to the task, simply say so and I will be more than happy to act as emissary with Maxwell. However, the wolf I have known all of these years would never allow himself to fall apart at a time when we needed him the most."

Rufus opened the door and stepped through. As he was about to shut it, Viktor called to him, "Rufus." He paused at the door, unsure what Viktor may say next. "I am…sorry." He sighed. "My father brings out the worst in me." He lowered his voice to almost a whisper, "I had no right to lash out at you like that."

"It is understandable, *mon ami*. But you must learn to control your emotions," Rufus replied softly. "They will be your undoing." Viktor nodded gently, his eyes pressed tightly together. "Prepare yourself. Your family returns shortly. They would rather you be happy to see them."

"It has been too long since I've been to the new world." Max looked out of the vehicle's windows. Spalding wound his way through the metro traffic from Wiley Post Airport, making the trip back to Tinker that much shorter. "Somehow, the buildings seem so much smaller than they appear on television."

"Watch a lot of American TV, I take it?" Darren asked him.

"Oh yeah. Satellite dishes are the bomb," Max replied. "I watch all kinds of American programming."

"Well, to be honest, most of the TV shows are based either in LA or New York. Much bigger cities. Oklahoma City is still kind of a cow-town compared to them." He laughed.

"The air smells different,'" Max said.

"That would be the cows." Spalding joked.

Max's sensitive nose could detect the petroleum industries, the cattle ranches, the many BBQ joints and steak houses. The mixture of scents to him was intoxicating and he liked it. He smiled to himself and thought of all the things he had been missing by hiding away in the small town of Avallon, France in his little Vickers house living vicariously through his television. "There is *life* here." He swooned at the tingling of his senses.

Spalding shot him a confused look through the rearview mirror and started to ask him what his comment meant, but Nadia drummed up conversation with him. "Grandfather, I think you will like Jack. He is a good man. A warrior, very much like you were. A leader of men."

Max stiffened at the mention of Jack's name and merely glanced at Nadia. "A good *man*, you say."

"Yes, he is a very good man." She beamed at him, wishing so much for his approval.

"He has not even shifted yet, correct?" he asked. "And yet, you have mated with him *and* are expecting a child?"

Nadia blushed and stole a glance to the driver, one of Jack's friends and co-workers who hadn't seemed to notice her grandfather's comment. If he had, he had no reaction as he continued to drive the large SUV through traffic. "Please, grandfather, say nothing to Jack yet of the child," she said in a whispered voice. "I only found out myself on my way to find you and have yet to tell him. I wish to wait until the time is…right."

Max studied her for a moment and then nodded. He didn't like it, but it was their business, not his. What did he care if she told the human that he had knocked her up?

"There it is." Spalding pointed to his right. "Our facility is in the back, away from prying eyes."

Max looked over at the large military complex spread over many acres. Inactive airplanes parked by the roadway on display for the world to see. He noticed the fence around the property and thought that it might keep out a human, but could never keep out a wolf. Perhaps it was only decorative?

"Are there places for wolves to run?" Max asked.

Spalding looked up the mirror again, his brows knitted in question. "Uh, no, not really."

"Grandfather knows that you are all wolves, yet contained by the bane," Nadia informed Spalding.

He visibly blanched. "Great. Another top secret classified military covert operation just thrown out to anybody..." he muttered.

"Relax, pup," Max growled. "I am wolf as well."

"I gathered as much, sir," Spalding sat upright at his voice. "No disrespect intended, sir."

He continued to drive them through the gates and on back to the southeastern portion of the facility to the oversized hangar where the Monster Squad called home. As Spalding approached the front doors of the hangar, the guards outside the hangar saw his approaching vehicle and opened the doors, allowing the SUV to drive up and inside the dark interior of the metal building.

Darren pulled the SUV all the way to the back of the building, past the numerous people packing away their gear and getting ready to move to Nevada. He stopped the SUV and shut off the engine. "Be it ever so humble..." he said as he stepped out. He opened the door for Natashia and Nadia. Max stepped out from the other side and looked around the facility.

Matt and Laura approached from elevator doors, smiles across their faces. "Tasha, I hope your trip was fruitful," Matt said.

"I believe you will be pleased, Colonel." She purred. She turned to Max and said, "Colonel Mitchell Matthews, may I introduce Maxwell Verissimo, my father-in-law." Both Matt and Max shot her a confused look, brows raised.

Matt extended his hand. "Matt Mitchell. I'm the Commanding Officer here, and this is Ms. Laura Youngblood. She's my Executive Officer."

Max took Laura's hand and poured on the charm. He kissed the back of her hand and his eyes never left hers, a soft smile across his lips as he did so, "Charmed." He whispered as he bowed to her. Laura felt a slight flutter in her stomach as his lips brushed her hand but she did her best to maintain her composure.

"Mr. Verissimo, it is very nice to meet you." Max nodded to Laura, his gaze penetrating her.

Finally he turned back to Colonel Mitchell, "Impressive place you have here, Colonel."

"Thank you. It's taken quite some time to get to this point but we're proud of what we've accomplished."

"Hunting people like me?" Max asked dismissively as Matt escorted them toward the elevators.

"Excuse me?" he asked, pausing by the doors.

"You *are* monster hunters, are you not?" Max stated accusingly.

"Yes. We are," Mitchell answered. "And if you were attacking humans and terrorizing small towns, then *yes*, we would hunt you down and kill you," he said with a cold smile. "Would you please step this way." He waved them through to the elevators.

184

Max smiled back at Mitchell and Matt knew it was a challenge. Two Alphas about to hike on the furniture and test who had the meaner growl. Matt also knew that if this was truly Viktor's father, then he was a much older werewolf and technically he should be the leader of a pack, but this was a military unit and by god, *he* was the designated leader and he'd see to it that his people were deployed as he saw fit.

As the elevator dropped to the lower levels, Max turned to Mitchell, "We will have much to discuss on how best to defeat the Sicarii."

Mitchell stiffened slightly. He knew that Tasha and Nadia had brought him back, but he wasn't aware of just how much they had told him. He wasn't used to civilians just spilling their collective guts to whomever they please. There had to be a 'need to know' and Matt wasn't convinced that Viktor's father had a need to know yet. "Well that is an issue I'd much rather discuss with Claudius Veranus once we've located him," Matt said dismissively.

The door opened and the group filed out, yet Max hung back and hovered near Mitchell. "He's been found," he said simply, then stepped out of the elevator and draped his arm around Nadia. "Show me this underground home of yours, pup."

Matt observed the man with his flippant attitude and really didn't think he liked him. He stepped out of the elevator and followed the group through the beginnings of the tour then interrupted. "We really don't have time for this. We are packing to go to another facility and won't be here for much longer," he informed them. "We really need to find this Roman

185

Centurion...this Claudius Veranus so that we can confer with him."

Rufus Thorn and Viktor came around the corner and Viktor stiffened at the sight of his father. After all of the centuries, he hadn't changed. A few more gray hairs in his beard, perhaps, but otherwise, exactly as Viktor had remembered him. Tasha and Nadia rushed to embrace him and he couldn't help but smile as he wrapped his arms around the two women he adored. "How was your trip?" he asked, then turning to Tasha, "Are you okay? Rufus said you sounded...sad?"

"I am fine," she said. "Honestly." She stroked the side of his face and kissed him deeply. Viktor held her tightly and melted into her kiss. The woman could melt steel with her kiss. Nadia hid her eyes and tried not to blush. When they finally pulled back, Tasha leaned into him and whispered into his ear, "But I have personal news for you later that you must promise to keep a secret."

He pulled away from her and studied her face. "What secret?" He probed her face for some clue, but found only a smile.

"I will tell you later." She poked him in the ribs to make him jump. "It's not my secret to tell."

"I do not..."

"Later."

"Ahem," Matt cleared his throat. "As I was saying, I appreciate your coming all this way, but unless this Roman, Veranus is somewhere nearby, or only you can contact him, I really don't see the point." Mitchell crossed his arms and gave Max a skeptical look.

Max chuckled and shook his head. "You don't need to search for him, Colonel. I am he."

Mitchell raised a brow and gave Max a skeptical stare. "Really?"

"Yes. Really," Max answered.

"Yeah," Matt answered. "Do you realize the odds of..." He sighed and shook his head. "Look, I appreciate your wanting to help. I really do. But we need the real deal here. If what I've been told is true, then we need to find—"

"Claudius Maximus Veranus, member of the Roman Tenth Legion, Captain of the Guard, defender of the Empire and holder of the Spear of Destiny," he proclaimed. "You are looking at him, Colonel."

Mitchell looked the man from head to toe, garbed in khaki shorts, Hawaiian shirt and sandals, Ray Ban sunglasses perched atop his thinning hair and wondered...*could he be telling the truth?*

"Father?" Viktor gasped. "What are you saying?"

Max turned and looked at Viktor, realizing that this was probably not the best way to tell his son that he was the progeny of a legend. Max lowered his eyes and shook his head slightly. "It's true Viktor. I changed my name after the legend of who I was outgrew who I *really* was," he explained. "I never wanted you to find out...at least, not this way, son."

Viktor squared his shoulders and shook his head. "And mother?"

He nodded. "She knows. I think that may be why her taste for power is bigger than her brains."

187

"Okay, look," Mitchell interjected, "I'm not exactly saying that I don't believe you, but...I don't believe you. It's just too damned convenient."

"Let me guess, you'd like a Roman Driver's License from around, say...I dunno, Zero AD?" Max laughed.

"That would work," Matt said stonily.

"How about something a little more tangible and a little harder to fake?" Max asked.

"What did you have in mind?" Laura stepped in closer.

"I brought my armor and my helmet." He turned to Mitchell and smiled. "And the Spear of Destiny."

"The actual spear?" he asked.

"The one and only." Max answered. "And...a little something else that might interest you a tiny bit more."

"What would that be?" Mitchell asked.

"The face of the Sicarii."

10

Jack waited in the mud hut with the other squad members, picking through the remains of the feast that was laid out in their honor. They had been there for most of the day while Loren the Wyldwood left with a small band of her hunters to meet with the other elders. Jacobs was outside playing catch with some of the children and trying to teach them the fundamentals of baseball, but they couldn't grasp the idea of hitting the ball with a bat and then running. Lamb offered to help, but his patience ran out early.

Jack found that waiting, even in the wonderful world of the elves to be the same everywhere. It simply drained you. It was like sitting in the waiting room of a doctor's office or a waiting room at a hospital. There was just something about waiting that sucked the life out of you. He had walked around their little village a couple of times and made small talk with many of the inhabitants. He'd skipped rocks across a still pond and spotted fish in the brook. He climbed a rope ladder and inspected a tree home in one of the larger trees and took a nap, but still, he waited.

Tufo came in and plopped down beside him, ripping a chunk from the loaf of wild grain bread and dipping it in the paste they had started calling Heaven-on-Earth Dip. He shoved it in his mouth and chewed it without tasting. Jack was sitting across from him and barely looked up when he plopped down. "If this takes much longer I think I'm going to go stir crazy," he muttered.

"It hasn't been that long, Chief," Tufo said. He glanced at his watch and tapped it. The numbers on his digital readout were jumbled. "What the…"

"Yeah, go figure," Jack said. "Time has little meaning in here. Could be hours, could be days…hell, it could have been months since they left."

Donovan, who appeared to be asleep on the bench in the corner of the hut, spoke up, "Fifteen hours, twenty minutes."

"How would you know?" Jack asked.

"Analog watch," Donnie said from under his boonie hat. "You should try one. I know they're difficult for anybody below second grade reading level to understand, but they're pretty reliable." You could hear the humorous sarcasm drip from his voice.

"Yeah, well…I happen to like digital, thank you," Jack shot back.

"And I like reliable," Donnie shot in return. He sat up and yawned. "But you're right. Time does feel…*different* here. I swear it feels like it's been a couple of days since they left."

"When Loren said they'd be back soon, I thought a couple of hours," Jack muttered.

Tufo ripped another piece of bread off and slammed it into the paste before shoving it into his mouth. Jack finally looked at him with questioning eyes. "What's with you? Homesick?"

Tufo glared at him and poured a cup of wine. "This mission sucks." He washed down the bread and cut a hunk of meat off the remaining carcass. "We should be out killing something instead of stuck in here sitting on our thumbs."

Donnie sat with his head hanging between his shoulders. He finally glanced up with a smart assed remark on his lips but held it. "Hey, where's your little pixie buddy?" he asked suddenly curious.

Tufo rolled his eyes and ground his teeth. "Don't ask," he growled.

"Oh, my God, Mark! You didn't burn her, did you?" Donnie asked, coming to his feet.

Tufo sighed and slammed his knife into the table. "No, dammit, I didn't burn her." He turned and glared at Donovan. "Now drop it, will you?"

Donovan's eyes narrowed on the Marine. "Did you kill her?" he asked accusingly. "Tufo, tell me you didn't kill the little sprite…"

"Oh, my God…no! I didn't kill her," he replied. "Now stop. Please," he said emphatically.

Jack began to chuckle and hid his face.

Tufo glared at him. "What?"

"Nothing, Gunny," Jack replied. His chuckling turned to laughter as he realized what Tufo had to do to get rid of the little pixie. "I didn't say a damned thing."

"You didn't say it, but you're thinking it!" Tufo yelled. "Stop it!"

Donovan's eyes lit up and he began smiling. "Aww, Gunny. Did you finally cave?"

"Oh for the love of…"

191

"Yup, he did," Donnie snorted. "Tufo's a pixie poker."

Jack lost it and burst out laughing, slapping his knee. Mark groaned and bounced his head against the table.

"Did you diddle Tink?" Donnie teased, then came up short when Tufo's survival knife found itself at his groin.

"One more remark, and you diddle *no one* ever again," he growled. "Got it?" Donnie backed away, his hands held in surrender, a smirk plastered across his face.

"Whatever you say, Gunny." He backed away to his bench again and sat down. He laid back down keeping an eye on the Marine the whole time. "Of course, Disney movies will never be the same again."

Jack lost it and fell to the floor laughing and Tufo put his head in his hands again, rubbing his temples. "Life isn't fair."

Lamb stuck his head in the door, "Yo, boss, looks like they're back."

Jack tried to regain his composure and collected himself from the floor. As he wiped at his uniform, he kept giggling to himself and tried to put the image out of his mind. Tufo came up beside him and said, "I blame *you*. You sent me out there, she attached herself to me, therefore, it's *your* fault. So keep your pie-hole shut about it."

"Aye-aye, Gunny," Jack said, a smirk still painted across his features.

As they stepped out of the hut and saw Loren and her party returning, he noted that their faces were grim. He didn't take that as a good sign. He prepared himself for the worst.

Loren approached him and he bowed to her and she to him. After their formal greeting, she escorted him back into the building and they resumed their seats. "I spoke with the elders of all of the Greater Elf tribes," she began. "Many felt that this was not their war, that this was the doings of mankind and the hubris of the vampire Sicarii."

Jack nodded. He knew what was coming next. They were on their own.

"But I explained to them that the vampire would not stop at burning the earth and enslaving *just* mankind. Our blood does strange and exotic things to vampires and they would stop at nothing to find our homes here in the Anywhere and enslave us all." She peered at Jack and he felt her gaze burn through him. "They have agreed to assist you in your endeavors, Chief Jack."

"That's great," he said. "When will your warriors be available to go?"

"On the morrow. If you like, you may stay here for the evening and leave with them."

Jack glanced at his squad mates and nodded. "That would be perfect, ma'am. We could make arrangements to fly them to our base once we have an idea the number of people we're talking about, and then arrange transport to—"

"You do not understand, Chief Jack," she interrupted. "We will take *you* where you need to go."

Jack gave her a confused look. "Ma'am?"

193

Her smile warmed him in ways he didn't even like to consider. He was a mated wolf, after all. "The doorway in which you entered our Anywhere...can take you where you wish to travel. You need only to tell us where that is."

"A portal," Jack said, more to himself than anyone.

"Yes, a portal. To anywhere in the world that you wish to be, within a short distance of course."

"Of course," Jack said, as if this were now common knowledge. "I would need to radio my people to find out exactly where we need to go. Is that okay?"

"We can open the portal to anyplace. Long or short distance to your people. If they are not there, then simply tell us where you think they will be and we shall try again."

"Sweet." Jack nodded. "I wish we had one of those things. It would sure knock down our response time."

Loren shook her head. "I am sorry, Chief Jack, the doorways to the Anywhere are only for the Elven People."

"I understand," he said. "But one can still wish, right."

"If one is to wish, then one should wish for victory in the upcoming battle, wouldn't you think?" she replied softly.

"Of course. Forgive me," Jack said, being brought back to their now shared reality.

"In the morrow, when the others come, we shall send you all to your place of choosing. For now, eat and rest. If you have need of anything, please let us know." She rose from her seat and left the building as regally as a queen.

Jack and his people prepared for a night in the gathering room. Here, where time had little meaning, he knew that it would be a long night.

Barbara Mueller had just finished loading the dishwasher and peered outside to the backyard. Bobby was practicing throwing his new football to one side of the yard, running as hard as he could to retrieve it then chucking it back to the other side. Barbara smiled and shook her head at her little man, unable to contain her pride not only in his dedication but to the obvious hundredth winning touchdown pass he made in his own little mind. She noted the dwindling light and slid open the rear porch door.

"Time to come in, Bobby. You need to wash up for dinner."

Bobby scooped up the football from the well-worn grass and slumped his shoulders, "Aw, Mom, do I gotta?" he whined.

"You bet your grass-stained little hiney you do," she said. "Upstairs. Bathtub. March." She ordered with a grin.

"But Mom, it's still light out." He glanced around at the darkness and then back at her. "Sort of."

"Now, mister. Supper's almost ready, and you have to scrub the gridiron off your body," she said. "You don't want your mac-n-cheese to get cold, do you?"

Bobby kicked at the dirt as he slowly worked his way in. He loved mac-n-cheese, but he hated coming in from his practice. The other guys had two weeks on him and he had a lot of catching up to do. He couldn't practice football from the bathtub and moms just didn't understand that.

He trudged up onto the deck and dropped the football into the seat of the lawn chair by the sliding door. He stuck his nose into the kitchen and sniffed. "Mom, can I skip the bath and just eat supper real fast? I think I could get a little more practice in before bed-time."

Barbara chanced a glance at him and chuckled. "Not on your life, mister. You got more dirt on you than you left in the yard." She carried the meatloaf to the table. She stuck a finger in his ear and wiggled. "I could plant potatoes in those ears," she teased.

"Mo-o-om!" he whined. "Don't do that. You just pushed it into my *brain!*"

"Bath!" she laughed, pointing to the stairs.. "Go!"

Bobby dropped his head and slowly trudged to the stairs. Just as he hit the middle landing, the doorbell rang.

"I got it!" he yelled, tromping back down the stairs, hoping to put off the bath a little longer.

"No way, José! Upstairs!" Barbara yelled as she flipped the kitchen towel onto her shoulder and walked to the front door. "Go! Shoo!" she said as she popped the towel towards his feet.

She went to the front door and peeked out of the side window. She saw two men in dark suits and sunglasses standing at her front step. At first she thought maybe they were cops, or Jehovah's Witnesses, but the little hairs on the back of her neck stood on end. She had an 'oh shit' moment as she thought of Robert, and then Bobby.

She glanced up the stairs and saw him peering around the corner. "Stay there," she whispered. "No matter what you see or hear, you don't come back down until I tell you to. Got it?"

Bobby nodded, fear suddenly creeping into his little eyes. "Pinocchio?" he asked.

"Maybe," she answered. Pinocchio was their 'danger word'. If they ever needed to send a message to the other that there was danger, the word to use was 'Pinocchio'. Barbara stepped back to the hall closet and pulled the pistol out of the holster that Robert had given her. She slipped it into the back of her jeans just as the doorbell rang a second time.

"Just a moment," she yelled. She peeked back up the stairs and breathed a sigh of relief that Bobby wasn't in sight.

Barbara took a deep breath and opened the door as she would for anybody at that time of night. She opened it slightly and used her foot to brace it so that it couldn't be forced open by anyone shoving on it.

"Barbara Mueller?" the closest man asked.

"Yes. Can I help you?" she asked cautiously.

"Yes, ma'am. We're with the DoD, and we've been sent to collect you and your son for your own safety," he replied.

She noted that both men appeared slightly pale, but thought it might be a trick of her porch light. The darkness of the evening had deepened and her porch light cast a bright white light that drained the color from everything in its glow.

"Can I see your identification please?" she asked. The man nodded with a slight smile.

He reached into his breast pocket and pulled out a flat black wallet and flipped it open for her showing an identification card and a badge. "I don't blame you for being suspicious, ma'am. You can't be too safe these days." He flipped it shut and slipped it back into his breast pocket. Barbara peered past him and noted a black van parked at the end of her sidewalk. The windows were tinted so dark that she couldn't see if anybody else were inside. The other man kept looking around as if expecting something.

"What about him?" she asked. The first man elbowed his partner and he turned his attention back to her. "Identification?"

He simply nodded and pulled his from his breast pocket and flashed it to her. He still nervously looked around, waiting for some unseen threat to strike. "Ma'am? We really need to get you and your son to safety."

"Safety?" she asked. "From what?" Barbara's hand snuck back and curled around the grip of the pistol in her waistband.

"I'm not at liberty, ma'am," the lighter haired man said. "We were just told to come and get you and take you to the base." She could tell he was already getting aggravated that she wasn't jumping and following his orders.

"I'm afraid I still don't understand. What base?" she asked.

"The military base, ma'am."

"You do realize that my husband and I are divorced, right? The military can't lay any claims to me or my son. And neither can my husband. We have a divorce decree." She was pushing the matter, buying time to milk information. She had to be sure, but she pulled the pistol from the back of her jeans and released the safety.

"Ma'am, please don't be difficult. This is for your own safety—"

"From what?" she demanded. "Safety from what?"

The man pulled back slightly, not expecting her to balk at his perceived authority. "From…hostiles and such and…"

"*Hostiles!*" she cried. "What the hell? Are we playing cowboys and Indians here? What the hell is a hostile?" she demanded.

The second, dark haired man who kept nervously looking around turned to the first man and said, "Fuck it, man, just grab the bitch and let's get out of here, will ya?" Barbara pulled the door open and fired two rounds to his chest and one to his head, then stepped back a half step and leveled the weapon on the first man.

199

"Who the hell are you people?" she demanded as she assumed a defensive shooting stance.

The first, lighter haired man shook his head and smiled at her. "Bullets aren't going to hurt us, lady." He opened his mouth and fangs descended in a threatening manner. "Come with me now and we may let you live."

"Look again, asshole. Your buddy isn't getting up." The vampire glanced down at his friend, prone on the front steps of her house. "Silver bullets, dumbass." Barbara put two in his chest right where his heart would be and watched him fall, his eyes still round with shock and fear with the realization that he was dead before he hit the floor.

Barbara stepped over the bodies and ran to the van parked outside her house. She threw open the driver's door and scanned the interior. There was nobody else inside and she slammed the door and ran back to the house.

"Bobby! Pinocchio!" she yelled as she ran to the hall closet and grabbed her bug out bag. She ran to the kitchen and made sure the burners were off on the stove and grabbed Bobby's football off the rear porch then back to the living room where Bobby had just come bouncing down the stairs. His eyes widened when he saw the two bodies on the floor and noted that his mom still had the gun in her hand.

"Mom? Did you shoot those two guys?" His voice was laced with excitement and tinged with fear.

"Yes, baby, I did. Get your coat and go to the car. Now."

"Where are we going?" he nearly yelled as she ran past him.

"I'm not sure yet," she said honestly. "Maybe to grandma and grandpa's, maybe to the cabin. Maybe to find your daddy."

Bobby nodded and grabbed his coat then ran into the garage. He threw his stuff in the back of the small SUV and climbed into the front and buckled his seatbelt. Barbara was right behind him, tossing her stuff in the back of the vehicle and catching herself as she tried to put the keys into the ignition. Her hands shook so badly that she could barely do it. Bobby reached over and placed his hand over his mom's trembling fingers and she looked over at her son, so much like his father, a natural calm in the eye of the storm.

"You can do this, Mom. I believe in you."

She forced herself to take a deep breath, then smiled at him and nodded. Then taking another deep breath, she slowly inserted the keys into the ignition and the SUV roared to life. She hit the button on the garage door opener and half expected a small army of monsters waiting for them as the door lifted, but let out the breath she'd been holding when she looked behind her and saw only the empty road behind her. She backed the car out and turned onto the road, facing the black van that delivered the attackers to her home. Fighting back the urge to scream at both the vehicle and the monsters that invaded her home, she put the car in gear and headed for the highway.

She drove for nearly a half hour before she pulled into a rest stop and dialed Robert. He didn't answer when she first called and the call went to voicemail, but just as she hung up, her phone chirped an incoming call. She looked at the caller ID and saw that he was calling back. She pushed the green button and nearly cried out when she heard his voice.

"Please tell me you just miss me," he said, his voice low.

"You were right Robert. They came. They came to our house," she sobbed. "They came to our fucking *house*, Robert!" She was about to lose it until Bobby reached out with his little hand and took her free hand in his. He squeezed gently giving her strength.

"Oh, my God, Babs, tell me you're both safe," Robert begged.

"We are," she said quickly. "I did just like you told me. I did it just like you fucking told me. To the letter, baby." She heard Robert sigh with relief.

"How many were there?" The nervousness obvious in his voice.

"Only two." She almost laughed. "Teach them to underestimate *me*!" She then laughed nervously and almost began to cry with the adrenaline pumping through her. "But, Robert…what do I do now? I just ran and left the bodies sitting on the front porch." She started to panic now, afraid the local law enforcement would be looking for her to arrest her and take Bobby away from her. Throw her in jail…hell, throw her *under* the jail!

"Did you see what they were? I mean…could you tell if they were vampires or…"

"Yes!" she said excitedly, but not wanting to repeat it in front of Bobby. She wanted to maintain his innocence as long as she could. "They were."

"No worries, baby. Come dawn, the sun will take care of the bodies. They'll be ash. Nothing left."

Barbara was trembling so badly she could barely hold the phone. "Robert, what do I do now? Where do we go?"

Robert blew hard into the phone as he tried to think. "If they found you at home, they can find your parents' house."

"Robert, they're on a cruise, we could lay low there. Nobody would need to know we were there," she offered. "They aren't due back for almost two weeks."

"No, the risks are too high," he said softly.

"What about the cabin? Would they know about Grampy's cabin?" she asked hopefully.

"I don't know, baby, they might." He paced with the phone thinking, she could hear background noises and the steady rhythm of his breathing. "I just don't know where the safest place for you to go is. I'd bring you with me, but all hell is about to break loose where I'm going and I don't want you and Bobby anywhere near this," he said softly.

Barbara felt hot tears pour down her cheeks as she thought of him marching off to war again and her chest trembled. "I love you so much," was all she could croak out, and it wracked her chest with pain to fight back the sobs.

"I love you too, Babs. So very much," he whispered. She heard him sigh into the phone then take a deep breath. "Listen, you have the silver ammo, right?"

She inhaled shakily and nodded. "Yes. I had it packed in my go-bag."

"Okay. Go ahead and go to Grampy's. It's in the middle of nowhere, you have four-wheel-drive, so you can get in and out easily. Also, you'll be able to hear any vehicles that come that way," he reasoned. "They keep it stocked with groceries and Bobby will have plenty of room to run around and fish and swim and..." Robert groaned. "Just be careful baby. Especially after dark."

She nodded again, knowing he couldn't see it. "I will, sweetheart. I promise."

"Tell Bobby I love him," Robert said softly.

"I will." And without thinking she said, "And Robert?"

"Yeah, baby?"

"When this is all over...when the dust is settled and you've saved the world and it's safe for us to go back to some kind of normal life and..." She choked up again, but regained her composure, "you and me?"

He expected her to say that they were done for good, that this was simply too much for any person to bear. He waited for her to drop the bomb that he knew was coming. He bit his lower lip and waited for the punch to the gut that he knew was already there, but simply hadn't been delivered yet.

Barbara cleared her throat so that he could hear her better. "You and me? Yeah. Together forever. I don't care if you *do* infect me," she told him. "In fact, I hope you do so we don't have to worry about it anymore."

Robert was dumbfounded. He held the phone closer to his ear to ensure he heard her correctly. "In fact, you and me can just move to Grampy's and once a month chase our tails and catch rabbits and deer and wake up naked in the morning covered in mud and rabbit fur and…"

"Barbara? Did you get hit in the head?" he asked.

She laughed into the phone and it felt good. Liberating, in fact. "No, baby. I just realized that some things are more important than playing it safe. So damn it, soldier, you come back to me, do you hear me?" she growled into the phone. "You come home alive. To *me*. So we can spend the rest of our lives together. Chasing our tails and doing it doggy style!" she laughed.

"Mo-o-om!" Bobby cried, poking her. "I'm right *here*."

Robert laughed when he heard Bobby, but had to sniff back the tears that welled up in his eyes. "You got it, baby. Do it doggy style. Make puppies and eat Alpo and the whole nine yards."

"Yuck, Robert. Okay, we won't go that far, okay."

"Well, I've had your meatloaf and…"

"Hey!" she laughed, "Way to ruin a tender moment, jerk!"

"I love you, Babs."

"I love you, too."

"Even your meatloaf."

"You are such a bad liar, Robert."

Dominic awoke from his drug induced sleep screaming. It took three orderlies and two members of Team Two to hold him down and strap his wrists and ankles to the hospital bed. The orderly was just injecting him with another dose of tranquilizer when he flexed and bent the rails of his bed. The two members of Team Two grabbed his arms again and held him down until the tranquilizer took effect and he relaxed.

As the orderlies gingerly stepped back, watching Dominic in amazement, the two Team members simply shrugged it off and one said in heavily accented English, "Steroids. You know how these American commando types are."

Dominic's metabolism was quickly burning through the tranquilizers and painkillers and his mind tormented him with the images implanted by the dark vampire. He twisted against his bindings as he sweated out the drugs, his mind racing against the images. There was something he had to do and his subconscious knew it, he just couldn't reach it. It was hidden behind a wall deep in his mind and he couldn't see behind it. He knew the vampire had gotten into his brain and scrambled his eggs, he just didn't know what he had done. The bastard had forced him to do things, to tell things that he wouldn't have told...Dominic ground his teeth and tasted blood in his mouth. Was it real or a memory that the bloodsucker had forced there, he couldn't tell. But his ears heard voices, scrambling and hectic and somebody was gripping his head. He fought against the grip, knowing the vampire had him again, preparing to bore into his mind once more.

Dom thrashed and someone forced something foreign into his mouth. He gagged and fought the urge to regurgitate as something was forced between his teeth...blood seeping down the back of his throat. Was he being forced to drink blood? The vampire's blood? Was the bastard trying to change him...surprise, surprise asshole, he was immune!

The voices around him settled and the grip on his head relaxed. Dom felt the pain in his mouth and wondered what had hurt his tongue. He bit down on the foreign object and felt it give like a hard rubber stop between his jaws. His jaws ached the moment he did it and the fog in his brain began to lift. He concentrated on the foreign object in his mouth, settling his body, relaxing and unclenching his muscles one at a time.

He tried to relax his mind, knowing there was something he needed to remember. What was he blocking that was so important and why was he just now remembering it? The pain killers and the tranquilizers were burning off again and he felt the knowledge slipping from him. He knew that something was there and it was getting further away, slipping deeper from his grasp as he became more and more lucid. There was something important that he had to find out...he just couldn't see it.

Dom sat up, his rheumy eyes open and searching. He noticed that his mouth was propped open with a bite-block and it was strapped behind his head. The two members of Team Two rushed to his side and he nodded to them. He mumbled something to them and they quickly took the bite block from his mouth. Dom sat up as straight as he could and spat blood to the side onto the floor. "Yuck, man that is nasty."

"You bit your tongue. They had to put the…thing in your mouth to keep you from biting it off," one of the members said.

The other stared down at him, his face twisted. "You were having some kind of fit," he said in heavily accented English.

"I need them to drug me up *good*," Dom told them, his eyes pleading with them.

The first one shook his head. "They are already concerned with the amount they have given you." He lowered his voice and gave Dom a knowing look. "They do not understand our metabolism."

"You don't get it," Dom hissed. "That vampire did something to me. He…*caused* something in my head and I can almost get to it when I'm under the influence."

The two squad members glanced around the room and then at each other. The first one laid a hand on Dom's chest and pushed him back down to the bed. "I will see what I can find," he said. "The doctors here will not give it to you, but if I can get my hands on the tranquilizers, I will give them to you."

Dom nodded and lay back while the EU Monster Squad member snuck down the hall. The second team member stood duty at his bedside, watching both the door and the window. After a few minutes, Dom asked him, "You guys been getting calls to a bunch of bullshit ops? Almost like you're being tested by someone who doesn't know how monsters act?"

The other team member looked at him and nodded. "Yes. We have had two such calls," he replied. "Both were...disappointing." He smiled at Dom.

"Vampires? Zombies? What did you have?" he asked, his throat rasping.

The team member unstrapped his arm and poured him a cup of water. "We had a small outbreak of newly made vampires. Both times, it was as if somebody had created these newborns and simply set them loose." He shook his head. "They were like shooting fish in the barrel."

Dom nodded after he washed his mouth out with the water and drank down some of the cool wetness to coat his throat. The chunk he bit in his tongue hurt now that he had taken a drink, and he almost regretted doing it. "We had similar things happen in the states." He reflected. "They didn't have a clue how to set up a real test the first couple of times, but the last one?" he shook his head. "That was when they nabbed me. They got us divided and overwhelmed me by sheer numbers." Dom thought back to the night they had been overrun and a cold shiver went down his spine. "It started out as maybe a half dozen to lure us in, then before we knew it, there was probably eighty of them swarming the house and another forty behind me. I got tackled and held to the ground while they shackled me." He shook his head again and gave a tight smile. "I can't wait to give them some payback."

"Very soon we pack it out to America. Then you can have your payback." The operator patted his arm reassuringly.

The door slipped open and the other squad member stepped in quietly. "It was not easy to find their tranquilizers." He held up the bottle of clear liquid and a syringe. "Are you ready to find whatever it is you are looking for?" He stuck the syringe into the bottle. He injected a large amount of air and then pulled the plunger back, filling the syringe with the clear liquid.

"As ready as I'll ever be," Dom said. He turned and looked at the other squad member. Dom opened his mouth and the man placed the bite block back into his mouth and Dom shut his jaw on it. The man secured it in place and Dom lay back while he reattached his hand to the strap at the side of the bed.

"Do you know what you are doing?" the second squad member asked. "Can you give him an overdose?"

The first man shrugged. "Did you see how much they gave him the last time? He said it was not enough." Then the man stuck the needle into the IV line and pushed the plunger on the syringe. He turned and watched Dom's eyes flutter and then close within seconds. "Hmm. Strong stuff."

"What if you gave him too much?" the second squad member asked.

"Then I gave him too much!" he whispered back excitedly. "I cannot take it back out of his arm!"

Dom felt the blackness ooze over him and the warmth of the drug envelope his body, his mind drifting into the ether. The last thing he heard before losing

210

touch with reality was, 'Then I gave him too much!' and yet, he didn't care if he had. This felt different than before when he was doped up. This felt wonderful and he felt like he was floating on a lake of warm darkness without a care in the world.

He could relax and rest and his mind could wander without the dark images flashing in front of his eyes. He felt himself sigh with relief as he relaxed. He opened his eyes in his mind and saw inky black water, calm and glassy, dark blue skies that were nearly black above him. He was floating on his back trying not to cause ripples in the serenity of the water. He slowly turned his head and could see the silhouette of an island not far from where he was, but he didn't care. He was too relaxed to care.

He sighed again and enjoyed the warmth of the water, floating along the surface like a leaf in a stream. Peace at last, he could finally rest. He was just about to glance at the island again when ghostly white hands burst from the water and grabbed him around the middle and began pulling him down, under the water trying to drown him. He knew exactly who those ghostly, cold white hands belonged to and he fought them as they pulled at him, grabbing at his clothing, ripping and slashing at his flesh to pull him to the bottom and hold him there until he too, was a corpse.

Savagely he fought back, pulling at the hands, kicking and shredding in return, punching with all of his might, struggling against the force that pulled him deeper and deeper into the inky blackness of the water. He felt when they passed the thermal layer in the water as it chilled him, or was that simply his life force

211

seeping from him as the vampire sucked his life energy away? Dom didn't know and he didn't care as he continued to fight, feet kicking at the unseen enemy below him, hands grasping, pulling, tearing and slashing at the enemy below him. When he finally broke free of the monster, he kicked for the surface of the water, his lungs burning for air. He shot forth from the surface of the water and gasped for oxygen, feeling the cooling effect immediately as he forced cold air back into his lungs, the darkness of the nightscape had turned to day, the serenity of the water restored to natural, but calm waves.

He continued to suck air as quickly as he could and kicked for shore. He could taste the salt in his mouth and didn't know what the hell was going on, but this felt as real as real got. The sea tastes real, smelled real and felt real. The sand under his feet felt real as he hit the beach of the small island and the seashells under his hand felt real. The sun on his back felt real and the gulls screeching at him for disturbing their scavenging sounded real. The waves crashing on the shore sounded real and the brine along the shore smelled as real as anything he had ever experienced before in his life.

Dominic didn't know what was going on and questioned if he was losing his mind. He fell to his knees on the sand, suddenly exhausted and confused. He looked to the interior of the island and noted that the jungle was teeming with plant life and birds. He knew that if he could find water, he could survive here...if it was in fact a real place. But he prayed to

whatever god there was that this was still a drug induced dream.

He tiredly pulled himself to his feet and trudged
off the water's edge and to the jungle's border. He
turned back and looked out at the ocean to see if there
was any sign of the vampire or a boat or any other sign
of how he had arrived here, but saw nothing but the
endless ocean. He glanced upward and saw the sun between the fronds of a palm tree's limb and knew that
had the vampire been real, its life would be forfeit in
daylight. Breathing a slight sigh of relief for miracles,
he stepped into the jungle to investigate this strange
new world he had arrived at.

11

The briefing room had been prepared and while the teams assembled, Mueller privately confessed to Colonel Mitchell what he did during his short leave time. Matt listened patiently and tried not to lose his cool when Mueller informed him that he had broken the cardinal rule of being with the Monster Squad and told his wife everything. And yes, for clarification, he meant *everything*. He also told Colonel Mitchell how he had swiped several dozen rounds of silver ammunition and equipped his wife with a comparable handgun in order to use the ammunition and showed her how to use it at the family farm.

Mitchell interrupted him and asked, "Do you have any idea what you've just done, Mueller?" Mitchell fought to keep his face from turning red. The cat was out of the bag and losing his temper at this point would do him little good. Curbing the damage caused by his operator's indiscretion might.

"I saved my family's lives, Colonel," Robert shot back quietly, keeping his voice low so that the others wouldn't know that their families were now under attack. "She just called me to tell me that two vampires showed up at our house at dusk 'to take them to safety'. When she questioned them about it, they got grabby and she put them down," he explained through clenched teeth.

Mitchell paled. "She was sure they were vamps?"

"Unless they were truly DoD and just needed a better dental plan, then yes, sir."

Mitchell nodded. He looked up and caught LT. Gregory preparing to enter the briefing room and waved him over. "Mueller's ex-wife and son were attacked at their family home by vamps. She put them down on her own." He didn't explain that she used stolen silver ammunition, no need to get too deeply into the details. "I want people sent to all immediate family members *now*! Surveillance only. Anything strange or out of place, they step in and take them out. Got it?"

"Yes, sir. Right away." Gregory ran down the hall and picked up a phone as Mitchell turned back to Robert.

"What you did was *completely* out of line, son," Mitchell began. Bob stiffened. He was prepared to take whatever punishment Matt dished out, so long as his family was safe. "But if you hadn't it could have gotten damned messy." He finished softly. "And your actions may have saved some of the other operators' families as well, *if* we get people in the field in time." Mueller simply nodded at him, unsure if he was off the hook or not. "What spurred this course of action?" Matt asked, not sure if he wanted to know the answer.

Bob took a deep breath and glanced over his shoulders to ensure nobody else was within hearing distance. "Dominic, sir. I couldn't take the risk he wasn't compromised."

"Good call, son."

Matt heaved a small sigh of relief. A small part of him felt it was because he had withheld the truth of the augmentation from the operators and felt guilty for having such selfish thoughts at a time like this. "Should have thought of it myself," he muttered. "Next time though, bounce these ideas off of me before you act, okay? We could have assigned someone to watch the families...ALL of the families. And not risk them finding out about the monsters."

"You mean not risk them finding out about *us*, sir?" There was no malice in his tone, but Robert knew exactly what Mitchell meant.

"No, Bob, I mean the monsters. We aren't monsters. We stop the monsters," Matt clarified. "If the day comes where any of us goes feral and starts killing innocent humans for the sheer joy of killing, then yes. Then we become the monsters and I pray to God that somebody else will hunt us down and put us out of our misery," He preached. "But until that time comes, we are the good guys. We protect the innocent from the evil. We are the first line of defense for the mommies and daddies who tuck their kiddies into bed at night and promise them that there is nothing hiding under the bed that will eat them in their sleep."

"Yes, sir."

"Let's get into the conference room. We have a lot to go over with this...Max character," he said with obvious distaste in his voice.

The two men entered the room and Bob found a seat with the other squad members. Colonel Mitchell went up to the front and checked to ensure that all the appropriate people were present then cleared his throat to get their attention.

"Okay, folks, let's get this started." He waited a moment while the noise settled and they turned their attention to the front. Mitchell nodded to Maxwell who was seated to the side and he rose and came up beside him. "This, if you haven't already met him, is Maxwell Verissimo. He is...well..." Matt glanced sideways at Max and shook his head with a slight chuckle. "Well, hell, it's complicated, wouldn't you say?" Max agreed, but maintained his position, waiting to be introduced to the group. "He is Viktor's father, Nadia's grandfather. So I guess that makes him your grandfather-in-law, Jack." The comment drew a few light laughs from the operators in the crowd. "Anyway, he is also the Roman Centurion we were hoping to find. And with that, I'll let Max explain the rest and tell his story."

Max stepped up to the podium and gripped both sides with his powerful arms and looked out at the crowd. He studied them for a moment then nodded. "Smells like a kennel in here," he said with a grin. He looked from face to face and found no humor in the faces of the soldiers in the crowd. He turned to Mitchell and murmured, "Tough crowd." Matt simply shrugged at him.

Max turned his attention back to the soldiers and essential support staff and straightened a bit. "Right, well, so much for ice breakers. As the good colonel said, I'm Max. Or as some of you have heard of me, Claudius Maximus Veranus." He didn't get the excited looks from the soldiers he halfway expected, so

217

he continued on. "I'm sure you've heard the story by now, one way or the other, yes?" He saw most of them nod or murmur to the affirmative, so he continued. "Well, for the most part, it's all true. I'm not sure what to add.

"I know that you are expecting some awe-inspiring speech, but to be honest, it has been far too long since I've held any position of leadership and it will take me a bit to get back into the swing of things." He glanced at Mitchell who simply watched him with a suspicious eye. "I'd like to be able to stand up here and tell you that there's some glorious plan inspired from upon high and that we will all be victorious and be bathed in riches and glory.

"But the truth is...war is not glorious. It is ugly. You know this as well as I do. Comrades are often lost and their praises are not sung by the people." Max glanced at Laura who turned away and sniffed back a tear. "We lose people in the fight against what we perceive as evil every day," he said quietly, "whether it is on a battlefield or in the very streets we live on by our civic protectors, and yet, those who will do evil never seem to run out of creative ways to keep forging on. They keep rising up amongst us and threatening everything that we hold dear." Max looked to Nadia and then Viktor who seemed surprised that his father would think of him so.

"While I wish that I could say, we shall flank the vampires and pierce them in the side, it really isn't that simple. I know simply from listening since I arrived that your Colonel Mitchell has a few surprises up his sleeve, but I honestly do not know if this will be enough

218

to thwart the enemy, for his true weapon isn't just sheer numbers, but an *idea* that somehow vampires are supposed to bring about the destruction of mankind." He paused a moment to allow the thought to sink in. "The idea that vampires are supposed to bring the end of humanity, the end of the world, if you will, is enough to continue on, even if he is vanquished.

"We don't need him to be a martyr, people…for his idea to continue to fester and grow among the vampire ranks." Max breathed deeply and continued. "We need to show *all* of them that any idea along these lines will be dealt with accordingly, and not necessarily with the true death. The worst thing that could happen to an immortal isn't *death*, but imprisonment."

"Hear, hear," Evan said from the rear. Max looked to him and simply nodded. Mitchell shook his head, shame evident across his features.

"Capture the Sicarii, bind him with silver and entomb him for eternity?" Max's features fell as he considered such actions. "That is a fate worse than death."

"How do you propose we capture someone with strength like he has?" Apollo asked. "This cat is supposed to be like…the grandpappy of all vamps. I thought if we killed him, all vamps dropped dead."

Max cocked his head and studied him a moment. "You really don't know do you?" he asked. "You've been hunting creatures of the night all this time and you don't know the difference?" He snorted derisively and shook his head. "Okay, you need to know the difference between Cursed and Damned." Max gripped the podium again. "Okay, folks, history lesson time.

219

"When it comes to wolves, the Damned are of *my* line. Damned by God himself. When you hear of natural born wolves, they are of the Damned line," he stated. "And before you ask, yes, a Damned wolf can bite a human and transmit the virus and make another wolf. That wolf is still a Damned wolf.

"A *Cursed* wolf on the other hand, is just that, a human who is cursed and becomes a werewolf. This was much more predominant a couple thousand years ago. In fact, back about...oh, say twelve hundred years ago, the wolf curse was so predominant that wolves were nearly hunted to extinction. And just as there are Cursed Wolves, there also used to be Cursed Vampires." Max looked around the room and saw eyebrows shoot up. "That's right. The Sicarii and myself, we were the first *of the Damned*, but not the first ever of our kinds. Prior to us, there were vampires and werewolves, but they were all of the Cursed nature.

"There is a history of vampires in China that go back a couple of thousand years before the Sicarii was ever thought of," He mused. "But, we are the first of the true bloods. Up until us, vampires couldn't procreate other than biting another human and same goes for wolves. We were the new breed." He looked around the room. "Any questions on the difference?"

Mueller stood up and asked, "Do the same things kill both kinds?"

"Beheadings, fire, wood chippers, etc...yes. Holy relics, silver, etc...not so much. Silver didn't come into play until the Damned," Max said.

"Where did the cross and holy water come into play then?" Sanchez asked.

"Hollywood," Max answered. There was a quiet wave of chuckling around the room as the operators relaxed a bit and learned a bit about both creatures. "No...seriously...Hollywood. And I think Stoker wrote some of that stuff too, but they were both wrong. Silver, stakes, beheading, blah, blah, blah that all worked. Silver especially. It's a very stout poison for both vamps and wolves."

Max inhaled deeply and blew out a cleansing breath. "But back to the point at hand." He paused a moment and stared off into nothing. "Look, there's more to it besides whether or not we just kill the Sicarii or not. While true, that if we could kill him, the grand majority of all the vampires in the world would probably fall over and turn to ash. And while you're thinking this is fantastic, why not just aim for that..." He shook his head as he tried to think of a way to explain the concept to them. "This is really tough, guys." He scratched at his beard. "Look, this may seem sort of...out there, to some of you, but bear with me." He stepped from the podium and slowly walked among them, reminding Mitchell of an old college professor that he had. "The world...the *universe*, is filled with opposites. Good and evil, black and white, cold and hot..."

"Blonde and brunette?" a voice from the rear asked.

Max turned to that portion of the crowd and smiled. "Sure. Why the hell not?" he chuckled. "Anyway, the point is, there has to be balance. Balance is the key." He turned around and slowly worked his way back to the front of the room, his presence seemed to

221

grow larger as he continued to explain. "Just as God gave His Son, it was because there was great evil in the world in the form of Satan. Good versus Evil. Light versus Dark. *Balance.*

"Like Yin and Yang, the balance must be maintained, otherwise a greater evil will rise up to take its place, because nature abhors a vacuum and when it fills that empty space it often fills it with something much nastier than what was there beforehand. And history has shown us that often, the perceived good that vanquishes an evil can often be twisted to become the new evil." Max shook his head, "This would not be good."

"Okay, you make sense, and I get that there are different kinds of vampires and wolves. I do get that, but let's say that we did kill this Sicarii, we'd be able to drop the sheer number of vampires in the world by, what?" Mueller pondered.

"Millions," Thorn finished for him.

Many of the operators turned to him with shock and amazement across their faces. Some even gasped at his response. "You're saying he'll be able to call up millions to his cause?" Spalding asked.

"*Oui,*" Thorn nodded.

"So why not drop this asshole and be done with it?" Mueller asked Max again.

Max shook his head. "Weren't you listening, pup? *Balance.* We must maintain balance."

"If we have to maintain balance, then you're saying for every one of theirs we kill, one of ours has to die, he'll win just due to the vast numbers he has," Sanchez shot back at him.

Max shook his head and lowered his eyes. "You're not grasping the larger picture." He scratched at his beard again and sighed. "Try not to think of this as a chess board with a set number of pieces. Think of this more as an energy field." He noted their confusion, but pressed on. "The Sicarii is very old and that, in and of itself, gives him strength. He also has a lot of people on his side, and that gives him strength as well. He's able to gather strength from their merely being available to him...like a *battery*! He has all of these little batteries that he can also pull power from!" he said, and noticed that the people in the room were suddenly on the same page as he was. "By our doing battle and taking away from him the little batteries en mass, we in effect drain him and make him more manageable."

"What about you?" Tracy asked. "Do you gain strength from the number of people in your group, or army or...pack? Whatever."

Max shook his head. "No. I wish it were that way..." he paused and reflected on what he was about to say, then thought of Victoria and her power hungry ways, and thought better of his comment. "Actually, no. I *don't* wish it were that way. I'm quite happy with the way things are now." He said, stealing a glance at Viktor. "I'm a warrior. A Centurion. A Lycan amongst Lycans and my skills have been honed over millennia. I am his Sentinel." Max said, his eyes turning steely. "While the Sicarii will lose strength as his numbers dwindle, mine will not. I may not increase in strength, but it will seem like it to him as his power dwindles."

"I mean no disrespect, sir, so please, do not take this question in the wrong manner." Hank slowly rose to his full height. "But what makes you think that you can handle Judah?"

Max raised an eyebrow as he studied Hank. "You know his true name?"

"When I heard that he was Judas Iscariot, I knew his true name," the Padre informed him.

"Interesting," Max responded. "I believe that of all of us, if any were to attempt to take him one-on-one, I would have the best chance of succeeding." He glanced around the room before settling back on Hank. "It wouldn't be the first time the two of us had fought."

Donovan rolled over and allowed himself a peek out the window of the common building. It was darker outside, but it never really got darker than what might pass for twilight in the real world. At first he thought it was because of all of the fires that the elves had going from their torches, their campfires and their cook fires, but he soon realized that as they slowly put their fires out and retired for the evening, it remained light outside. The twilight was simply a side effect of the dimensional world they were in.

Donovan sighed heavily and pulled the light blanket up again, trying to get comfortable. "I can't sleep."

Jack was sprawled out on the floor, his bedroll spread out under him. He opened one sleepy eye and glared at Donovan. "Because you slept all day while we were waiting for them to return." He rolled over, turning his back to Donnie. "Shut up and maybe you can catch a few zees."

Donnie sighed heavily again and tried another position. "This doesn't feel right, Chief. According to my watch it should be morning."

"Your watch is broken," Jack murmured. "It's dark outside."

Tufo rolled toward Donovan and gave a 'Psst!' as quietly as he could. Donnie turned to him, his eyes wide awake. Mark made a motion toward the door and Donnie nodded. Both men slipped out and left the others to sleep.

As soon as they slipped far enough away from the group, Donnie asked, "Sup, Gunny?"

"I couldn't sleep either. Thought maybe we could get some air." His eyes shifted toward the treetops where the grand majority of the Greater Elves lived.

Donnie nodded and they strolled through the main pathway toward the brook. "Something on your mind?"

"Nothing major," Tufo said. "Just thought I'd ask you about your encounter with your Sprite."

Donnie nodded, a slight smile crossing his face. "Figured you'd get around to that sooner or later."

"You did, did you?"

"Oh yeah," Donnie said knowingly. "Feeling the effects are you?"

"What do you mean?" Tufo asked, knowing exactly what Donovan meant.

Donovan looked at him sideways and kept walk-ing. "The *longing*? The desire to have her back?" Tufo feigned ignorance in his reaction, but Donovan knew better. "It fades with time, Gunny."

Tufo simply nodded as they continued to walk. They reached the brook and Donovan picked up a rock and tried to skip it. He failed miserably. "How long does it take?" Gunny asked him.

Donovan shrugged. "Everybody's different." He bent down and selected another stone. "Some a few days, others weeks." He looked at Tufo and raised an eyebrow. "I've heard that some people never really get over it."

"Fucking great."

"Yeah, they should print a warning label on the little pixie bitches." Donovan laughed and tossed the rock causing a large splash.

"Damn straight they should," Gunny shot back. "Do not stick your pecker in here!"

"Or you'll want to keep doing it!" Donnie laughed.

"I know, right? Damndest thing, too," Mark said, lowering his eyes. "You feel like shit for doing it, but, man...those pixies sure as hell know what they're do-ing." He stared off toward the horizon.

Donovan got a glazed look across his eyes as his memories carried him back. "They sure do."

"How do they—"

"I have no idea," Donovan answered before he could ask. "I spoke with a shaman who knows about pixies, or sprites, or spriggans or whatever the hell you want to call them. He thinks there's something that

226

they secrete that makes you desire them so that you don't stop in the middle of it."

He gave him a puzzled look and Donnie shrugged. "You saw how she damn near bit Lamb's finger off, right? Could you imagine if you pissed her off by not finishing the job once you started?"

Tufo cupped himself and his eyes shot wide. "Yeah, probably a good thing they have that addictive juice then, huh?"

"Oh, yeah. It gets you past whatever trepidations you might have once you start."

Mark picked up a rock and skipped it across the brook. Donovan stared at him and shook his head. "Show off."

"Lots of practice. I *was* retired, remember?" Tufo shot him a shit-eating grin.

"Speaking of, when Dom gets back...what are you going to do? Go back to being a spotter?"

Tufo's face clouded slightly and he looked away. "I don't know." He shrugged and then turned back to him. "To be honest, I don't think Matt will give me much choice."

"Mitchell? Why would he keep you out of the muck?" Donnie asked. "You held your own before, didn't you?"

"That was then, wolf boy," Tufo said sarcastically. "Now? I'm just old and slow compared to you juiced up youngsters."

Donnie nodded, understanding completely. He knew a lot of operators that woke up one day and got their walking papers from higher up. Orders that stated they were being put out to pasture simply

227

because they had reached a magic number that the powers-that-be decided meant that they couldn't do their job any more. He didn't agree with that at all. "Maybe you could hang around as a technical advisor or something?"

Tufo shot him a scornful look. "Me? A technical advisor?" He threw another rock, hard, not even trying to skip it. "I don't know enough about the ins and outs of how you boys operate in theatre. It wouldn't work. Besides, I'm a field agent," he finished, slightly less angry.

Donnie nodded and turned to head back to the common building. "Well, maybe we can find a place for you. I mean, hell…we wouldn't have found the Greaters if it weren't for you."

"Yeah," Tufo said with sarcasm. "I could be your token human."

"Come on, man…work with me here. I'm trying to keep a positive outlook."

"Well, *I'm* positive. Positive that my old wrinkled ass will be kicked to the curb again once Dom is back safe and sound," Tufo said bitterly.

Donovan wrapped an arm around Tufo's shoulder and pulled him in as they walked. "The fat lady ain't sung yet, buddy."

Tufo snorted a laugh. "The only thing that will keep me in this uniform is if I'm killed in action, bud."

Donnie shot him a surprised look. "We don't even tease about shit like that, Gunny."

"I ain't teasing either, brother," he said. "Just do me one favor, alright?"

Donnie studied him a moment as they paused under a large oak. "What's that?"

"If I do bite it in battle...if I don't make it? Do NOT send me home. My old lady would take too much joy in digging me up just to kill me again," he said, his features set in stone. "I'd rather have a Viking funeral anyway."

"Seriously? Where the hell am I supposed to find a Viking ship to send you off on?"

Mark gave him a sardonic smile. "Dumbass, it doesn't have to be an actual Viking ship. Just any old boat will work. Just toss my shield and sword on there with me and set the damn thing on fire...push it out into the bay."

"Gunny, Oklahoma City doesn't *have* a bay. And we're moving to Groom Lake for the big 'battle of all battles'. That's in the desert. Again, no bays."

"Oh, for fuck's sake, forget I said anything, will ya?" he said totally exasperated. "You'd think a real friend could find a way to see his dead buddy off the way he wanted but all you got is excuses. Fine."

"No," Donovan laughed, "no, if that's the way you want to be sent off, by God, I'll find a way."

"No, just drop it."

"No, I'm not going to drop it. I'll find a boat. It may be a freaking tuna boat or a row boat or maybe a tug boat, but I'll find you a boat."

"Forget I said anything." Tufo marched back to the common building.

"No, I can't forget it," Donnie said, trying to be serious. "If that's the way you want to be sent off, then I'll make sure that's the way you are sent off. Hell, I may not even wait 'til you're dead. I bet I can find a boat here in Canada…a dinghy!"

Tufo shook his head. "Everybody's a comedian."

"Just trying to help a buddy out," Donnie said, still smiling.

The little messenger stepped gingerly into the old cathedral and glanced nervously first to the second story window for the dark vampire that he called 'master', then to the courtyard. He finally spotted him by the broken altar, staring up at the fresco of Christ, his head tilted, studying the painting. He quickly stepped to the dark vampire, afraid to inform him of the bad news that had just worked its way across the seas to them, but he knew that he must be told.

"Master? I come bearing grave news," the little messenger said, his legs trembling as he approached.

"Tell me, Puppet," the dark one said as he pointed to the painting on the wall. "Do you think they would care to know that their paintings were all wrong?" He ignored the little vampire.

"Master?" he asked, unsure what he meant.

"The humans. Do you think they'd care that their depictions of Christ are all wrong?" he asked. He pointed to the painting with one long finger. "He looked nothing like this. Or any of the other paintings I've ever seen of him," he remarked absently.

"I…uh…perhaps…er…perhaps *you* could paint them one that is more accurate?" the little messenger asked, confusion crossing his own features.

"Me?" the dark vampire chuckled. "I am no painter, Puppet."

"But you could tell the painter what he looked like, yes?"

The dark one continued to stare at the painting and sighed. "I suppose I could," he remarked. "But why give them hope?" he said.

The little messenger was confused and had almost forgotten why he had come to find the Sicarii. "Master, I come bearing grave news."

"Yes, Puppet. I heard you the first time." The dark one finally stepped away and turned his attention to the little vampire. "Please, Puppet. Enlighten me."

The little messenger dropped his eyes to the floor and lowered his head. He truly did *not* want to tell his master this news, but he knew that he needed to know. "Those we sent to collect the family members? They returned with sorrowful news, Master." He waited for his dark master to explode with anger, or at least surge his power over him, but it did not come. He lifted his eyes and peeked at him and saw that he only waited, his face was one only of expectation. "They, uh…went to the homes of the hunters, but the hunters had no family, sire. All but the one with the ex-wife…and she was prepared. She killed the two vampires who went there."

The little messenger cringed and waited for his master's fury, and yet it did not come. Slowly he released his tension and noticed that his master's brows

231

were knotted in concentration. "She was prepared for our visitors?" he repeated as he stepped away, tapping at his chin as he gave the information thought. He shook his head and slowly smiled. "Mr. DeGiacomo was quite clear that nobody was to know of their mission, nor of the existence of our kind. How could she be prepared for two visiting vampires?" he mused. "Somebody broke the rules, Puppet," he said in a sing-song voice.

"You are not upset, Master?" the messenger asked.

The dark vampire turned on him, his face puzzled. "Of course I am upset, Puppet, but one cannot rip asunder the messenger over a little spilled blood! It would be uncivilized." The dark one paced slowly. "However, the other hunters not having family...this is curious.

"It is impossible that Mr. DeGiacomo could have lied to me...not while under my control," he mused. "So perhaps the other hunters lied to him? About their families still being alive?" He spun back to face the messenger, "Or where they currently reside? Or if they ever existed at all!" He laughed; more to himself than from the humor of the situation.

"So, Puppet, our plan to hobble the human hunters by holding captive their loved ones has fallen flat."

"And the ex-wife may well report our attempt to capture her and her child to the hunters."

"Of course she will," he spat. The dark one sat on his favorite pile of rubble and tapped his chin again. "How can we use this to our advantage, Puppet?"

"I don't see how, Master," he said. "As you know, I'm no master tactician, but I see no way that we can use this to our advantage."

"Let me think, Puppet. If there is a way to use this foul-up to our advantage, I will find it."

"I'm sure that you can, Master," the messenger said with full confidence.

The dark one turned to look at him and the messenger fidgeted in his place. "Was there anything else, Puppet?"

"Only that our people were successful in placing electronic tracking devices on most of the cargo carriers of the hunters in England, the EU, and South America." The little messenger smiled.

"Very good Puppet." The dark one smiled. "What of the American hunters?"

"We, uh...weren't able to get past security, Master," he said quietly. "Not *yet* at least. They are still in place and have not given up yet."

"Very well, Puppet. Inform me once they all have been put in place." He dismissed him with a wave.

The dark vampire sat upon his rubble and considered the possibilities with the hunter's family. So the woman escaped and killed two seasoned vampires doing it? Not an easy task. Being prepared is one thing, but killing two seasoned field agents is another. The Sicarii stepped up to his second floor window and gazed out at his city again. He needed to clear his mind and allow the answer to come to him. Thinking too hard clouded his thoughts, and clearing his head of thought allowed new ideas to flow into him. Nothing cleared his head as well as gazing out upon his city from the open window, the night air blowing cool upon his skin.

For more than two millennia he had found ways to turn negatives into positives. He knew that every cloud had a silver lining, he just had to find a creative way to turn this into one. He had the opportunity to nab a hunter's family member and she gave him the slip...if only he could find her again. All the better if she were with the hunters now. But then, he wouldn't be able to use her if she were dead. Perhaps, after he and his army killed her husband, they could find her and the child and use them to promote the breeding programs...use the child as future stock and the mother now?

No sense in micro-managing the small things. Those would be the problems of the farmers. His was simply to deliver the world a massive dose of death and destruction and nurture the flames of devastation as creation itself was turned to ash. He felt the corners of his mouth tug as the smile pulled at him and he realized that as the mental image of the end of the world flashed through his mind, it was the only time in the last two thousand years he had truly been happy.

12

As the work crews continued to pack away their gear and load the trucks Matt oversaw the tasks and checked off on different groups as the trucks pulled away from the hangars and left for their different cargo planes. He had just finished signing off on the last truck when Lieutenant Gregory came up behind him. "Sir, there's a Colonel Anderson on the line for you."

Mitchell nodded and headed for the elevators to go to his office. "Tell him I'm on my way to the phone." Mitchell hurried to his office, not wanting to keep the base commander of Groom Lake waiting any longer than possible, but wanting a quiet place to speak with him.

Mitchell entered his office and picked up the receiver. He punched the button before he was seated at his desk. "Colonel Anderson, thank you for calling," he said as pleasantly as he could, knowing the other full bird would *not* be happy about the circumstances. "I'm terribly sorry to keep you waiting."

"Quite all right, Mitchell," Anderson said on the other end. Mitchell tried to picture the man in his mind and simply couldn't do it. His voice was as nondescript as one could imagine a voice to be. "General McAfee filled me in...well, as much as he could, really." Matt could tell that Anderson hoped for a little more information, but Matt wasn't about to give it to him over the phone.

"Colonel, I can assure you that the need for your facility is real…and temporary. As soon as we arrive I will be more than happy to fill in any blanks that the general couldn't," Matt offered. "But under the circumstances, with phone lines the way they are, I'm sure you understand my hesitation in divulging any more information than absolutely necessary."

There was a brief silence on the line before Anderson came back. "I do understand, Colonel," he stated plainly. "General McAfee told me…*more* than I think he probably should have," he said somewhat cryptically. "However, we were speaking in person at the time and I must say, sir, that I have a bit of trouble believing what he had to say."

"That is understandable," Matt replied with an internal groan. If McAfee let the cat out of the bag, he might have a harder time selling the need for Groom Lake to the base CO than he expected. "But I can assure you, Colonel, it is a very real threat."

"That is what the general said as well." Anderson cleared his throat and then asked, "Is it true that you and your teams have been battling these…*types* of terrorists…for over ten years now?"

"Very true," Mitchell informed him, unsure of what else to add. "And, as I stated earlier, our need for your facilities will only be temporary." Mitchell felt this might be the time to test the waters on the availability of Groom Lake's security forces. "Colonel, if I might ask, what military and security forces do you have at your disposal that we might be able to put to use for the upcoming endeavor?"

Anderson paused a little longer than Mitchell liked, and when he came back on the line, he didn't directly answer Matt's question. "Mitchell, did McAfee explain to you how this was going to work?"

Matt stiffened in his chair and reached for his scotch out of habit. He sighed as he poured himself a double and skipped the ice this time. "No, Colonel, he didn't explain anything to me. He simply stated that Groom Lake would be made available."

Matt heard Anderson chuckle slightly over the phone and his earpiece crackled as Anderson obviously shifted his phone about. "Allow me to enlighten you somewhat. You and your team have *full* access to this facility, and you and I both hope that you are successful in your little *endeavor*." He paused and Mitchell knew that Anderson was about to drop a bombshell on him that he wasn't prepared for. "You have your reasons for wanting to be successful and so do I...well, besides the obvious ones."

"I'm sure," Matt added dryly.

Anderson chuckled again. "For certain. I'm sure that the good general informed you that I'm a career man?"

"Oh yes," Matt replied. "He most certainly made a point of—"

"Good. Then it won't come as a surprise to you that I held out a bit on him." Matt could almost hear Anderson smiling through the phone. "You might say I balked on him. Dangled the carrot, so to speak."

"Mm-hmm. And what did the 'carrot' cost the general?"

"Why, my star, of course. As soon as you and your…hunting party are done saving the world, I pack my bags and report to the Pentagon," Anderson stated quite happily. "While you and your teams? You inherit Groom Lake. Or, whatever's left of it."

Matt sat there a moment, his mouth hanging open and his scotch held in his hand. He wasn't sure how to respond to such a statement. After a moment, he set his scotch on his desk and before he could gather his thoughts to reply Anderson said, "No comment, Mitchell?"

"That isn't what I wanted, Anderson," he said quietly. "I only needed to borrow—"

"That's *General* Anderson," Anderson interrupted. "Rather, it will be soon enough." He chuckled again.

Matt forcibly swallowed the bile that rose in the back of his throat and quickly swallowed the scotch on his desk. "I suppose congratulations are in order."

"I certainly played my cards right," Anderson said coyly.

"You certainly did," Matt agreed, but not for the same reasons.

"So, Mitchell, when do you and your teams plan to arrive?" Anderson asked.

"In the morning. I'll be needing as many hangars as you can make available."

"Yes, McAfee gave me a short briefing of your needs. All classified projects are being pigeon holed into as small an area as we can manage, all non-essential personnel are being sent off base and all contracted security forces are being called in," he stated. "You do realize that our security teams are all contracted people, don't you? We have Wackenhut contracted out here. Most are ex-commando types, or wanna-bes, but they are pretty hard-core. We really don't have many active duty military out here. But what we do have are all at your disposal."

"I'll take whatever I can get," Matt said. "Especially military people who have technical expertise."

"Those, we have," Anderson replied with a joyful lilt in his voice.

"Then I suppose I'll be seeing you tomorrow, Colonel."

"Looking forward to it, Colonel," Anderson replied.

As Matt hung up, he poured himself another scotch and called for Laura on the two-way. He kept thinking about what kind of officer would sell his own command for a promotion and it made his stomach turn again. He had half a mind to send Anderson packing the moment he got to Groom Lake, but as soon as the thought crossed his mind, a darker thought crept up behind it...*wouldn't it just be too damned bad if something fatal happened to the general-to-be during the altercation in the desert?* Matt shook his head and wondered where that thought came from, but the growl that came from deep in his chest reminded him exactly where the thought had originated from. His wolf thought it and he allowed it to surface.

An evil smile crossed his features and Matt had to erase the thought from his mind. He was an officer as well and he wouldn't allow such thoughts to manifest in his mind. He'd rather a scumbag like Anderson get promoted than have his blood on his hands.

Matt stared at his map of the U.S. across his office and the area where the Groom Lake base was located. He pondered the possibilities of running the operation from the facility, then realized, if the entire Groom Lake facility was turned over to him…he wouldn't be able to run the operation anymore…he'd have to be a base commander!

For a moment, Matt almost panicked as he thought of losing the teams and being stuck with administrative duties that he did *not* want, but then he pushed away the thoughts and refused to allow the fear to grab him. He reminded himself that he was still an officer first and the Monster Squad CO second. If McAfee arranged this, then there was a reason. He was sure that he could contact the Oversight Committee and get things changed if he absolutely needed to, but…this was unheard of. Usually base commanders were Academy men who were half a step from earning their star if they hadn't already. He wasn't an Academy man. He had no intentions of ever rising up past full bird and the very thought of moving anywhere beyond where he was now…hadn't crossed his mind in the past ten years.

Laura knocked on his door and pulled him from his thoughts. "Enter." He poured her a drink to go with his third.

"You bellowed, oh great one," she teased as she slipped into the chair opposite him.

"Just got off the horn with Colonel Anderson at Groom Lake," Matt's face was solemn.

"Oh, shit," Laura groaned. "Let me guess. We can have the base over his dead body?"

"Oh, no...better," Matt said, his face taut. He slid her drink toward her.

"Do I want to know?" she asked as she sipped at the amber fire water.

Matt reclined in his chair, holding the scotch to his chest and stared at her. "The bastard held the base over the General's head and basically blackmailed his way to his General's star," Matt informed her. "We save the world from mindless bloodsuckers and that little weasel gets made into a military leader of men. Can you believe that?"

Laura shook her head and downed the scotch. "Un-fucking-believable," she hissed.

"Believe it." He said. "And you want to know what else?"

"Oh no. There's a part two?" she moaned. "Wait...pour me another." She slid her glass over and Matt poured the drink.

"I'm glad you're sitting down." Matt said. "Whatever's left of Groom Lake after we save the world..."

"IF we save the world, you mean."

"IF we save the world, you are correct." Matt nodded to her. "Well, whatever is left of the base? You are looking at her *new* base commander once the dust is settled." Matt's mouth was a tight line.

Laura's eyes rounded with shock. "Are you serious?"

"Deadly."

"Matt! That's freaking great!" she cried out as she stood up. "We have our own base now."

"In the middle of a flippin' *desert!*" he shot back. "There's *nothing* to do out there."

She shot him a look that would have broken a concrete wall. "Matt, nobody ever leaves the base now."

"Because there are actually things to do here, Laura. We have no idea what is out there. From the satellite photos I've seen…there's nothing there. People leave every night by plane. Or bus. But the point is, they LEAVE. There's nothing there," he explained. "I can't expect my guys to move to the middle of nowhere and be effective. They need down time to do…stuff. They might want to go to a baseball game."

Laura scoffed, "It's a Triple A team, Matt."

"It's a good Triple A team," he argued. "And we have basketball…"

She nodded, "Yes, there is that. So, we bring in the stuff they like. You're the new base commander. You can do stuff like that, remember?"

"But I'll be responsible for *everything* out there. I may not be able to CO the Monster Squad anymore," he said quietly.

"What is that supposed to mean?" Her faced twisted into a quizzical look.

"It means," he replied, "that you may have to take over as CO of the squads." His eyes reflected the sadness he felt.

Laura's eyes rounded again, but this time from fear. "Oh, no. No, no, no…Matt, no!" she repeated. "I'm not…I can't do that!" she said, backing up away from him.

"Laura you're the perfect pick," he said, getting to his feet.

"No, you don't understand," the color draining from her face, "I've been…under a lot of stress lately. I've actually been thinking of maybe…moving on."

"Moving on? To what?"

Laura groaned and looked away, unable to meet his eyes. "Anything." She shook her head. "Matt, I don't know how much longer I can do this."

Matt sat there and studied her. He knew that she had been having problems, but he needed her to pick up the slack and take the reins on this. She was his right hand man. But he didn't want to pile on more than she was ready to handle.

He slowly approached her and placed a friendly hand on her shoulder. "Listen, right now we don't know what the situation will be out there. It may be that I can do both," he lied. He knew better, and so did she. Groom Lake was a busy, black budget, high-dollar military operation and it would take all of his attentions to keep it going. "Just think about it. And if you honestly don't think you can handle it, that's okay too. You're my friend and I want what's best for you, you know that."

"I know, and I truly appreciate the offer." But they both knew that she wouldn't take him up on it. She was biding her time. "I'll consider it." She turned to face him and he saw the concern and worry in her eyes.

"Okay. But one problem at a time. Right now, we have to finish getting everything loaded onto the transport planes and ready to go by morning."

"Roger that, sir."

"Make sure that our guests understand that we'll be leaving at sunup. Mr. Thorn needs to make arrangements," Matt said. "I don't know if he has something that is light proof that he can be flown in or…"

"I'll see to it."

Paul Foster hung up his phone and turned to his enforcers. "Pack up everything. We are leaving this area and heading to Nevada. Our Master will be texting us GPS coordinates to a military base. As soon as we get them, send them out to *everyone* and inform them to get there as soon as possible. Time is of the essence."

The enforcer nodded then turned toward the trailer where Damien had been locked away. "What of him?"

Foster's shoulders slumped and he stepped over to the trailer. He placed a hand against it. "He has been silent for how long?"

"Days," the enforcer replied.

"Get him out and check on him. If he is still…unstable, destroy him," Foster said quietly.

The enforcer opened the trailer and Foster stepped back, holding a hand to his nose. The stench of the dead woman's body was nearly overpowering. Damien sat in the far corner of the trailer cradling what was left of her corpse in his lap. He held a hand over his eyes to block the dim light that came from the open double doors. Foster stepped to the rear opening and peered into the gloom. "Are you calmed down?"

Damien looked up at his maker and held the woman's skull in his hands. "She won't wake up," he sobbed.

"Of course she won't. She's dead," Paul stated flatly. "You killed her."

Damien slowly stood on wobbly legs and the woman's corpse slid away from his lap, her skull still in his hands. He looked down at the rotting remains and simply stepped over them, firmly grasping her skull in his hands.

"Damien, we need the trailer. You can come out if you'll be good, otherwise, I'll have you put down like an untrustworthy dog. Do you understand me?" Foster stated matter-of-factly.

"Yes," Damien replied softly.

"Come on then."

Foster noted the lack of flesh on the corpse and the apparent bite marks about the bones. "Did you eat her flesh, Damien?"

"Only parts of it."

"You do realize that only ghouls eat the flesh of the dead."

"She wasn't dead to me." He looked into Paul's eyes. Damien's eyes were searching for some unseen meaning but Paul saw nothing behind his. Damien's eyes were void of that spark that indicated that he was still there.

"How much of her did you eat?" he asked, not sure he really wanted to know the answer.

245

"The naughty bits. And the fleshy bits. And some of the crunchy bits," he said with a smile that never reached his dead eyes.

Foster cringed inwardly but allowed no outwardly showings of his emotions. He knew that Damien's mind was as close to being lost as he could be and not be retrievable. It was said that when vampires feasted on dead flesh rather than blood, they became ghouls and ghouls were just a half step above zombies both in intellect and in actions. They lost their minds, their abilities and their taste for blood. They'd sometimes be found digging up corpses in graveyards, especially those graveyards that catered to the religions that frowned upon embalming since formaldehyde would sour their stomachs.

Damien staggered toward the rear of the trailer and bits of the young woman fell from him with each step with a wet and sickly plop and stuck to the trailer floor. Damien's feet squished through various mucks and blood and shit and intestinal fluids and the flies were horrendous. Paul noticed maggots clinging to his clothes and crawling slowly about in his hair. His own dead flesh shouldn't be prone to maggots, but if he became a ghoul, then all bets were off.

Foster helped Damien step down from the trailer and nearly gagged at the dead flesh clinging to his clothing and the rot and blackened goo dripping from him.

"Get him to a bath and burn his clothes," he ordered. He pointed to the inside of the trailer. "Dispose of...*that*. And pressure wash the inside of the trailer. We'll be needing it, and I don't want anything of mine

246

put in there. Use bleach if you have to. But get rid of the smell." He fought back a gag. "It smells like a horde of zombies were in there."

He walked Damien to the rear of the warehouse and had two of his female vampires prepare him a bath. Damien did not want to give up the skull in his hands and Paul had to promise that they were going to wash it for him and make it pretty. Damien acted as though his psyche was very damaged and Foster treated him with kid gloves. He whispered to one of the women, "Boil that skull, strip it of all flesh and then acid wash it. Buff and polish it if you have to, but make it shine for him." He turned to another of the females who were about to strip down and scrub Damien, "As soon as he is cleaned up and dressed, get some blood into him. Maybe if we can get some fresh hemoglobin into his system, we can salvage what's left of his mind." She merely nodded as she continued to undress.

Foster wasn't exactly sure why he was trying to keep Damien alive any longer. With his father dead, his connections in Washington were limited, but he had this nagging feeling that Damien would be important one day and keeping him alive would be in his best interests. He couldn't put his finger on why he felt this way, it just seemed like the right thing to do at the time. As he watched the damaged vampire stagger off to be scrubbed clean and made presentable, he wondered if he weren't making a big mistake keeping the little bastard alive.

The text came in from Rufus and Paul studied the coordinates. He forwarded them to his enforcers who in turn forwarded the information to all the vampires in their legion. Word was spreading as fast as electronics could forward it. By the end of the night, every vampire in their army knew where to assemble, and they had less than twenty-four hours to be there. For those who were stateside, it shouldn't be an issue. For those traveling from overseas, it might be slightly problematic, but they would do what they had to.

Plans were made and blood was stored for the journey and upcoming battles. Weapons were forged and armor fitted. Vampires and familiars made ready to either kill or die trying, and most weren't even sure what their cause was. They knew only that their masters ordered them to make ready and lay life and limb on the line for blood honor, and each was more than willing to do so.

Viktor stormed into Natashia's room as she finished packing her few belongings. She had only arrived when she was sent back out to find Max, with the intent of gleaning information to point her in the direction of Claudius Maximus Veranus, but her things had been somewhat scattered as she had repacked for her trip to Europe and now she found herself trying to get her things ready to move once more. Viktor allowed the heavy door to slam into the wall as he entered the room, his breathing coming in huffs and his eyes, dark.

"Why didn't he tell me?" he growled.

"I'm assuming you mean your father," Natashia responded as she continued to refold and pack her belongings.

"Of course I mean Max. Who else would I be speaking of?" he barked.

"Perhaps you should ask him rather than barge in here and yelp at me like a wounded pup," she snapped.

Viktor's eyes narrowed at her. He was used to her speaking her mind with him, but never with such a sharp tongue had she ever lashed back at him, especially when he was obviously so angry.

"What did you just say?" he growled slowly at her.

She turned and gave him a droll look. "I'm quite certain you heard me, my love." She placed her hands on her hips and stared him down, daring him to move against her. "All of this time you've held nothing but animosity towards your father when he expected you to step up and take your rightful place amongst the pack."

"You know I couldn't do that," he said through gritted teeth.

She leveled her stare at him, her eyes slowly turning amber. "You could have if you truly wanted to reign," she said. "You chose to allow your mother to maintain control. You allowed a *bitch* to be alpha of the pack and you tucked tail when she branded you *outcast*."

Viktor's eyes widened with shock at what his Tasha had just said to him. It was as if she were channeling his mother. He couldn't believe his own ears to hear such things from her mouth. "How could you expect me to stand against my own—"

"I'd expect you to be the Alpha!" she practically screamed. "You are a Lycan of the First Order!" she demanded, slamming her fist against the table. "You should have stood up to her as your father intended."

Viktor felt her knock the wind from his sails. He couldn't believe what was coming from his own mate. She had surely turned against him. It had to be Max's doings. The time they spent together had poisoned her mind, turned her heart against him. He shook his head as he backed away from her toward the door.

"You don't know what you're talking about—" he started to say just as he backed into someone solid. He turned to find Max standing in the doorway, watching the two of them. "What are you doing here?" he growled.

"She's wrong, you know," Max said softly.

"What are you talking about?" Viktor asked, stepping away from him and backing into a corner where he could keep a watchful eye on both Max and Tasha.

"Tasha," Max answered. "She's wrong." Max shrugged as he entered the room and pulled a chair to him and sat in it. "I never expected Victoria to turn against you, nor did I expect that she would go against my orders."

"What difference does it make now?" Viktor asked, his voice a mix of hate and despair.

Max shook his head and turned his eyes to the floor. "Son, you've always been so damned proud, but you simply can't see the forest for all of the trees, can you?"

"Make sense, old man," Viktor growled.

"Oh, you don't want to challenge me with your growl," Max said. "I may have tried being a pacifist, but if I'm about to go back into war, I'm not going to roll over and show my stomach to anyone, least of all you." Max gave an evil smile, daring his son to try something. "Remember who *trained* the Lycan, my boy."

"How am I wrong?" Tasha asked. "What else could he have done then if not stand against Victoria?"

"He could have challenged her, yes. But he need not destroy her." Max said. "To meet a challenge doesn't mean you have to kill to win."

"But it's written—" Tasha interrupted.

"No, it's not," Max cut her off. "Who told you this?"

"Victoria," Tasha answered.

Max threw his head back and laughed heartily. "She played you, son!" he practically yelled. "She knew that you wouldn't kill her, so she convinced you that you would have to kill her to remove her from power." He shook his head again. "I think when next you two meet, perhaps you should take her up on her offer and see how quickly she backs down."

"And if she chooses another to act as her proxy?" Viktor asked.

Max's eyes narrowed on him and his lip curled. "Then do what you have to do, but take that which is rightly yours," he snarled. "Then beat your mother's ass and teach her a lesson."

"Won't you be coming back to the pack with us once this is done?" Tasha asked.

Max stared off for a bit and then shook his head. "No. My time leading the pack is done," he answered softly. "I have other interests now."

They sat in silence for a few moments before Viktor spoke, "Why didn't you tell me?"

"Tell you what?" Max asked. "That I'm Claudius Veranus?"

"Yes."

He smiled at him. "And what would you have done had you known?"

Viktor thought a moment and shook his head. "I don't know. But I still feel that I should have known who you were...who I am. Who *we* are."

"We are wolves, son. Where we come from...makes little difference. It's what we do with ourselves that makes us the men, and the wolves of legend," Max said. "You can live your life as quietly or as grandly as you choose. You know the risks of both. The quieter you live your life, the longer you may be allowed to live and the more mundane your existence. The grander you live your life, the more you run the risk of being hunted down by others with little understanding and the greater your risk of being killed." He stood and placed the chair back and turned for the door. "As for me? I choose to live my life keeping the balance. God has placed me here to keep the Sicarii in his place. I am the Sentinel. I am the Captain of the Guard of the *Legio X Fretensis* and I keep watch to ensure that, should he rise and threaten the world, the hand of God is ready to smite him back to his proper place."

"And who is there to keep you in your place?" Viktor asked.

Max smiled at him and gave him a wink. "You are, my son. You are."

Jack was shaken awake from a very restful sleep and looked up to see Kalen rousing him. The common building was practically glowing from the unearthly light outside that must be what passes for early morning daylight in this dimension. He felt as though he had slept for ten hours and his body almost ached from the too long slumber. He stretched, listening to his joints protest and pop. He peered about the room as the rest of his squad woke and gathered their gear.

Horith approached him and spoke quietly, "The others will be arriving soon. Perhaps we should make meal and prepare to leave."

Jack gave him a thumbs-up and gathered his things, placing them back in his pack. The table had been reset for breakfast and Jack was amazed that such a meal could be prepared and set without waking him since he was such a light sleeper. He grabbed his radio and checked for any kind of signal. He soon realized that wherever they were, radio signals were a definite no-go. He turned it off to save the battery and put away the radio then grabbed a quick bite. Perhaps once the others began arriving and the doorway was open, he could radio back to HQ and find out where Mitchell wanted them to muster.

Jack grabbed an apple and a heavy bread roll made from some dark grain and strolled out among the large trees again. The morning air greeted him and he noticed a slight breeze, something that had been missing since they first arrived in the Greater Elf ward. The draping limbs of the trees gave a slight swaying motion in the breeze and Jack's memory noted that something seemed *off* about the little village. He strolled through the pathways and while everything appeared the same, it just felt somewhat askew to him. He couldn't put his finger on it, but it felt different.

He continued to stroll along the pathways and noticed a lack of children, a lack of the elderly, the tree homes were closed, doors and windows shut. Jack stopped and turned in place looking up at the tree houses and noticed that the trees themselves had drooped their limbs as if to protect the homes in their branches. He shook his head slowly as he took it all in. An eerie feeling cut through him. It was as if the forest itself knew that something was about to happen and wanted to protect its wards.

Jack turned back toward the common building and encountered Kalen speaking to a number of the warriors in his hunting party. As Jack approached, Kalen sent them on their way and turned to him. "The others will be approaching soon," he announced as he turned to walk with Jack.

Jack stopped and held him lightly by the arm. He pointed to the trees. "I noticed the trees and the lack of people. It's as if the trees are trying to protect them."

The other nodded. "It is the Wyldwood. She has brought about the change and asked the forest to help protect us in case we are not successful."

Jack tried not to show his amazement at her ability to do such things, but he failed. "Impressive," he whispered.

Kalen smirked and shook his head. "She can do much more if the need is there," he stated simply. He swept his arm wide to encompass the entire area. "She can move all of the trees to a safer area to avoid fire. She could coerce the forest animals to bring food to the people inside their homes if needed." He lowered his voice to a whisper and came in close to Jack's ear, "She could even convince the brook to flow up a hill to bring its waters to the people." He nodded his head as if to convince Jack he weren't stretching the truth.

Jack turned and gave him a quizzical look. "Can she only do those things *here*, or can she do them out there in the real world as well?"

It was Kalen's turn to give a quizzical look. "They are one and the same."

Jack laughed. "Oh, no, buddy, they aren't. Things are definitely *different* in here."

Kalen's brows knitted in thought and he glanced around the area. He spotted Horith and whistled. A moment later the slightly taller twin was standing with the two men and Kalen spoke to him in Elvish. Horith answered in the same language and Kalen nodded in acknowledgement. Horith turned to Jack and stated, "On the *outside*, the Wyldwood is slightly limited in her ability, but she can do a lot of the same things." He pointed to the sky and the surroundings. "But in here, the aura feeds her strength so what she does isn't as stressful on her." He smiled at Jack. "Does this make more sense now?"

Jack was nodding. "Yeah, actually, I think it does. In a strange sort of way, I think I understand." Jack looked around at the magical place and smiled. "Almost like this place feeds her batteries no matter where she goes and if she's here, then she's sort of plugged in."

The twins looked at each other and shrugged, the concept of electricity not really sinking in. Jack just smiled again and patted Horith's back. "I think I got it. Right or wrong, I think I understand."

Jack noticed a group approaching them through a haze of morning fog off in the distance. What appeared to be a hunting party soon emerged from the feathering wisps and showed to be one of the arriving groups of warriors from another tribe of Greater Elves. Their members wore different leather armor and their faces were painted, reminding Jack of American Indians from old western movies of his childhood. If not for their pale skin, light hair and slightly pointed ears, he would have thought that he was watching a war party of Comanche or Apache arrive straight from the 1800s. They carried bows and spears, clubs and many other handmade weapons that he didn't recognize as anything but lethal.

Horith broke away from Jack and trotted to greet the newcomers. He embraced many of them and spoke in hushed tones. Their faces were grim, but happy to see an old friend. Perhaps under different circumstances, the reunion would be more joyous. Jack almost didn't hear Tufo approach him as the two observed the newcomers greet their hosts. "They just get here?" Mark asked.

"Yeah." Jack responded. "Appeared like ghosts out of the mist." He turned to Tufo and shook his head. "It was kind of eerie how a group that large could be so silent."

Tufo nodded. "Sweet. Let's hope that kind of stealth comes in handy against bloodsuckers." He handed Jack a package that was wrapped in a fine cloth. "A gift from Loren."

"What is it?" Jack asked as he untied the string binding it.

"Your eyes only, buddy," Tufo said. "Not my place to know, I guess."

Jack hefted the weight and it felt solid. He unwrapped the many layers of the silken cloth and looked at the gift inside. It appeared to be a large rock, roughly twice the size of a softball and made of some type of crystalline quartz. With hues of yellow and pink running through it, it was stunningly beautiful, but he couldn't imagine the significance of the gift.

Jack nudged Tufo who glanced at the shining rock. He gave a low whistle. "Nice paperweight, pal. You should be proud." He smirked.

Jack shook his head slowly. "Somehow, I doubt seriously that this is just a paperweight." He glanced around at the camp with the bowing trees protecting the inhabitants, the foggy mist that hadn't been there before and the way the sunlight made everything glow strangely. "No, there's something to this thing." He wrapped it carefully back up.

"Meh, with our luck it's a dragon egg or something," Tufo muttered.

"Uh, no. Dragon eggs are *much* larger and scaly. They look like—"

"I really don't care," Tufo interrupted. "I'm just saying that it's probably something that will come back and bite us in the ass." He nodded toward the warriors assembled in the village center, then pointed off in the distance. "There are more coming."

Jack peered into the mist and saw another group merging out of the fog. He didn't know if his mind was playing tricks on him or if the fog was growing thicker, but as the group emerged, the fog was so thick he could barely see the bodies as they stepped out. "I wonder if they're using the fog to mask their numbers as they travel?" he thought aloud.

"If they are, it's a pretty neat trick," Tufo said.

Donovan approached the pair from the rear and asked, "What's with all the fog? I stepped out just a bit ago to piss and it wasn't like this...where did all these people come from?"

"Elf back-up, I guess," Tufo muttered, popping a nut into his mouth.

"They're the warriors from the other districts," Jack said. "They're supposed to be arriving this morning."

Donnie nodded. "Any idea how many?"

"Nope, didn't ask," Jack said. "Beggars can't be choosers."

Tufo shot him a sideways glance. "Who says we're beggars?" he asked quietly. "Their asses are on the line, too, ya know."

Jack simply nodded and continued to stare as the number continued to grow exponentially in the village square. He couldn't be sure, but he knew there were multiple hundreds milling about, talking in hushed and quiet tones. He couldn't pick up a single word of any conversation, but he noted more than a few quizzical and a few unfriendly stares in their general direction. "I think we're being sized up."

"Let 'em," Tufo grumbled. He tossed a nutshell on the ground and turned his back on the crowd. "I still say screw 'em," he growled, his temper flaring with the offhanded stares. "All of this other-worldly crap is for the birds. We don't need their help. We got enough firepower to level the blood suckers. Drop a couple of MOABs on 'em as they come sneaking in and let the pieces fall where they may. End of story."

Jack hiked an eyebrow at him and chuckled slightly. "Right. And let the cleanup crews deal with picking up the pieces from a million or so vampires when they're scattered over a couple dozen square miles of Nevada desert?" he asked. "That's mighty nice of you."

"Meh, let the buzzards have them." He smiled. "From what I understand, the virus won't cross over to animals anyway. It would be good for the environment. Feed the wild critters, fertilize the fields, who knows? Maybe we could get something to grow out there if we scatter enough of their bone meal across the fruited plains."

"And *that* is why you'll never be in charge, Tufo," Jack smiled.

"Oh, hell. If I were in charge, I'd have had you boys injected with tracers a long time ago." He said straight faced. "As soon as they nabbed Dom, I'd have dropped a fucking nuke on their asses."

Jack's face went slack as he realized that Tufo had both a good idea, and that he'd sacrifice Dom in a heartbeat. He searched Mark's eyes to see if he were joking, and he simply couldn't tell. He was about to tell him that he was a heartless son-of-a-bitch when Tufo added, "But not before I sent you boys in balls-to-the-wall to pull Dom's ass out of the ringer." He popped another nut into his mouth and turned back to the growing crowd of elves. He shook his head. "Sure wouldn't be recruiting a bunch of bleach-blonde Indians to go on the warpath with me."

Kalen left the growing group of warriors and approached Jack. "Do you know yet where we need to go?"

"I need to radio my boss and find out, but I can't seem to reach him from here."

Kalen simply nodded and led him back to the entrance of their domain. He pressed along the sides of the stones again and pushed it aside, revealing the very same place they had entered. Jack stepped out and sent a radio message, meanwhile Donovan ensured that the team got everything packed and ready to move out. He was certain that they would be leaving soon and while they were overloaded, he noted that the warriors carried only their weapons and a few small leather pouches tied to their waist. He hoped that wherever they went, they had provisions to handle them all.

13

Dominic trudged through the jungle, fighting through the thicker areas and climbing up to the highest ground he could find until he finally broke through to a clearing. As he stood in the bright tropical sunshine, he could hear water rushing through the dense jungle underbrush. He strained his ears, slowly turning his head until he was able to pinpoint the direction of the sound. He pushed off in the general direction and found himself at a freshwater pool fed by a beautiful waterfall.

He fell to his knees and sunk his head into the cool, fresh water, letting it soak into his uniform top and saturate his hair. Finally, he pulled his head out and cupped his hands to drink from the cold, fresh water until he satisfied his thirst. Dom sat at the water's edge and took in his surroundings. If he didn't know better, he'd think that this could be a tropical paradise, but the familiar tickle in the back of his mind reminded him that this was still all in his head, a comatose dream induced by the drugs administered by the Team Two members.

He reached into the water and sifted his hands through the sand in the water, feeling the grains and small rocks shift between his fingers. He watched small fish dart off as the mud below clouded the water and quickly washed away. Dom sighed and focused on the plant life surrounding the little pool and tried to imagine them going away, but they wouldn't. The island breezes blowing the tops slightly, the sun playing across the fronds made them feel so realistic to him.

He slowly got to his feet and made his way toward the waterfall, peering upward to the top. He saw how the water cascaded from the top of the islands mountainous peak and worked its way over the edge to crash here into this little pond before washing away to the coast. He had no idea what the purpose of this dream was or what he was supposed to do next, but all of his training had taught him to seek high ground to ascertain the layout of the land.

He was just about to look for the best way to begin scaling the mountain when he heard a noise in the underbrush that sounded distinctly like someone approaching. He quickly scooted from the water's edge and took cover behind a low palm to see who might be sharing the island with him when the islands other inhabitant burst through the shadowy jungle. Dom squatted lower to the ground, his hands resting in the soft earth below him and his fingers instinctively curled into the soil below him, feeling the coolness of the shaded earth. Although his eyes watched for the island's newest inhabitant, his mind thought that the ground certainly felt real...it felt *right*.

Dom's attention shifted and although he couldn't immediately see who the other person was, he quickly approached where Dom had been squatted by the water's edge and he was able to see his back. Whoever it was he was dressed in khaki shorts, a light Hawaiian shirt and deck shoes. He was a large man with grey hair and his skin was tan, as if he had spent a lot of time in the sun. He studied where Dom had been at the water's edge and drank and stood up to look around. Dom watched the man put his hands to his mouth and yell, "Hello!" into the jungle. Dom was no fool, though. He didn't move. He still wasn't sure if this was real or his imagination, but he trusted nobody. The man kept turning, scanning the area, but Dom couldn't see his face. He cupped his hands again and yelled, "Dominic! Where are you!"

Dom was shocked. Whoever this was, he either was expecting him, or knew he was here. He toyed with the idea of stepping out from behind his cover, but he just couldn't allow himself to do it. The experience on the darkened sea with the vampire who tried to drown him was still pulling at the back of his mind and he didn't trust anything or anyone right now. He kept watching the grey haired man intently and when he turned and Dom finally saw his face, he nearly fell over.

He could see his face clearly now…the crow's feet around the eyes, the dark hairs intermixed with the grey, the scruffy stubble of unshaven beard. The broad chin with the cleft in it, the dark brows and dark eyes that he had stared into so many times during his childhood…he was looking at the face of his grandfather, lost at sea when he was barely ten.

With a fearful shake in his hands, Dom pulled the fronds away from his hiding place and stepped out into the open. The old man turned his head toward him and smiled, the slight gap in his front teeth flashing at Dom and sending a chill up his back.

Dom took another tentative step toward him and was shaking his head in disbelief. "This can't be. You died…"

"I know, boy," the old man said still smiling at him. "Nearly twenty years ago." He stepped toward Dom and the specter definitely left prints in the sand. "Yet here I am."

Dom froze in place and continued to slowly shake his head. "You died. Grammy got the report from the Coast Guard."

"I know, boy." The old man stopped and slowly the smile faded from his face. He shook his head and his features saddened. "But somebody's got to lead you back home."

The little messenger hurried to the antechamber where the dark vampire awaited news for any movement of the human hunters. He had sent search parties out to look for the ex-wife that had escaped capture as well, but no sign of her had yet to show. She hadn't been using any credit cards or they could have tracked her down, so wherever she had gone, she was either using cash, or had no need for money. The Sicarii was pacing behind the bank of computer operators who worked diligently trying to trace her whereabouts.

They had followed some of her movements by hacking into traffic cameras, but lost her once she got into a rural area. They were now going through government records to see if there were any land holdings in the direction she was headed and tracing her histories to see if she had any college friends who may have relocated to an area in that general direction.

The little messenger burst through the door excitedly. "Sicarii! I have news of the hunters," he yelled, breaking the silent ticking and tapping of the computer hackers who never looked up from their work.

The dark vampire stopped his pacing and turned to the little messenger. "Yes, Puppet. Tell me something that will please me," he responded softly.

"They are on the move, Master," he said excitedly. "Planes are departing from all areas and heading in one general direction."

The dark vampire leveled his gaze at the little vampire in anticipation. When the little vampire stood there and simply stared at him, the dark one sighed heavily and responded, "*Where* are they going, Puppet?" he asked impatiently. "Why do you make me ask when you know I want the answer?"

"Oh! Forgive me, Master," The little vampire apologized. "I didn't mean to displease you. I was simply—"

"Puppet!" Sicarii growled. He took a moment to compose himself. "Simply tell me. Where are they going?"

The little vampire lowered his eyes to the floor. "I'm not sure, Master," he answered softly. "At least, not exactly." He looked up again and noted that his master held a droll look upon his face. "They have begun leaving in their planes. The planes here in the EU and in England and South America are all headed to the United States, but we're not sure exactly where." Then he added quickly, "Yet! But we should know soon, Master." His little legs began to tremble so he added, "And we were able to get tracers on two of the American planes and one of them has taken off as well, Master. It is headed west by southwest. So…maybe Arizona? Southern California?" he offered. "We really don't know yet."

"But you will soon, I understand," the dark vampire finished for him. "As soon as you know exactly where they are going, let me know. Until then, do not interrupt me." He shooed away the little messenger with a wave of his hand.

"Yes, Master." He bowed and scraped his way back out of the computer room and stood in the hallway.

The little messenger sighed heavily and looked at his hands. They were still shaking from fear. Every time he went near the master, his entire body trembled from fear of his immense power. He didn't know why he did it, but he did. His master had never made a violent move toward him and his mind told him that he was safe, but his body quaked with fear every time he came close.

He trotted back to the communications room and waited for word on where the planes would land, hoping that it wasn't anytime soon. It had gotten to the point that it was taking longer and longer for him to recover from his meetings with the Sicarii.

HEATH STALLCUP

Back in the computer room, one of the vampire hackers shook his head and whispered a quiet, "Damn."

The dark vampire turned to the tech and asked, "What is wrong?"

The vampire cracked his knuckles and sat back in his seat a moment. "Master, I cannot be certain, but I think I may have found the woman."

The Sicarii stepped toward the computers and leaned over his shoulder. "What is this place?"

The vampire clicked a few buttons and the picture on the screen enlarged. "This is the military base where the human hunters are stationed. On a hunch, I decided to hack into their security cameras. I timed it for someone who drove straight through, stopping only for fuel and checked the times around then for a vehicle like hers. I searched an hour prior and three hours after and almost to the minute, here is a vehicle matching hers...to a 't'. Of course, from this angle, we can't see the driver well and we can't verify the license plate, so I'm not positive, but...it's an awfully large co-incidence."

The dark vampire nodded his head and leaned back. "Pull up the security camera footage of the vehicle when she left her house." The technician pulled it up and it was a grainy black and white still from a low quality camera. The vehicle year and make was the same and it was obviously a light metallic color, but both images were black and white, so verifying the color was near impossible. The Sicarii stared at the two still images for what seemed a long time before he stood back and asked, "Was the direction she headed in the same general direction to the military base?"

After a few clicks on the computer, one of the other techs piped in, "It *sort of* is. It's in the same general direction, but only if she were trying to avoid getting on the freeway at the closest ramps."

The Sicarii nodded. "Smart one, this girl. She probably suspected that we would have agents waiting for her at key locations should she evade her captors," he said softly. "*Very* smart, indeed." He stood straight and nodded. "Very well. Shut down the search. She's most likely at the military base with her ex-husband. Which means that the hunters know that we tried to abduct her." He glanced around the room. "Good work."

As the first cargo planes departed, Mitchell picked up his briefcase and started for the main doors of the hangar. He noted the dark SUV with the limo tinted windows parked within. Rufus and Viktor were about to get in when Rufus stopped and motioned to him. "Colonel, would you be so kind as to join us on our jet?"

Matt studied him a moment and considered the options. "You're flying out of Wiley Post?"

"*Oui*. And Max will be joining us," he answered. "It will give us a chance to…discuss matters, before we reach Nevada."

"It's a pretty short flight, Mr. Thorn. What exactly did you hope to accomplish during it?" Matt asked, shifting the briefcase to his other hand.

Rufus raised an eyebrow and stared at Mitchell. "Have you considered, Colonel…the Sicarii will be attacking on the full moon, *oui*?"

"Yes, I am aware of this," Matt responded.

"And does this Groom Lake facility have a silver barred cage for you?" he asked simply.

Matt froze in place with fear. He had been so preoccupied with facing down the vampire and his horde that he had forgotten about his own problem and when it occurred. He glanced back over his shoulder and tried to calculate how long it would take to tear out one of the sets of silver bars and transport them. His brow broke out in a cold sweat and his palms turned clammy when Max came up behind him and placed a hand on his shoulder. "Relax, Colonel," he said softly in his ear and Mitchell automatically felt his heart rate slow and his breathing come under control. "That's just one of the things we'd like to discuss on the plane." Max motioned to the SUV. "Care to take a plane ride with us?" Matt stared at the SUV and noticed that Viktor didn't seem too happy about it, but, he never seemed very happy.

He radioed to Laura and informed her that he would be taking the civilian flight with Thorn and Verissimo and that she was to finish supervising the loading of the last cargo plane then hop that flight. She gave him a "Roger, sir." Mitchell hopped into the SUV with the others. Max climbed in behind him and smacked the roof to let the driver know they were ready. The SUV pulled out of the hangar and began to make its way through the base. Max cleared his throat as he looked at Thorn. "You realize, it wasn't that long ago that simply being this close to a vampire would have sent me over the edge. I would have tried to kill you regardless of your actions."

Thorn nodded thoughtfully. "Then it is very good that you have put such things behind you, oui?"

"Actually, Tasha filled me in before we got here." Max gave him a toothy grin. "She tells me that you're a better man than most...men."

Thorn chuckled. "I shall take that as a compliment."

"It was meant as one."

Mitchell interrupted their conversation, "Why would you have tried to kill him regardless of his actions?"

"He's a vampire." Max stated simply.

"And you're a werewolf." Matt shot back.

"True. But wolves can choose. Vampires *have* to feed on blood." Max explained. Thorn remained silent as he spoke. "It wasn't until Tasha explained to me about the *Lamia Beastia* that...well, to be honest, I wouldn't have believed it had I not met him."

"And you can tell simply by meeting him?" Mitchell asked incredulously.

Max looked at Mitchell as if he had fell on his head. "Can you not *smell* the difference?" Thorn remained still throughout the conversation as if he

270

weren't present. "He smells of mutton and beef and...goat?" He turned to Rufus. "Is it goat?"

Thorn simply nodded his head and gave a soft, "*Oui*."

"And you can smell what he eats on him?" Matt asked, still unbelieving.

Max chuckled and shook his head. "Mitchell, for a wolf, you have an incredibly dull nose."

"I try to use my *other* senses as well," he said sarcastically. "Besides, I've never had a very good nose," he added in a somewhat more quiet voice.

Max nodded and reached out for Rufus' hand. "Do you mind, Monsieur Thorn?" Thorn shook his head and raised his arm to Max. Matt felt stupid and even embarrassed for Rufus as Max held his arm under his nose to him. "Take a deep smell."

"Deep. Pull it deep into your sinuses and let it roll around in the back of your head then tell me what comes to your mind."

Matt felt foolish, but sniffed deep of Rufus' arm. At first he only smelled the detergent of his linen coat, then a musky cologne that smelled of sandalwood and pine. Then...there it was. He could smell it...it smelled of...*death*. He pulled again, deep into his sinuses and he could smell it, *under* the smell of death, he could smell something that reminded him of wool...of sheep. A scent that smelled of beef, raw steak. And a musky scent of...a goat popped into his mind. He turned to Max, his eyes wide in astonishment. "And you could smell this from a distance?"

"Easily," Max said, releasing Rufus' arm. "Thank you, Monsieur, for your assistance," he said to Thorn.

"How is that…possible?" Mitchell asked.

"Practice," Max told him. "Every time I go outside, I see something at a distance and I try to scent it. Sometimes I'll close my eyes and sniff and try to identify something and then open my eyes and see if I can see it."

Matt nodded and sat back thinking about what Max had just shown him. "Does this have anything to do with my lack of foresight and the silver bars?"

Max shook his head. "No, Colonel, it doesn't. What it does have to deal with is your needing to hone your skills as a wolf."

Matt nodded as if he understood, but he didn't see how that helped him with his immediate problem. "I see now how I've let certain aspects of my…condition…slip. And I realize that I should be honing the skills that come with this condition, but I really need to address the here and now and the more pressing matters of—"

"Colonel, if it were actually a *pressing* matter, we would have already seen to it," Viktor interrupted. Matt turned to him, but he was staring out of the deeply dark tinted window. Viktor slowly turned to look at him. "You won't be needing your silver cage on the full moon," he said simply.

Matt was shocked. "And what do you propose we do with me during this particular moon cycle? Chain me with silver?"

Max smiled at him and shook his head. "Colonel, you will be in close proximity. When any wolves are in close proximity, we are *pack*. And needless to say, I AM the alpha wolf, yes?"

272

Mitchell thought about what he was saying at the moment. "Are you saying you'll be able to control me?"

"Like a newborn pup. Yes, sir," Max responded. "You'll do exactly what I say, whether you want to or not."

"You do realize that I'm not a natural born wolf, right? I can't control what I'm doing, full moon or not."

"And you realize that it doesn't matter, right?" Max replied. "Cursed or Damned, natural born or bitten, all within the sound of my voice will hearken and heed the call."

Matt inhaled deeply and let it out very slowly. "It still feels like we're taking a very big chance here."

"We are not, I assure you," Viktor stated. "It is not the first time that an alpha wolf has used his call to control a lesser wolf during the moon."

Matt nodded, deciding not to take offense to the 'lesser wolf' comment. "Okay. As long as I don't hurt anybody."

"Oh, you'll hurt plenty of people. Any vampires who get too close to the humans, I expect you to rip them asunder and lay waste to all," Max said, his smile evil.

Matt's gaze shifted from Max to Viktor and then to Thorn. "Present company excluded, of course."

"I do not plan to be present where the humans are, Colonel," Thorn stated. "I intend to lead my people into battle against the forces of the Sicarii."

Matt sat up straighter. "Now hold on just a minute." The other three sat back and simply looked at him. "I don't know what you three have cooked up here, but let's not forget something here. This is still a military installation and a military engagement. And whether you like it or not, *I'm* the military leader here." He allowed his statement to sink a moment. "Now, Thorn, I realize that you will have people on the ground and that you want to lead them into battle, but you need to keep in mind…we have a satellite that we intend to deploy that will saturate the battlefield with high intensity UV radiation. We intend to turn night into day.

"Max, I understand that you intend to go after the Sicarii yourself because you think you're the only one who can handle him mano-y-mano and while I think that's all noble, you need to realize that you're going to have a handful of special-op commandos backing you up, not to mention a couple hundred thousand vampires who are laying it on the line as well.

"And you." Mitchell pointed at Viktor, "well, honestly, I have no idea what it is you think you're going to do, but you all three need to get it in your heads that we need to work together. We may well go at this as a three or four pronged attack, but we need to coordinate everything." Mitchell eyed them all as he sat back in his seat. "Look, fellas, I'm not trying to piss in anybody's Post Toasties here. We just need to go at this logically. We need to figure out what resources we have available and utilize them to the best of our abilities."

Matt glanced at his watch. "We'll be at the base in a few hours and we can get settled in and I can get some info from Anderson. He's the base commander there. They may even have some resources there that we're not aware of. But once we have an idea of *everything* that is available to us, then we can start formulating some plans.

Max started to argue but held his tongue. He closed his mouth and nodded. "I agree, Colonel. Let us hold back on making specific plans until we know exactly what resources are available and then try to come to some agreement on how best to utilize them."

Thorn simply nodded at both men and remained quiet. His thoughts were on the *Lamia Beastia* and how many would probably be sacrificed in the upcoming battle. He cringed at the thought, but he also cringed at the thought of *not* fighting the Sicarii.

"By the way, thank you," Matt said to Max.

"For what?"

"For being able to control my…inner beast," he said, somewhat sheepishly.

"There is a lot you could stand to learn, Colonel," Max said.

"I know there is. I just haven't had time."

"He's been too busy hunting and killing his own kind," Viktor said, venom dripping from his words.

Nadia and Natashia loaded into the small Jeep and prepared to leave. They planned to take Max's jet to Groom Lake for him so that once the battle was over he could depart straight from there. Max decided to fly over with Viktor and Rufus and asked his daughter-in-law and granddaughter to ferry over his luxury jet for him. As they prepared to leave, they saw Laura lugging the last of her bags to a Humvee.

"Ms. Youngblood, are you preparing to leave as well?" Nadia asked.

"Just loading the last of it," she huffed.

"Would you like to ride over with us? We are taking grandfather's plane to him. He is flying over with Rufus and father."

Laura glanced around. The only people left were the skeleton security crew. Matt had told her to catch a flight on the last cargo plane but she really didn't look forward to being belted down to a folding chair in the back with the crates. "I, uh...should probably take the cargo plane."

Nadia could tell that she didn't really want to and pressed her a bit further. "It has *very* comfortable leather seating. And a liquor cabinet. And sodas. And chips. And other...refreshments." Nadia blushed. "I'm sorry, I do not know how to entice you properly." She threw her hands up. "But it truly is a very nice plane and there are more than enough seats," she pleaded.

Laura glanced at the Humvee again. She gritted her teeth and pulled her bag off the back and put it with her other two. She slammed the tailgate shut and pounded on the back. The Hummer started up and pulled out of the hangar. Laura slung a bag over her shoulder and tried to lift the other. "Lead the way."

Nadia smiled and grabbed her other bags as if they weighed nothing and tossed them in the back of the Jeep. "It will be such fun!" she said. "Just the three of us."

Laura looked over Nadia's shoulder and saw Natashia standing at the door of the Jeep appearing bored. "Hurry, Nadia. The pilot is waiting."

"A moment, mother," she yelled. "Ms. Youngblood is coming with us. Won't that be fun?!"

"Peachy," Natashia muttered.

Laura cringed at the thought of being stuck with Natashia, but held her thoughts to herself. She took one last look around the hangar, feeling as though she were forgetting something. She grabbed one of the security staff and double checked the duty roster before signing out. She noticed that hers was the last name to be signed out so she was assured that all personnel were en route to Nevada, other than First Squad who were still in the field. She handed the clipboard back and sighed, taking one last glimpse at the hangar, hoping that they all would be returning safe and sound.

"We really need to go. The pilot is waiting," Natashia said as she climbed into the Jeep. Laura nodded absently still staring into the hangar, the nagging feeling that something was being forgotten lingering in the back of her mind.

"I'm coming." She climbed in the back seat.

Sanchez strapped in to the transport plane and waited for the plane to start its take off procedures. Hank unbuckled and moved over next to her. "I have something for you." He buckled in next to her.

"Yeah? What's that?" she asked hoping for another box of doughnuts. "Will it make my ass fat?"

Hank smirked and shook his head. "No, I'm afraid I didn't get a chance to get into town before we left."

"Too bad, Padre." She nudged him with her shoulder. "Those fat pills were the bomb."

Hank reached behind him and pulled out a bundle that was wrapped in a wool blanket. He carefully unwrapped it and handed it to her. "Usually there's a ceremony for this, but considering the circumstances…"

"What is it?" she asked, her brows knitting together.

"Your first katana."

Maria unwrapped the blanket and revealed a shiny black scabbard with a leather belt attached to it. Her mouth dropped open and she found herself at a loss for words. "Oh, my God, Hank…I don't know what to say."

"You don't have to say anything." He lifted the sword and placed it into her hands. "You've earned it."

"No, I haven't." Her eyes began to mist as her emotions ran wild.

Hank snorted at her. "Oh, yes you have. Trust me on that one." He looked her directly in the eyes. "I've never been one to believe in reincarnation or previous lives or…well, any of that. It just goes against my beliefs," he explained. "I understand that a lot of cultures choose to believe it and many religions are based on it, but for me, it just never fit. But you? The way you handle a sword and the way you fight? I can't help but wonder if you weren't a Samurai in another life." He smiled at her.

"Hank, I don't know what to say," she said, her eyes tearing up. "This is the nicest thing anybody has ever done for me."

"Somehow I doubt that," Hank replied. "And a simple 'thank you' is fine for me. Besides, it's the least a teacher can do for his best student."

Maria continued to admire the sword and slowly pulled the blade from the scabbard and studied the blade. Then she turned and smiled at him. "Hey…wait a minute. You said your 'best student'! I'm your *only* student!" she laughed.

Hank chuckled and nodded. "Touché."

Maria fought back a sniffle. "Thank you, Padre." She slid the blade back into its scabbard. "It's beautiful."

As the plane's engines whined and began to rise in tempo and the craft slowly gained speed along the runway, Spanky nudged Apollo and asked, "Don't tell me the Padre is moving in on your woman, buddy."

Apollo had been watching the presentation of the blade with more than just a little interest. He tried not to let it bother him, but if the truth were known, he was more than just a little jealous of the time the two had been spending together. It seemed that Sanchez had less time for him because she was too busy knocking swords with Hank in the practice room. Apollo gritted his teeth and tried again to shake it off. "Naw, man, they been practicing hard lately. Padre just hookin' her up with a solid blade, man…that's all." He peered at the two again and watched Maria run her hands along the long black scabbard, the awe in her eyes and the pride on Hank's face as he observed her caressing the damned thing. Apollo closed his eyes and leaned his head back against the bulkhead of the plane. "Naw, he's just hooking her up so if she ever run out of ammo again she can still protect herself. It's all good."

Spanky watched Maria and Hank as they continued to talk and discuss the sword and he gritted his teeth. He looked at Apollo and his easy demeanor. Darren shook his head and let out a sigh. "If you say so, bro. But if it were me, I wouldn't be so comfortable with another man getting all sweaty with my gal."

Apollo laughed without opening his eyes. "If they was knocking boots, I might be jealous brother, but they be knocking wooden swords."

Darren continued to watch the two and blanched when Maria reached over and took Hank's hand in her own and squeezed it. He quickly turned and looked at Apollo who still had his head leaned back against the wall, his eyes closed. He breathed another sigh and shook his head. He sincerely hoped it was platonic. The squads didn't need any kind of romantic drama, especially now.

14

It took a little creative work on Jack's part to explain where they needed to go, but once the Greater Elves figured it out, they opened the Doorway to Anywhere to an area just outside the base proper at Groom Lake. First Squad went through first in case anybody from the Groom Lake command were nearby, but the place they exited was nearly three hundred yards away from the largest building. As the warriors began filing out, so did the fog. But once the fog cleared, the warriors were gone, camouflaged into their surroundings to the point that unless you were using heat vision, you probably couldn't see them. As Jack looked around, he wasn't even sure if they'd show up with IR. He shook his head as he and his team worked their way toward the facility.

They didn't get far before two Jeeps rushed up on them, contracted security closing on them rapidly, weapons drawn. First Squad started to take a defensive stance but Jack ordered them to stand down. He showed his hands as the security personnel advanced on them.

"We're with the new command," Jack tried to explain, but the security contractors didn't want to hear it. They ordered the men on the ground, their weapons tossed to the side.

Jack smiled and told them that simply wasn't going to happen. As the point man with the security force brought his weapon to bear and was preparing to fire, it was knocked from his hand by an arrow out of nowhere, his backup security forces suddenly wrestled to the ground, their weapons taken from them from unseen intruders.

Horith seemed to appear from a shimmer of heat above one of the security personnel. He looked toward Jack and asked, "What do you want done with them?"

"Just bind them for now." Jack noticed the disappointment in the elf's eyes. "We'll need every man that can fire a weapon later." He turned back to his team and directed them onward. They worked their way toward the buildings in front of them and lurked in the shadows. "It may be a while longer before the others show up and until they do, we may not be very welcome," he said in a low voice.

Ing pointed back toward the security forces. "Won't they be missed?"

"I'm sure they will, but there's not much we can do about that right now." He turned to Lamb, "Monitor all the frequencies you can and see if you can pick up the one they use. If we can listen in, it will give us a heads-up."

"On it." Lamb broke out his scanning radio gear and plugged in his ear bud. He turned to Jacobs, "Bring me one of their radios. Maybe I can narrow this down." Ing turned back to where the elves had the contract security personnel hogtied and pulled a portable radio from one of their belts. It looked like a walkie-talkie, but he knew better. This unit was a state

283

of the art Motorola with rotating frequencies and built in scramblers. He hustled back to Lamb and handed the unit over. Lamb took one look at the radio and shook his head.

He tapped the chief on the shoulder and gave him a no-go signal. "This isn't going to work, boss. Even if we could pick up their frequency, we couldn't hear them. This thing has a hundred and twenty-eight bit encoder. Without the code to input, we're dead in the water."

Jack sighed and had him secure his gear. "Fine. We lay low until the planes start arriving. Scout us a building." Donovan started forward when Kalen stepped in front of him. He too seemed to appear out of a heat shimmer and stopped him dead in his tracks.

"Allow us, Chief Jack."

Horith appeared next to him, his jaw set. "We can move more freely about. We will find you a building to hide in and let you know." Then both elves fell back into the shimmer and blended with the environment before stepping into the shadows.

"What I wouldn't give to be able to do that..." Donnie muttered.

"Me too," Jack added. He turned back to the rest of the squad, "We hold tight until they return."

The squad laid low in the shadows for a while, counting the minutes until more security personnel showed up to engage them when Kalen reappeared at their rear. He gave a low whistle and waved them back behind the hangar. Crouched low and staying in the dwindling shadows, the squad moved with him and down three buildings to an open rear door where

Horith stood, holding it open. Once inside the coolness of the building, the squad spread out in two-by-two fashion ensuring the building was indeed empty, many of the Elven warriors closing the rear.

They converged back at the rear, reporting the building clear. Jack had them stand down and secured the doors. The building appeared fairly empty, large crates stacked toward the rear and nearly to the ceiling. The men hunkered down and waited for something…anything to happen. Always alert but taking rest when they could, simply happy to be out of sight of any passersby.

"Any idea how long we'll have to wait?" Tufo asked.

Jack shook his head. "They were bugging out when I radioed in. It could be hours before they actually start landing, or they could start landing any minute. I don't know exactly when they began." He glanced around the large hangar and noticed there were no windows. "We'll just have to keep an ear out for any planes landing and new activity."

"Did you notice the place looked like a friggin' ghost town out there?"

Jack nodded. "They were supposed to evacuate all non-essential personnel. I guess they did."

"Gives me the creeps," Tufo said as he pulled a chunk of beef jerky from his breast pocket. He offered Jack a piece and tore off a piece to give his mouth something to do.

"At least we know security is still active," Jack responded.

Tufo snorted. "Unless those clowns were all that's left." He said hooking a thumb toward the contracted security forces tied up along the wall. They did not appear happy.

Jack shook his head. "Somehow, I doubt it. This place is too high-dollar black budget to just leave a handful of rent-a-cops left to protect it." His comment left the security forces faces turning red with anger but at the moment, Jack didn't care. He motioned Tufo to follow him with a hook of his jaw. They approached the security forces and Jack eyed the men sitting along the side wall of the more or less empty building. "Which of you is 'in charge' of this group?" he asked.

They all sat silently, the gags still in their mouths, venomous gazes turned toward him. "I don't think they like you, Chief," Tufo chuckled.

"They don't pay me to win popularity contests, Gunny," Jack said through the side of his mouth. He turned back to the men on the floor. He gave an exaggerated sigh and said, "Look, guys, you might think we're the bad guys, but we aren't. We are a forward scout party for the new temporary command. Surely your base CO told you about the new command that was coming here?" He looked to each man for some kind of recognition in their eyes and found nothing but more anger. He shook his head. "Fucking officers." He turned to Tufo, "Can you believe that they didn't even tell their security people that the base is being handed over to a new command?"

Tufo shot him a sardonic grin. "Sounds about right. Bastard is probably polishing his big fat brass."

286

Jack smiled. "Probably." He turned back to the men again. "Look, fellas, this can go easy or this can go rough. Which would you prefer?"

One of the tied men mumbled an epithet that even through the gag was recognizable. Jack simply nodded and glanced at Tufo who shrugged. "Fuck 'em, Chief. They're Alpo."

Jack casually reached down and grabbed the man who cursed him and the man next to him. He lifted both men completely off their feet and held them, one in each hand. Their expressions changed from anger to shock as the man before them displayed amazing strength. He pulled them each to his face and growled at them, "I want to be *real* fucking clear about something, *gentlemen*. We *are* taking command of this base, and when we do, you *will be* working for us." He said in a deep, low voice. "I don't give two shits if you believe me now, but once the change of command takes place, if *any* of you fuckers give me shit and try to get revenge because we got the drop on you today…I'll rip your heads off and shit down your windpipe." The look in his eyes was absolutely feral and both men knew true fear. "Do you understand me?"

He was met with frantic nods, sweat having popped out on their foreheads and the stink of fear emanating from both of them. He let go and let them both fall to the floor then turned to the others whose looks of astonishment had replaced their anger as well. "Are you going to give me grief?"

He was met with a choreographed shaking of heads, eyes wide from each of them. "Good." Jack turned and went back to his group, Tufo on his heels.

287

"A little heavy handed, don'tcha think?" he whispered.

"If it gets the message across, so be it," Jack muttered. "I don't want to risk any of them taking pot shots at us when the chips are down because they got their feathers ruffled this morning and their egos bruised."

Tufo bounced the idea around and nodded. "Makes sense, but wouldn't it make more sense to just give them a lower priority assignment once we're closer to zero hour?"

Jack stopped and turned to face Mark. "Right now, we don't know for sure what assets we're going to have or how thin we're going to have to spread ourselves." He pointed back to the men being held along the wall. "We may very well need each and every one of them at a high value position and for the life of me I don't want to worry about whether or not I can trust that they won't try to put a bullet in the back of one of my operator's heads."

Tufo rubbed at his chin and stole a glance back at the men. "Give me a second with them, would ya?"

Jack studied him a moment. "What are you thinking?"

Tufo grinned at him wickedly. "Classic good cop-bad cop."

Jack shook his head. "Mark, we can't afford—"

"Trust me, Chief." He turned his back to the men along the wall. "I won't do anything stupid."

Jack thought a moment and sighed. "Carry on, Gunny. Just be smart about it."

"Aye-aye, Chief." Gunnery Sergeant Mark Tufo strolled over to the men along the wall and hunkered down in front of them. He eyeballed the men and shook his head. "Sorry about the boss. He tends to lose his temper pretty easily." He reached over and pulled the gag out of one of the men's mouths. He pulled his canteen out and offered the man a drink of water. The man eyed him warily and took a small sip. "Don't worry, bud. It's only water." The man took a second small drink and nodded at him. Mark recapped the canteen and nodded to him. "You in charge of these guys?"

The guy eyed him a moment and shook his head. "No. I'm just a security officer."

Mark nodded. "Well, I apologize for having to do this. We just don't want to get our asses shot off by people who are supposed to be on the same team." He noticed the security officer giving him a disbelieving look. "Yeah, I know. I can only imagine what you fellas must be thinking. A group of armed military bust in and tell you that they're taking over, but nobody said anything to you." He sighed and sat down on the concrete floor in front of him. "It doesn't make sense right now, but I promise you, what he said…" he indicated with a thumb over his shoulder, "it's all true."

"Right," the guy deadpanned.

"Yeah," Tufo agreed. "Well, you'll find out soon enough, I suppose." He glanced over at the other security officers. "Any of you guys want a drink?" He shook the canteen and they all either ignored him or shook their heads. "Okay, well, if you change your minds, just let me know."

"What do you plan to do with us?" the ungagged man asked.

"Do?" Tufo responded. "Nothing. We're just waiting on the rest of our command to show up and then you'll be free to go."

The bound men shot him disbelieving looks. "So you break in to one of the most secure facilities in the world, overtake our security team and then declare that you'll let us go as soon as your backup arrives?" the man asked.

Tufo snorted. "It's not back-up. This base is being...borrowed for a short time," he said.

He glanced at Jack who was directing Jacobs and Lamb in low tones across the hangar. Tufo didn't want to let too much out of the bag right off, but he didn't want to appear to be keeping secrets from the men that they may well end up counting on when the chips were down.

"Look, it's complicated, okay? But let's just say that there's a huge fight coming and logistically, this base was necessary to fight it. Our bosses pulled some mighty big strings to procure it and...well, here we are. The rest are on their way." Mark shook his head when he thought about it. "To be honest, I think it's a pretty chicken shit way of doing things if your base commander didn't already fill you in about it."

"Well, he didn't," the man spat, shooting Tufo an angry stare.

Mark simply nodded. "I understand. And I'd be just as pissed as you are if I were in your shoes." He smiled apologetically at him. "Actually, I'd be even more pissed."

"Somehow, I doubt that," the security officer said.

"Trust me on one thing though, once you get the full story, you'll probably understand," Tufo said as he started to get up. He glanced back at the shimmering figures moving about the hangar. "Then again...you might not."

Dominic stared at the old man that he knew as his grandfather when he was a child. He slowly approached him and poked at him tentatively. He felt real under his fingertip and the old man slowly smiled. "Yeah, I'd probably do the same thing." He turned his head slightly askew and cast Dom a sidelong glance. He outstretched his own hand and touched Dom's shoulder, his eyebrow raising. "Damned if you don't feel real, too."

"Maybe because I *am* real, Lou."

"To you!" the old man stated. "Last thing I knew, I was fighting like hell to keep my trawler from capsizing. Then somebody that looked like my father was telling me that I had to get my ass back *here* to help you get back to home," he said, his arms crossing his broad chest. "You mind telling me exactly how you got here, boy?"

Dom shook his head. "Grumpy, I have no fucking clue where *here* is..." He received a hand upside the back of his head that startled him.

"Son, I have no idea how old you may be now or how big you think you are, but if your mother heard something like that come out of your mouth, she'd wash those words out with lye soap," he said solidly. "I'll allow hell, damn and occasionally shit if the situation calls for it. But unless you're drunk and fornicatin', you don't talk like that."

Dom rubbed at the back of his head and stared at his grandfather. "Jesus, Grumpy, what gives?"

The old man drew his hand back again and gave him a wild look. "You better be praying, son."

Dom threw his hands up in surrender, "Okay, okay!" He stepped back and honestly appraised the old man, a slow smile crossing his face. "I'm starting to believe you're really him."

"You better believe it, boy," the old man replied. "Now answer my question." The old sailor demanded. "How did you end up here?"

Dom shot him a pleading look. "Grumpy, I don't know where 'here' is."

The old man shook his head. "Son, you're in Purgatory."

"What the…" Dom trailed off. "How did I get here?"

"That's what I just asked you."

Dom shook his head. "I have no idea."

"Was you killed?"

"Huh?" Dom's confusion was compounded by his situation, but it didn't help that he didn't understand what his grandfather was asking. "What do you mean?"

"Was you killed?" he asked again slowly. "Is your body lying in a ditch somewhere dead or near dead?"

"Oh...no!" Dom registered now what he was getting at. "It's such a long story, Grumpy." He sighed. "So very long...and I don't think you'd understand if I told you."

"Try me," the old man said.

Dom sighed heavily again, unsure where to start, so he started at the beginning. He told him everything, the augmentation, the abduction, the brain rape by the vampire, being in a hospital bed...everything that led up to him being *here* on this island. But he had no idea how a tropical island could be Purgatory. Louis DeGiacomo listened intently and tried not to judge. This was his grandson, after all.

When Dom finished his story the old man began to pace slowly in the sand along the fresh water pool. "Some of what you told me makes some sense," he began. "The whole darkness and then it was light. That was probably you being given too much drugs and then either your body fought it off or the doctors brought you back." He turned to Dom, "You *died*, boy. And you came back. But either a part of your soul or all of it or...I dunno. Most of it. Something. It ended up here. This is your personal Purgatory. YOU created this."

"What?" Dom cried, "Why would I create this?"

"Everybody's Purgatory is different. This is yours." Lou looked around and smiled. "I have to admit. It ain't bad. I could live here."

"I need to get back," Dom said. "But...there's *something* I need to remember. Something that damned

293

vampire stuck in my head and it's important. I just can't quite…reach it."

Lou nodded. "I know. I can feel it in you." Dom shot him a curious look. "Don't ask me what it is, son. I have no clue. I couldn't tell you that any more than I could tell you what you ate for breakfast this morning. It's just something I can feel."

Dom nodded, not sure he believed him, but simply accepted. "Okay, so how do I get out of here?"

"No idea." Lou plopped down in the sand. "No flippin' idea," Lou repeated as he picked up a rock and heaved it across the pool.

Dom stood there and stared at the back of the old man's head. "How can you say you were sent here to help me if you have NO CLUE how?!"

Lou shook his head. "I don't know," he admitted. "I told you what I know. I was trying to keep my boat from sinking…I'm guessing I failed because the next thing I know my Pops is telling me that I have to come help *you*. And then here I am."

"Sweet Mary, mother of…Grumpy that was twenty years ago." The old man shot him a dirty look. "You passed twenty years ago," Dom explained.

"Boy, do you really think that time has any meaning on the other side?"

"I…don't. I…I guess I never really thought about it."

"Well, I can tell you that it doesn't." Lou picked up another rock and rather than throw it, he held it and rubbed it between his fingers. He held it up to his eyes and studied it a moment. "Everything feels so real here."

294

"I take it that it didn't feel real where you were?"

"I was only there a moment," He said quietly. "I mean…it only felt like a moment. Like…I had *just* got there. Literally just got there. And my Pops says, 'You gotta go help Dom, he's in trouble. Help him get home.' And then >poof< I'm walking on this island and I'm thinking to myself that was one helluva dream, except…I knew it wasn't a dream. I can FEEL it inside. I know that it wasn't a dream. Like I know my own name. But for the slightest moment I thought that maybe my boat went down and I washed up here, but…there are no tropical islands in the Atlantic, right? So…it wasn't a dream. Except it sort of *is* because you dreamed this up because it's your Purgatory."

"Okay, now you're screwing with my head, Grumpy."

"Screwing with your head? Try being me…realizing you've been dead for twenty years and that everybody you know is either dead or about to be."

"Yeah, that would be heavy, but it still doesn't tell me how to get out of here and back to where I'm supposed to be."

Lou shook his head. "How am I supposed to know? Maybe you click your heels together and say 'there's no place like home' three times?"

"What?" Dom was beginning to think that the old man had really lost it.

"Don't tell me you've never watched the *Wizard of Oz*?" he asked astonished.

"Uh…no. I don't think I have," Dom admitted.

"Boy, there is something fundamentally wrong with you."

Dom sat down beside his grandfather and laughed. "Yeah, I guess there is."

The two of them sat in silence for a while and just watched the waterfall. They listened to the sound of the birds, the wind and watched the water, enjoying the peace and the sunshine for a moment, neither saying anything while Dom sifted the dirt and the sands between his fingers.

Lou turned to Dom after a while and said, "What if I am supposed to help you remember what it is that you can't remember?" he asked. "Whatever it was that the vampire stuck in your head."

Dom shrugged. "I don't know. Maybe."

"Well hell, boy. It can't hurt to try."

"No. It certainly can't hurt to try."

"Worst case scenario, you remember it, and at least you'll be ready should we DO figure out how to get you back."

Dom smiled at him. "Sounds like a heckuva plan to me, Grumpy."

"Okay then. Let's get started." He shifted on the ground to face him. "Tell me again everything you remember, and this time, don't leave out any details."

"Master!" yelled the little messenger as he trotted into the cathedral. "Master! I have news!"

The dark vampire entered from the side entryway going into the courtyard and surprised the messenger, causing him to almost fall. "Puppet? What do you have?"

"Master, the computer technician that found the woman on the cameras…he was mistaken." The little messenger was almost beside himself with excitement. "It was not her!"

The Sicarii merely raised an eyebrow waiting for him to go on. But like most times, the messenger did not catch on. "And?"

"Oh! Forgive me, Master," he stammered. "Um, well, he checked the cameras at the military base each day and the same car enters at almost the same time each day!"

The Sicarii shook his head, not understanding. "Master, it is not her. It is simply someone driving the same kind of vehicle." The messenger scrambled to open a folder and pulled out a grainy photo. "See? He was able to get a picture of the driver on another day and it is a man!"

The Sicarii stared at the photo for a moment and handed the paper back to the messenger. "They are still looking for her then?"

"Yes, Master. I have asked that they redouble their efforts to find her," he stated proudly.

The dark vampire nodded. "Very good, Puppet," he stated simply. "You have done well."

"And, we have discovered that the runaway woman's parents are on a cruise ship, Master." The little messenger all but sang. "We are arranging for someone to intercept them and——"

"I don't think it necessary to interrogate them. If they are on a cruise ship, one could simply 'meet and greet' them," he said with an evil smile. "Funny how people on vacation just *love* talking about home." He turned to look at the little messenger. "Their property, their pets, their kids…*grandkids*."

The little messenger's eyes grew larger as he smiled along with the dark vampire. "Yes, Master. As you will, so mote it be."

"Tell me, Puppet, have you learned yet where the hunters are all going?" the dark one asked.

The little messenger lowered his eyes. "Not yet, Master. They are still in flight."

The dark one simply nodded and waved the messenger away. He stepped back to his courtyard and considered the possibilities. If the woman hadn't gone to her husband, then perhaps the human hunters didn't know of his intentions yet. Or if they did, they weren't aware of his attempt to abduct her. He wouldn't know until he had her…but he *would* have her. He would notify his enforcers to use however many assets they had in the United States as necessary, but he would have her. If they had to use bloodhounds to scent her out, they would track her down.

He looked to the moon and could almost count the days until the next full moon by its shape in the sky. A little over a week left until he turned the largest army in the history of the world upon its human inhabitants. And once he had the woman, he would be able to use her against her husband and cripple the human hunters from the inside. Although he doubted seriously that they could ever cause him any real threat, he would rather hedge his bets and have an insurance policy. The one hunter that he had in custody for a brief time turned out to be far stronger both physically and mentally than he had ever dared hope and he didn't dare risk allowing himself to underestimate them again.

He turned to the sky and bowed his head. He prayed once more the same prayer that he prayed every night since his creation. He hoped beyond hope that *this* time, God would answer his prayer and remove the curse that damned him. He prayed that God would take pity on him and restore him to his humanity. He prayed that if God wouldn't do any of these things that He, in his almighty wisdom, would see fit to relieve him of his life so that he would no longer have to suffer on this earth, a monster.

The dark vampire fell to his knees on the cobblestone courtyard and prostrated himself before the heavens and begged God to end his life before he could unleash his fury.

"Colonel Mitchell, we're being told that we're entering a no-fly zone, sir," the pilot said over the internal communications.

Mitchell stood up from where the four men were seated. "If you'll excuse me, gentlemen, I better go take care of this." He went forward to the cockpit and donned a radio headset.

"They're threatening to send up fighter intercepts if we don't divert our course, sir."

"Get me on the radio." When the chatter came up on the radio set, Mitchell keyed the coms. "This is Colonel Mitchell from Air Base Tinker. We're just one civilian transport plane in a fleet of military…"

"I repeat, you are entering a no-fly zone. Divert course now or we will shoot you down."

"And *I* repeat, that this is Colonel Matt Mitchell of the United States Air Force. The new Base Commander for Groom Lake. Maybe you better clear things with Colonel Anderson before you go making threats, son." Mitchell seethed underneath but did his best to maintain a calm demeanor.

"Wait one, civilian transport."

Mitchell waited a moment before the voice came back and ordered the pilot to enter into a holding pattern outside the outer markers. The pilot gave back an affirmative on the radio but informed Mitchell that they didn't carry enough fuel to hold for very long. They could only maintain a holding pattern for maybe forty-five minutes at the most. The pilot had expected to just shoot down here and land then put the plane away.

Mitchell waited for about five minutes before he radioed the tower to ask what the holdup was. It turned out that Colonel Anderson didn't bother to tell anybody to expect company. He just sent non-essential personnel home and the base was operating under a skeleton crew and nobody could find the good colonel.

Mitchell did his best to control his temper. He got back on the radio and informed the tower to contact the Pentagon and go through General McAfee. He would inform them who the new base commander was...then they could clear the flight to land along with all of the following flights incoming from Tinker Air Force base and all of the other incoming flights that would be inbound from all over the world. Mitchell could hear the tower operator's voice quiver somewhat once he dropped McAfee's name, but it didn't take long before clearance was granted.

Matt pulled his cell phone and called McAfee's office and prayed that he would accept the call. To his surprise, the General answered his own phone as soon as it rang. "Sort of expected you'd be calling, Mitchell."

"Sorry to bother you General, but it seems that Anderson is MIA.",

"Well, he's sort of on his way here." The general almost sounded apologetic.

"He's *what*?!" Matt all but screamed into the phone.

"Seems he felt that whether you were successful or not, he wanted his damned star. Said he wasn't a necessary part of the equation."

Mitchell seethed with anger as he heard the words come through his phone. "General, do me a favor please." Mitchell said as nicely as he could muster.

"What's that, Mitchell?"

"Contact whatever transport Anderson is on and have his ass shipped right back out here. On the double." Matt could almost hear the general smiling through the phone.

"What reason should I give *Colonel* Anderson?"

"He hasn't done a formal change of command, of course," Mitchell stated. "I have no fucking clue what is what out here. That doesn't seem the proper procedure for handing off one of the military's shiniest black op bases, does it to you, General?"

There was only a slight pause before the general chuckled into the phone. "Consider it done, Mitchell." He guffawed. "Anything else?"

Mitchell ground his teeth together as he fought the urge to ask the General to plant a foot in Anderson's ass before he sent him back. "I think that will just about do it, General. I'll see to the ass chewing once he gets here."

"He won't be happy."

"I don't give a shit, General. I almost got my ass shot off by my own fucking people because that moron forgot to tell them that we were coming," he growled. "Maybe I'll forget to tell them that *he's* coming and see how he likes it."

Matt heard the General chuckle a little more into the phone before he said, "Just mail the pieces back to the Pentagon, son." And then he hung up.

As Matt put his phone back in his pocket the pilot turned to him and said, "Remind me never to piss you off, sir."

Matt turned to him and chuckled. "Don't pull a bonehead move like that one and you'll be just fine.

Taxi us inside one of the empty hangars so we can get the doors shut for Mr. Thorn. It's still daylight out. You'll probably have to radio the tower to find out which ones are empty."

"Roger that, sir."

"Jack, it sounds like planes landing." Tufo jogged back from the doors.

"Can you tell what kind?" Jack asked.

"The kind that fly in the air," he answered in a smart-assed tone. "Dude, I was a Marine, not Air Force. I blew shit up for a living."

Jack shook his head and rolled his eyes. "Lamb, you and Jacobs recon and see what kind of planes we have coming in and report back."

"Aye, Chief."

Lamb and Jacobs slipped out the back door and made their way between the buildings, staying low and in the shadows. They watched a civilian jet land and taxi toward them, base personnel coming out of an underground building across the way and heading to the hangar next to theirs. They crept back into the shadows and waited while the rollup doors were opened and the plane taxied inside. Ing worked his way back to the rear of the building and checked the rear doors of the hangar but they were locked. He double clicked his coms and worked his way back to where he left Ron who was spying C-130's lining up to land on the dual runways.

"Looks like they're ours," he said into the lip mic.

"Okay, let's get ready to meet and greet," Thompson said. "Back inside."

Lamb and Jacobs worked their way back into the hangar and shut the door behind them. "How are we going to do this boss?"

"I guess we just open the doors and let them know we're here," Jack said.

"And if for whatever reason these aren't our people?" Tufo asked.

Jack shrugged his shoulders. "They're due. If it isn't them, then we surrender until our people show up."

"What about those guys?" Mark asked, indicating the security forces.

"Untie them," Jack said. "No sense in keeping them bound any longer. Whether they're our people or not, it's about to get real."

Tufo nodded and walked over to the security forces. "Okay, guys. On your feet." He helped each of them get to their feet and untied them, keeping a watchful eye on each of them to make sure they didn't make a stupid move and try to jump him.

"We want our weapons back," the mouthy one said.

"All in due time," Mark replied.

"Why not now?" he asked. "I heard your leader. If this isn't 'your people' then you'll be surrendering anyway, so why not just give them back to us?"

Mark shot him a shut-the-fuck-up look. "You'll get them when we say you get them," he answered through gritted teeth. "Don't push me on this or…"

"Or what, tough guy?" the smart-mouthed one asked, bowing up.

"Gunny," Jack said without raising his voice. Mark continued to stare the man down. "Gunny, come get the door."

"Yeah, be a good dog and do what your master says," the mouthy one snickered. Mark paused and shook his head. He forced himself to take a deep breath and walk away.

"He isn't worth it, Mark," Jack said once they were by the roll-up doors.

"Maybe not, but I'd feel better if I handed him his ass."

"Like I said, we may well end up needing these guys—"

"For what? To drop smart assed remarks at the blood suckers?" Mark quipped. "'Cuz that's about all they're good for."

Jack peered back at the group milling about at the rear of the hangar. "Probably, but if nothing else, we can use them for bait," he said smiling.

Mark gave him a double take. Slowly he smiled and said, "I like the way you're thinking."

305

"So truly, you've never allowed him to feed from you while you made love?" Nadia asked her eyes still full of wonder that Laura and Evan were lovers.

Laura smiled and shook her head, her face tired from the constant blushing. "No. Even if I wanted him to, Evan would never try."

Tasha still appeared bored from the constant questions and answers, but occasionally she would seem to have her curiosity piqued, but she quickly quelled her emotions and went back to pretending boredom. "Nadia, please, give Ms. Youngblood a break from the constant questions." She gave her daughter a dismissive wave. "Some things are meant to remain private."

"No, really. It's okay. I understand that some things must seem truly bizarre to the uninitiated, or even—"

"Wrong," Natashia stated rather drolly.

"Mother!" Nadia interjected.

Laura was taken somewhat aback by her quip. "I suppose one might think it...wrong," Laura explained. "But if you truly knew Evan, you'd know that he isn't like most vampires."

"Think of Rufus, mother."

"I could never have feelings for Rufus," Natashia stated flatly. "He smells of death."

"It is not just his scent though, mother. Think of *him*. He is kind, gentle and he has a good heart—" Nadia explained.

"He has a *dead* heart," Natashia interrupted. "A heart that will never beat again."

Laura sighed and shook her head. "I can't expect someone else to understand."

"I do," Nadia said. "The heart wants what the heart wants."

Laura smiled at her and Nadia smiled back. Natashia rolled her eyes at the two of them. "Oh please. A *real* man at least has a pulse. He has more than just body heat, he has a real *fire* inside of him." Her eyes glossed over as she thought of Viktor. "He has strength and vitality. Broad, rippling shoulders, large arms and a huge—"

"Mother!" Nadia exclaimed. "I think we get the picture."

Laura's face flushed again as she fought *not* to form a mental image of what Natashia described.

"I cannot help it, my dear," Natashia stated. "I am simply explaining that a real man is a real man. Not something that used to be a man and now is simply…dead flesh reanimated," she said with obvious distaste.

"To each their own, I suppose," Laura replied.

Nadia turned back to Laura, "Still, I have heard many say that the bite of a vampire is intoxicating. That the bite alone can induce orgasm."

Laura was shocked. "No…no. The bite contains the virus. It can cause one to turn into a vampire just as easily as blood being introduced into the body."

Nadia looked at Laura as if she were stupid. "Who has told you this?"

"I…er…well, the research we've done has shown that the same virus that is in the blood is in the mouth and that—"

"Non," she interrupted. "There may well be a virus in the mouth, but it is not the same as that in the blood. Have you compared the two?"

Laura sat there a moment and thought about whether the two were ever tested to see if they were the same. "I honestly don't know. We just assumed…"

"You know what they say about assuming," Natashia said in a sing-song voice, her eyes staring out the window.

Laura rolled her eyes. "I'm not a research scientist so I don't know for sure. I just know what they have told me. Avoid being bitten and avoid getting blood in any cuts, eyes or in your mouth."

Nadia giggled. "It is not that simple. The body has to be under stress in order to create a vampire."

Laura turned her attention to her. "What do you mean?"

"Either the body has to be bled down and put under stress, or…some kind of outside source of major stress put on the body and *then* the vampire blood introduced. You cannot simply introduce vampire blood to a healthy human body and turn it into vampiri. Otherwise, what would stop a vampire from bleeding out into a local human water source?"

Laura thought about that a moment. "Wait a moment…but…that very thing happened once."

Nadia shot her a questioning look. "What? When? How could this have happened?"

"A very long time ago. One of our hunters…he came from a very small border village. A group of vampires hit the village and killed a lot of the residents. One of the vampires ended up falling into the town well and bled out. The few survivors drank from the well and…well, they were turned. They had to be destroyed."

Nadia thought for a moment. "So, the town was ravaged by vampires and people were hurt? Then a wounded vampire sought refuge from the sun in the town well and bled into it, the people drank from it and they in turn, were turned into vampiri? Yes?"

"More or less, yeah. So, if it doesn't work that way…"

"The people were placed under a unique stress with the attack? Some, if not all were injured in the attack? And then they drank from this well?" she asked.

Laura began to understand. And this made more sense why Hank and the small handful of residents who didn't turn…who probably *also* drank from the same well, were safe from the effects. "So there has to be a major stressor, or injury *before* the virus is introduced to the human host?"

"Yes," Nadia said, "and it comes from the blood, not from the mouth."

"The virus in the mouth is different?"

"Very different," Nadia explained. "The one on the mouth…it is more like a drug. It makes the person not care that it is being fed upon. It kills the pain of the bite. It makes you feel happy, content, and in many cases quite sexually fulfilled," she said with a smile.

"How do you know all this?" Laura asked.

"I live with vampires," Nadia stated flatly. "They tell me everything."

309

"I thought the vampires you live with drank only the blood of animals?" Laura asked.

"They do," Nadia replied. "But they didn't always. There used to be a time when they, too, fed on humans. They knew no other way."

"Much like we wolves, Ms. Youngblood," Natashia stated. "There was a time when werewolves craved the flesh of humans more than anything else." Her eyes had taken on an almost feral look and it gave Laura a chill. "Once a wolf gets the taste for human flesh...it's nearly impossible to break her of it."

"What happens if a wolf *does* get a taste for humans?" she asked, not sure if she wanted to know the answer.

"Usually, the wolf is hunted down and killed by other humans," Natashia answered. She gave her a smile that didn't quite reach her eyes. "That is precisely why we teach our young from an early age to hunt only other animals when they shift. Gives them the scent of animal blood to sniff for when the moon calls them. Teaches them how to hunt and kill something with *four* legs rather than something with two." She smiled again, this time the smile definitely didn't reach her eyes. "It's also why we take them deep into the woods and away from *humans* when the moon is near."

"I see," Laura said.

"Do you?" Natashia asked, shifting forward in her chair.

"Excuse me?"

"Do you see?" Natashia asked again. "Do you have any idea what it might be like to worry that a

310

human might hunt down and kill your only child because she might do something during a full moon that she has no power over?"

Laura was taken somewhat aback by the question and was feeling really uneasy by Natashia and her attitude. "Actually, no. I suppose I don't."

"I didn't think so," She practically growled. "You have no idea what it's like to—"

"Mother!" Nadia warned. Natashia shot her a look that Laura wouldn't want to be on the receiving end of, but to her credit, Nadia did not back away from. "Ms. Youngblood is our guest and we will not behave this way."

Natashia glared at her daughter a moment longer then sat back in her chair. She muttered something about 'monster hunters' under her breath that Laura didn't catch but judging from the look that Nadia shot at her, she assumed that Nadia heard every word. There was a ding and the pilot came over the speaker. "We'll be making our approach here in just a moment. Please make sure that your seatbelts are fastened and all unsecured items are stowed away. Thank you."

Saved by the bell, Laura thought as she fastened her seatbelt. The conversation had gone from uncomfortable but tolerable to downright frightening in a very short time. She wondered before the flight what Jack saw in these women. Other than her physical attributes and Nadia's wonder at everything...she didn't know if she would ever be able to put up with Natashia's moodiness and nasty disposition. The sex must be mind-blowing for him to marry into such a messed up den of...Laura chuckled at herself. She had thought 'den', and they were wolves. Yeah, she realized she must be stressed if something that stupid made her chuckle.

15

"So that's it?" Lou asked. "That's all you got?"

Dom rubbed at his temples, his head hurting. "Yeah, Grumpy, that's all I have."

"Nothing you might have left out?"

"It would take a hundred lifetimes to tell you *everything* that vampire shoved into my head. I hit the highlights."

Lou sighed heavily. "Boy, we don't have a hundred lifetimes. We have to get you back to your people so you can stop this bloody bastard."

Dom shot him a withering look. "How come you get to cuss and I don't?"

Lou gave him a lopsided smirk. "Who's the grandpa here, squirt? Who's the salty sea dog? Who's the sailor and who's the Army grunt?"

"Who's dead and who is still kicking, ya old fart?" Lou smacked him on the side of the head again and Dom yelped. "Hey! Dammit! Knock it off. I told you I have a concussion." He rubbed at the side of his head and closed his eyes against the pain.

"Yeah, well that's your real body in the real world," Lou shot back at him. "Here, you ain't got no concussion but if you keep back talking me, you're going to have your hand on your head and a lump under it."

"I don't remember you being such a hard ass before," Dom whined.

"And I remember you being a sweet-natured ten-year-old," Lou shot back. "Now look at you! You're as big as a bear and whine like your little sister."

Dom gritted his teeth as the old man berated him. He clenched his hands into the damp sand and dug his fingers into the coolness. He could feel the grains between his fingers and it felt so real. The breeze felt real and the scents from the island plants smelled real. The spray that the breeze blew from the crashing waterfall that would occasionally mist them and cool them in the sun felt real as well. So why was his brain telling him that this couldn't be real.

Dom sighed and looked up at his Grumpy. "Why couldn't we just stay here?" he asked softly.

"What?"

"Seriously. Why can't we just stay here?" he asked. "I've missed you so much, Grumpy. We could fish and eat fruit and...look. We have plenty of fresh water. Who knows? Maybe a boatload of pretty girls will wash up here one day and we could—"

"Stop it, boy." Lou got to his feet. "You still don't get how this whole Purgatory thing works, do you?"

"What do you mean?" Dom asked getting to his feet as well.

"This isn't forever, son. If you don't figure out whatever it is you got to figure out...you don't just stay here. You *have* to move on," Lou informed him.

"What do you mean move on?" Dom asked, desperation seeping into his voice.

Lou avoided his eyes. "This is just a weigh station. This isn't permanent." He swept his arm to indicate the island. "You may have created your own little version of heaven here, but this isn't the final destination. If we don't get you back to where you belong, you have to go on."

"Go on?" Dom asked, afraid of the answer. "To where?"

"Where do you think?" Lou said. "The other side."

"The other side?!" Dom cried. "The other side of what?"

"Don't play stupid on me, boy." Lou finally met his eyes, his face stoic. "You know exactly what I mean."

"Heaven?"

Lou's features hardened. "If that's where you're intended to go, then yes."

Dom's face fell. He could feel his guts tighten. "What do you mean, if that's where I'm intended to go?"

"I don't know where you're headed, boy. That's above my pay grade." Lou sighed. "I was just sent here to get your ass back home."

Dom felt his knees weaken and he plopped back into the sand. His hands went instinctively to the dirt and he grabbed a handful of it. It felt *so* real in his hands. He squeezed it tightly and he could feel the individual grains biting into his flesh. He could feel the small rounded pebbles, washed smooth and made round by thousands of years of water rushing over them, smoothing them, polishing them and now he squeezed them in his hand until they left indentions in his skin.

He breathed in deeply and exhaled slowly. Once, twice, three times, trying to calm himself. It was one thing to prepare yourself to die for your cause, but quite another to question where your eternal soul may end up. He had never questioned that before. But now...here he sat. In Purgatory with his dead grandfather and neither had a clue where he might end up if he ran out of time.

Dom nodded, finally accepting his fate. "Fine. Let's do this."

"Do what?"

"Whatever the hell we have to do to figure this out."

Lou smiled at his grandson. "That's the DeGiacomo spirit. Never give up."

Dom smiled back at him. "Hell, Grumpy, I have one foot in the grave with the Grim Reaper on my ass and I ain't giving up." He stood up and clapped his grandfather on the back. "I got my Grumpy again. Who could possibly stand in my way, right?"

Lou shot him a questioning look. "You do realize I sunk my own boat, right?"

"Yeah," Dom said slowly. "Thanks for the encouragement."

"Master! Master!" The little messenger yelled as he ran down the hallway. "We know where they are going!"

The little messenger burst into the cathedral but the dark vampire was not to be found. The messenger ran into the courtyard, but again, the Sicarii was not there. He turned and ran back down the hallway and threw open the door to the computer room.

"Master!" he cried out, but with a quick look around the room, the tall dark vampire could not be found. "Have you seen the Sicarii?" he asked of the computer technicians.

One of them looked up from his work at the keyboard and simply shook his head no then went back to work. The other was going to mess with the messenger and say 'yes, I have seen him, he's about six foot tall, dark complexion, dark hair, dark eyes, lots of power' but decided that the messenger probably would not appreciate his sense of humor. He, too, simply shook his head. The little messenger scampered out of the room and down the hallway again. As he rounded a corner at full speed he nearly ran into the Sicarii and two of the enforcer vampires. The little messenger slid to a stop and fell on his back in front of the dark vampire who stared at him.

"Yes, Puppet?"

"We found where they are going, Master," the messenger stated excitedly. Once again, the dark vampire waited for the messenger to continue and decided that, rather than ask, he would simply continue to wait until the messenger realized his mistake. It took an awkwardly long time.

The two enforcers finally stepped forward and one of them said, "Say something, you blithering idiot, or I'll cut your fucking head off!"

"What?" the messenger asked. "Oh?! Forgive me, Master! I've done it again! I'm so sorry...I...er...they...I mean, the human hunters, they've all gone to Nevada! They are all landing as we speak."

"Nevada?" the Sicarii asked. "What could possibly be in Nevada?"

"I have no idea, Master," the little messenger answered, not realizing it was a rhetorical question. "As you know, I do not have a tactical mind as you do."

The dark vampire turned to his enforcers, "You two, with me." And the three of them marched off to the computer room leaving the messenger in the hallway. When they entered, the Sicarii ordered one of the computer operators to pull up the tracer on the planes. "Where in Nevada are they?"

"It looks like they're in the middle of nowhere." The tech stated.

One of the enforcers elbowed the other and he smiled. "Area 51."

The Sicarii turned to the enforcer and raised an eyebrow. "What did you say?"

"Area 51." He pointed to the map of Nevada that was pulled up. "This is about the right spot for where it should be. It's a top secret military base in the middle of nowhere. I think it's supposed to be a part of Nellis, but I'm not really sure."

"How do you know this?" the dark vampire asked.

The enforcer blanched. "I, uh, like to read magazines, Master."

"Magazines?" the Sicarii asked.

The other enforcer smiled and said, "UFO magazines, Master." He stifled a snicker.

The dark vampire's face fell. "You're telling me that *this* is the base where they put the UFOs that all of the crazies talk about?"

The first enforcer turned stoic. "Yes, sir."

The dark vampire turned back to the screen and looked at the beacon that was flashing on the screen. Surely there had to be some mistake. Were the human hunters hoping to use some kind of *alien* technology to stop him? He looked at the screen and studied it. "Why is there no base showing here on the map?"

"It is top secret, Master," the enforcer informed him. "Although most of the population knows it exists, the government refuses to acknowledge it. That is why so many believe that there are UFOs out there."

The Sicarii felt a laugh begin to form in his belly as he imagined the human hunters attempting to stop him using other-worldly technologies! Silly humans, God himself refused to stop him. In the Sicarii's mind that meant that his actions were preordained and already written as the cause of the fall of man.

"If the human hunters all wish to gather in one spot...to put all their eggs in one basket, so to speak, then who am I not to come along and break them all for them?" he said softly. He looked up at the computer techs. "Spread the word to all my people. We assemble here, in Nevada. The Blood Apocalypse begins here."

Colonel Mitchell hit the ground running. He arranged to meet with the project leaders who were still on base, military personnel and the captain of the security contractors and in his new office...just as soon as someone showed him where the hell his new office was. The moment Laura touched down, she was put in charge of getting their personnel on the ground and commandeering what buildings were available and getting the squads set up. He needed a list of assets that were available to him ASAP. Matt was introduced to a Major Flemings, military attaché to the numerous civilian contractors and from what Mitchell could tell, one hell of a sharp cookie. She quickly ran him through the basics of what was what as far as the different military aspects of the base and explained that the civilian contactors pretty much took care of their own stuff. Mitchell got the distinct impression that Flemings was one he was going to be going to quite often in the near future.

Once everybody got off and running he pulled Flemings aside and had a heart-to-heart talk with her. "Major, I understand that Anderson pretty much bailed on everybody without so much as a kiss my ass before he headed out the door…"

"That was pretty much his M.O. when he was CO here, sir," she stated flatly.

Mitchell sat back in his chair and nodded. "I figured the man was a turd when I spoke to him, but I never would have thought that he would have run his command like that as well."

"Permission to speak freely, sir?" Major Flemings asked.

Mitchell eyed her and cracked a smile. "Always, Major. I expect my officers to be able to speak their mind." She eyed him cautiously before she spoke.

"With all due respect, sir, Anderson is an Academy man who wanted nothing more than to get his next promotion. He didn't care whose neck he stepped on to get it either, sir."

"I'm well aware of that, Major."

"Are you also aware of the fact that he didn't actually run this base, sir?" She squared her shoulders. "I did," she stated rather proudly. "I made it run like a Swiss watch. For all intents and purposes, this base was *mine*."

Mitchell smiled more broadly. "I am so happy to hear you say that, Major."

She shot him a questioning look. "And why is that, Colonel?"

"Because, to be honest, I have no flippin' clue how to run a base like this," he stated. He rose to his feet

321

and walked around his desk. "And to be honest, I have no *desire* to run a base like this." He sat down on the edge of his desk and looked her square in the eye. "I've got bigger fish to fry and more important tasks at hand.

"Now, Major, please don't think I just want to hand the whole kit and caboodle over to you and simply say 'here ya go, it's your mess now so you handle it' without some kind of recognition and restitution."

Flemings' brows rose up. "I'm listening."

"You keep doing what you've been doing. I'll do what I need to do. We work together to make it work. I'll pull whatever strings I have to pull to get you promoted and as soon as it's possible, we get you made the Base CO all proper like."

Her mouth set in a disbelieving line. "Right," she quipped. "I do your job for you and you're going to hang me out to dry."

Matt gave her a hard look. "Major, I'm going to pretend that you didn't say that. I will, however, give you the chance to meet my XO and my people. Talk with them and find out from them the kind of man I am. Once you've done that, if you don't believe my offer, I'll leave it up to you. You can stay and continue your job just as you've always done, or you can put in for the billet of your choice."

She sat back in her chair. "You're serious, aren't you?"

"Major, as I've already stated, I have much bigger fish to fry and the last thing I want to do is have to push papers around trying to run a military facility like this. McAfee pulled this deal out of his ass for some unknown reason…maybe he thought he was doing me a favor, maybe he thought he was doing Anderson a favor. Whatever his reasoning, I don't want the job. You do. I'll do whatever I can do to make it official," Mitchell said. "That's the best I can offer."

She studied him for a moment before she stood and extended her hand. "Deal."

"You don't want to talk to my people first?" Matt asked.

"Nope. Anybody who offers that already knows what they're going to say. Besides, if you welch on the deal, I can screw this up for you far worse than you could ever screw things up for me." She shot him a sardonic smile.

Matt thought about what she said then shrugged. "You're definitely right about that."

"Okay, Colonel, what can I do now to help you get settled in?" she asked.

"We don't have time to get settled," he told her. "We have to move fast and hard. We have a lot of shit to do and little time to do it." She shot him a questioning look and he nodded. "Right. You and yours have no idea why we're even here…I need to fill you in." He sighed heavily and motioned her to take her seat again. "I'm going to fill you in first, but then we need to call a base-wide conference of key personnel and do this once. Since you are basically my right hand man—"

"Woman," she corrected.

Matt looked at her a moment and informed her, "I don't stand on PC crap, Major. If you have a problem with that…"

323

She smiled at him and shook her head. "No, sir, not if you don't."

"Good," he said. "I'm very relieved to hear that." He thought a moment and smiled. "I guess I've been lucky. My XO is a woman, but she's just one of the guys for the most part. Thank God she doesn't stand on PC crap either."

"Sounds like my kind of girl."

"I think you'll like her," Matt said. He paused a moment then glanced around. He leaned in close and lowered his voice. "Okay, I gotta ask, because I know my boys are gonna ask."

"What's that, sir?"

"Is there any *alien* stuff out here?" he asked quietly.

Flemings actually snorted as she shook her head. "No, sir, there isn't any alien stuff out here."

Matt actually looked a little disappointed. "Damn, I was actually hoping there was."

The Major glanced to the sides and lowered her voice. "Rumor has it though…that about thirty years ago? There *was* alien stuff out here. It all got shipped out to Wright-Patterson, though. Hasn't been any seen since."

Matt stared at her. "Are you serious?"

She nodded. "I ran across a very old file cabinet in one of the underground bunkers that had some of the old files in it," she said. "Pretty interesting stuff in there."

Matt sat back and stared at her. "I don't suppose you still *have* those files, do you?"

She gave him a stoic look. "That would go against protocol, Colonel."

Matt smiled at her. "Can I have a copy?"

She never flinched. Matt kept smiling. "Come on…I'm the new CO after all."

Finally the ends of her mouth slowly curled into a smile. "I'm sure a copy might find its way into your IN basket."

"Good man, Major," he said. "Er…woman. You know what I meant."

"Yes, sir," she said. "Now, you were going to fill me in on exactly *why* you're here?"

Matt leaned back in his chair. "Yeah…about that," he said. "Do you like scotch?"

16

Tufo escorted the security forces out the front doors of the hangar with the rest of First Squad on either side and behind them. They watched as more and more planes continued to land and taxi to the sides of the runways. Crews offloaded gear and trucks carried stuff to empty hangars in a flurry of beelike activity. A forklift drove by with a tech on it who stopped and backed up to double check to make sure he was seeing what he thought he was seeing. "Chief?"

Jack looked up and saw one of the techs that he had left at Tinker operating the lift. "What's up?"

"How did you get here, Chief? I thought you were in Canada?" he asked.

"We took a shortcut," Jack smiled.

"Oh." The man was unsure how exactly to take his answer. "Colonel's in his new office. Concrete building on the other side of the tarmac there with the flags in front. You may want to check in."

"Thanks Walters," Jack said. He turned to the security forces. "Looks like the change of command has taken place. Jacobs, return their weapons and give them the keys to their Jeeps."

"Aye, Chief." Jacobs hurried to retrieve their weapons and keys and Jack turned to the security forces again.

"Remember what I told you fellas. Time is coming where we are going to have to work together. If I can't count on you, you're no use to me." He shot them a look that put fear into most of them.

"So you're just letting us go?" the smart-mouthed one asked.

Tufo stepped up. "Yup, despite my better judgment. But I am curious how you boys knew we were even out there. There's no cameras back there."

"Ground sensors detected movement…" one of them started to say when the smart-mouthed security officer punched him in the chest.

"Shut your pie hole, dumbass," he fired off. "Just because they're letting us go doesn't mean we have to feed them any intel."

Tufo sighed. "Yeah, just because you fucking *work for us now* doesn't mean you should actually play nice, now does it, ass-hat?"

"Stand down, Gunny," Jack said. "Contract personnel are easily replaceable."

Tufo turned and stared at the smart-mouthed one who had paled a bit with that comment. "Yeah. Replaceable. I like that idea."

Jacobs came trotting up and handed the security forces back their weapons. Most checked them and placed them back in their holsters, but the smart-mouthed one held his a moment longer than Jacobs liked. He could tell that the man was seriously thinking of doing something stupid and Ing knew that even if he didn't do it now, odds were that he would do something stupid later. The man hesitated a moment longer, then placed his weapon back into his holster without checking it and snatched the keys from Ing's hand. "With me." Was all he said as he turned toward the back of the hangar and stomped back toward the Jeeps.

Ing approached Jack and said quietly, "That one is going to be a problem, boss."

"I know. But we can't do anything about it right now."

Tufo came up on the other side. "I understand wanting as many people as we can get our hands on that can carry a weapon, but some people are just plain liabilities, Jack. That asshole is a liability."

Jack nodded. "I know." He turned and watched the man throw the rear door open and heard it slam against the metal wall. He watched him stomp out the back and heard the Jeep roar to life throwing gravel as he spun away. "We'll deal with him when the time comes."

"Bait?" Mark asked.

"Or something," Jack responded.

Laura exited the hangar quickly, looking for the C-130 that she knew Evan had flown in on. She watched as it landed and crews headed that direction unaware that the cargo was light sensitive. She grabbed the nearest transport, commandeering it and headed in the direction of the taxiing plane. She pulled the two-way radio and tried to raise the CDO but no-body was answering. She cursed under her breath and reattached the radio to her belt. She urged the driver forward, hoping that Evan had found a shadowed area to hide in as the rear cargo deck lowered in front of her and crews began offloading cargo with lift trucks.

Just as she ran up the rear loading ramp of the plane, her radio squawked to life. "Mitchell to Youngblood, come in." The voice sounded of static in the interior of the plane, but she pulled the radio and responded.

"What's your twenty?"

"I'm on the tarmac greeting Dr. Peters' plane." She tried to keep the tremor out of her voice and hoped she did as she searched through the numerous crates and packages still strapped to the deck of the plane's cargo hold.

"Very well. I'm forwarding you a layout of avail-able buildings and hangars with a suggested key for logistics. When you find Dr. Peters' crate, have him and his equipment taken to his...'location' and set up as quickly as possible. Copy?"

Laura paused a moment to ensure she heard cor-rectly. "Matt, did you say 'when I find his *crate*'? Over."

"That is correct. He crated himself. Said he could sleep on the trip," the static-filled voice returned.

Laura heaved a sigh of relief and braced herself against a large box to her side. She placed her forehead against the box and allowed herself to laugh with the flood of emotions that flowed through her body. A crewman approached her from the rear. "Ma'am? We need to get the plane offloaded and clear the area."

She turned and glanced at him, realizing her eyes had watered. She wiped her eyes, her face still smiling. "Sure. I'm just happy everything made it okay," she said. Her PDA chimed and she pulled it. Glancing at it she pulled up the logistics key and saw the building where Matt wanted to put Evan's lab. It was an underground bunker with no windows and she smiled. "Crewman? Can we get everything labeled with prefix 7-16 taken here?"

He looked at the PDA and nodded. "Yes, ma'am. That's right across the tarmac. Southwest of here a little bit, shouldn't be a problem at all."

She smiled at him and patted his shoulder. "Let's make it as quick as we can. A lot of this is scientific equipment that needs to be powered back up as soon as possible."

"We'll double time it, ma'am."

"Thank you." She turned and left the plane to allow the crew to do their jobs without her looking over their shoulders. Laura looked around the tarmac and saw three more planes offloading gear, crews scrambling to move the crates and equipment in order to get the planes stowed and out of the way. She closed her eyes and sighed to herself, allowing one long moment to gather her thoughts.

She opened her eyes and marched off to the next plane to orchestrate setting up their operation. She had truly hoped that Matt would do his best to keep everything under one roof, but since their operation was six levels deep under an oversized hangar, it would be nearly impossible to find any one building large enough to do so. Not until he assumed command and moved everything over from Tinker would he be able to consolidate the Monster Squad and make Groom Lake their home.

She approached the first scene just as they finished offloading the equipment and she scanned the numbers painted on the crates. She ran her finger along the manifest and saw that this all went to the armory. She went back to her PDA and found the armory was now in a steel reinforced concrete building at the end of the complex, next to what would become the new training facility. She directed the crews there and headed to the next area. The heat was starting to build on the tarmac and she wished she had a tall drink of water just as she saw Tufo and Jack approaching along with the rest of First Squad, smiles spreading across their faces.

"Where the heck did you come from?" she asked.

"Canada," Jack said.

"Via a rock," Tufo added, a smart-assed smile crossing his features. "Helluva mass transit those Elves have."

She shot him a curious look as if he were drunk, but ignored his comment. She watched Jack give him a slight elbow and Tufo turned a bit more serious. "Well…it's good to see you again." She was still not sure how to take their just showing up. "You should probably check in with Mitchell and then we could definitely use a hand getting set up."

"Yes, ma'am," Thompson replied. "That's where we were about to go when we saw you."

She pulled out her PDA again and slowly turned, her finger outstretched until it settled on a larger concrete building with a single American flag out front. "I

331

think that's the Headquarters Building," she said. "Looks like his office is probably the ground floor…first office on the right."

"Thanks, boss." Jack turned to go. He stopped and turned back. "By the way."

"Yeah?" She looked up from her manifests.

"There's about three or four hundred Elf warriors in that hangar over there," Jack said, hooking his thumb over his shoulder. "Pretty nice guys, but…"

"But what?" Her eyes grew large at the thought.

"I wouldn't let anybody mess with them. They're a little more on the serious side."

Jack entered the Headquarters Building and made his way toward Mitchell's office. He was pretty sure he was headed in the right direction because he could hear Mitchell chewing somebody up one side and down the other before he even got near the door. He slowed his pace and debated hanging low in the lobby until Matt was through with whatever problem had arisen but the door flew open and two men came storming out, their mood reflected by their faces, and their faces showed that they were *not* happy. As the two came around the corner and the first man passed him, Jack began to realize why when he recognized the second man as the smart-mouthed security forces member that they had subdued upon arriving.

Well, he didn't waste any time tattling, did he? Jack thought as he hiked an eyebrow at the fellow who stormed past him. Jacobs and Lamb held the doors open for them as they stormed out of the building and Tufo smiled and tipped his cap to the men as they marched away.

Donovan shot Jack an interesting look. "I think somebody told on you."

"*Us,*" Jack corrected. "Remember, we're a team."

"Oh, yeah, *now* we're a team once you land us in hot water," Donovan teased. "I see how you are."

Jack shook his head and prepared for an ass chewing. He approached Mitchell's door and knocked. "What now?" Matt barked then looked up to see Thompson waiting just outside the door.

"Should I run and hide, or is it safe to enter?" he asked.

Matt picked a stack of files off of a chair across from his new desk. "Come on in, Phoenix." He sighed. "Sweet Jesus…we haven't been here thirty minutes and already they're treating me like I own the fucking place."

"What are you talking about? I thought you made it clear that this was all temporary and…"

Matt shot him an exasperated look. "You didn't get the memo?" he asked sardonically. "Once we win this whole vampire World War Three, *I* become the new base CO," he stated with exasperation.

Jack's jaw dropped. He was nearly speechless.

Matt pulled a hand down across his face and wanted to scream. Jack leaned forward and asked, "Are you for real here?"

333

Matt's eyes lifted and he stared at Jack a long moment. "As a heart attack."

"So...the move here isn't temporary?" he asked. "Or is the squad losing you?"

"Hell no!" Matt barked. "Where I go, the squads go." He leaned back in his chair and looked around for his other bottle of scotch. When he couldn't find it, he got frustrated and threw a stapler at the trash can. "Damn it. I can't find anything around here."

Jack stood up and poked around a few boxes until he found what he knew the colonel was looking for and held it up. He heard the man give an audible sigh and he poured two glasses. "So what then, Skipper? You going to run this place *and* the squads at the same time?"

Matt tossed back his drink and enjoyed the burn before he addressed the question. "Honestly, Chief, I had hoped that Laura would pick up the reins, but..." he lowered his eyes, "she's been looking for a way out for quite a while now."

Jack was shocked. He honestly thought that Laura loved working with the teams. "Okay, so what other options do you have?"

"Well, there's this major here that claims she's been running the show for the ass-hat that abandoned it rather than do an actual turnover to us...but..."

"But what?"

"But my gut is giving me fits. And I've learned to trust my gut," he said. "I'm sure she probably could run the show on this end and leave the squads to me and all would probably be just fine."

"Well, there ya go, Skip."

334

"Think about it, Jack. When is our busiest times of the month, and when can I absolutely NOT be there?"

Thompson nodded with understanding. "I got ya. But you do realize that we have more than enough qualified duty officers to pick up that slack, right?"

"It's not the same and we both know it."

Jack sat there a moment and slowly started to smile. "Skipper, I have an idea."

Matt looked up at him and gave Jack a very uneasy stare. "Why is my gut twisting on me, Jack?"

"Well…you may not like it at first, but it really is a good idea, especially if you think about it logically."

"Jesus, Jack, my gut just did a flip flop and I have this ungodly urge to mutter 'oh shit' and you haven't said a goddam thing yet," Matt said, his sixth sense buzzing at him like a bee in a bonnet.

Jack's smile widened and he threw back his own scotch. He set the glass on the Colonel's desk and placed his hands on either side of the desk as he smiled at him. "I got the *perfect* replacement for Laura."

"Oh, shit…"

"No, now, hear me out," Jack said.

"I had to say it. Never go against your gut."

"Tufo."

"Fuck me…" Matt groaned.

"No! Listen to me, Matt. He's perfect for the job!" Jack argued.

"How the hell can you say that, Chief?" Matt argued. "He's an arrogant, self-centered, son-of-a-bitch that goes off halfcocked—"

335

Tufo yelled from the Lobby, "I can hear you, ya know."

Matt stopped mid-rant and looked at Jack. He leaned forward and whispered at him, "You brought him with you?"

"The whole team's out there," he said. "But that doesn't change the fact that he's perfect for the job, Matt and you know it. AND, it wouldn't require him to go through augmentation, AND he's proven he can work as a negotiator, AND..." Jack paused as he recalled Mark's comment about the tracking devices and then nuking the head vampire. "And, he's a pretty sharp guy, Skipper. Maybe a little more brutal than I thought he'd be, but he's damned sharp."

Jack leaned back in his chair and stared at Mitchell. "You said yourself that he was probably the closest thing to a best friend you had back in the day and the guy was one hell of an operator."

Matt inhaled deeply and let it out slowly. He never took his eyes off Jack and he studied him. "I've always taken your input as equally important as Laura's Jack, you know that," he stated. "There was a reason you were made Team Leader of First Squad." Matt stood up and poured himself another drink. He poured Jack one and reached for a third glass. "Tufo!"

"What?!" came the yell from the hallway outside.

"Get your old, wrinkled ass in here," Mitchell barked.

Mark sauntered around the corner and leaned against the doorway. "You bellowed, oh great one?" he said slowly.

336

Matt sat back down and slid the third drink across the desk. "Clean out that chair and have a seat."

"What for?" Mark asked, eying Mitchell suspiciously.

"Long term employment opportunities," Matt said.

"This is total fucking bullshit!" the security officer yelled as he threw a radio across the security office. It just missed the bank of monitors showing the different locations where cameras were running twenty four hours a day and manned here in the 'man-cave' by Wackenhut's top-notch security personnel around the clock. The man behind the banks of monitors flinched when the radio bounced off the enclosure but never removed his eyes from the screen.

"Calm down, James." The captain of the contracted security forces was doing his best to calm the man, but he knew it would do no good. Most of his men were either ex-military commandos or SWAT team members or some other form of elite fighter or they wouldn't have gotten this billet. With those kinds of men came large egos and those egos were sometimes easily bruised. "Anderson bailed on us and left the base to this nitwit Mitchell. We can't help that."

"That doesn't give his people the right to just slip past all of our defenses and not explain to us *how*!" the man screamed. "We need to know where the weaknesses are so we can strengthen them and I want to know what the fuck they were using to make those half-naked guys disappear and reappear like that...they could be any fucking where."

"We're going to figure it out and we're going to get some answers, but blowing your top and demanding answers from somebody like Mitchell isn't the way to do it," Captain Roberts said, trying to make his voice soothing. Logic rarely worked when one of his best had his temper flared and James McDonald's temper wasn't just flared, he was past the boiling point. "We're going to have to use kid gloves with this guy if we want to get answers."

"Fuck that!" McDonald spat. "We ought to just go in there, cuff the bastard and beat the answers out of him. I guaran-damn-tee ya that me and the boys could get some answers out of that full bird if you'd just let us do our fucking jobs."

Roberts pointed a finger at him, "Your job is to do what *I* tell you to do. Do you understand me?" He jabbed the finger into his chest to emphasize his point. "Do you?"

McDonald glared at him, his eyes wild. "I got you," he said quietly. "I don't have to like it though."

"No, you don't," Roberts agreed. "The time for liking it comes later," he added, an evil smile crossing his features.

James glanced at him, unsure that he caught his meaning. "What do you have in mind?"

"Payback, of course. Nobody breaks into *my* base, abducts *my* men and then tells me to stand down over it," he threatened. "Not unless they want their dick slammed in the door."

"Now that's what I like to hear." McDonald smiled, calming down somewhat. "So what do you have in mind?"

Roberts shook his head slowly. "I don't know yet." He turned and watched all of the activity on the monitors. "But we're recording everything that these bastards are doing." He pointed to the screen. "This isn't just some standard run-of-the-mill change of command here."

"Then what is it?" James asked, studying the screens.

"I don't know," Roberts answered. "It's more like…an invasion." He tapped the monitor at the top. "Look at all this shit they're moving into the underground bunker. Who needs that much crap? And who are all these new fucking people? We don't have any of their files, their security clearances, their service jackets, health records…nothing. It's like they just blew into town and the new sheriff tells me to mind my own fucking business and guard the gates?!" He glanced at James again. "Fuck him. I'm going to get to the bottom of all this and when I do, I'm going to throw a monkey wrench into their works that will make the Titanic look like a dinghy sprung a leak!"

James laughed and clapped his captain on the back. "That's what I wanted to fucking hear." He sat up straight and squared his shoulders. "Finally, somebody with some *balls* around here."

Max tossed his bag onto the bed of the room he had been given. He didn't bother to look around or check out his surroundings. He knew that time was now their enemy. He needed to call to the others and have them come here, to this place and for some the distance would hinder the speed in which they could respond. He walked back outside, his mind already preparing for what he must do, preparing to reach out to all of those like himself, his children, children of the wolf.

He walked out into the hustle and bustle of the different crews still moving the squad's gear, unpacking, setting up, preparing…he moved past it all as if they weren't even there. His eyes searched, looking for the proper place. He could feel it, but he couldn't find it. He closed his eyes and let the energy of the place flow through him. `

He felt his body being pulled to the west and his feet moved him in that direction. He walked past the different buildings, the hangars, the cafeteria, the machine shops, the repair shops, the manufacturing facilities, the contractor's buildings until he found the spot his body was responding to. When he found the spot, he raised his arms and began to hum, low and deep from within his belly, the pitch and timbre slowly rising until it was audible to those nearby, though few paid any attention. To the few that did, it appeared that he may be meditating or practicing some form of yoga, but to the wolves on the base, they began to feel something stir inside them...

Each of the augmented operators felt a restlessness stir inside. Mitchell felt his wolf call to him stronger than when he found himself staring at the photo of the girl in the ice. Each of them felt an overwhelming desire to stop what they were doing and answer a call...a call so deep and basic that they would do anything to answer it. One by one they all stopped what they were doing and followed the sound that they felt more than heard. From the four corners of the facility, they found themselves each heading past the different buildings, the hangars, the cafeteria, the machine shops, the repair shops, the manufacturing facilities, the contractor's buildings until they found the spot that the call was coming from. They found Max.

They formed a circle around him, staring as if entranced, one by one falling to their knees, their eyes never leaving him. Tufo had followed Jack out and even tried to get his attention a time or two but had realized that something wasn't right when Jack didn't respond. He stood there with the others now, mouth agape as he watched the monster squads all fall prostrate to the ground before this bearded guy in sandals like some kind of wacked out modern-age guru. He was about to draw on him when Matt walked by and stood in front of the group. He seemed mesmerized by whatever was happening here and Mark wasn't sure if this was a good thing or a bad thing. His mind raced from bad to worse thoughts as he saw all of the people who now surrounded this guy...the squad members, their CO, Jack's wife and in-laws...then he realized...Max was 'calling' the wolves. From wherever they may be, he was calling them *here*.

Mark holstered his weapon and waited, keeping an eye for any outside threats to what was happening. He waited a few more moments when just as suddenly as it had begun, Max stopped humming and all those around him seemed to suddenly wake up from whatever held them hypnotized. The group slowly came around and seemed disoriented at first, unsure of how they got there or what had actually occurred, but they knew that something was different. They still felt...*something*...a pull that made them want to come here, even though they *were* here.

Matt got to his feet and tried to clear his head. He seemed to have the most difficulty as he had tried the hardest to fight it, and his disorientation was taking longer to recover from. Max approached him and laid a hand on his shoulder. "You're feeling fine, aren't you, Colonel," he stated more than asked.

Just as soon as Max said it, Mitchell felt right as rain. He cleared his throat and faced Max. "Yes, I am, thank you." He glanced around at the others and asked in a low voice, "What the hell just happened?"

"I've called the others," Max said, keeping his voice low. "I couldn't do it without affecting all wolves." His eyes betrayed him and Matt saw the sadness in them.

Mitchell simply nodded. "How soon?"

Max shook his head. "As soon as they can. They cannot fight it," he stated. "As you noticed."

"Even though you've stopped?"

Max nodded. "The seed has been planted. It will only continue to grow. As it does, the pull will grow stronger as well."

Matt looked at the others who were starting to break up and try to go back to what they were doing before the interruption. "What of them? Of us?" he asked. "Of me? Will it continue to affect us all like the others? Continue to grow?"

Max shook his head. "You are already here. The effects will wear off shortly." He patted the colonel on the back. "You've already achieved your goal."

Matt nodded, trying to understand. "Very well," he stated. "Keep me abreast of the numbers and we'll do our best to house them as they come in."

"As you wish, Colonel."

Matt turned to leave and then caught himself. "Oh, and one more thing."

"Yes, Colonel?"

"Next time you do something like this, let me know first, okay? A little heads up would have been nice."

Max's eyes grew wide with realization then he bowed slightly. "Apologies, Colonel. Next time…if there ever *is* a next time, you will be informed beforehand."

"Thank you," Matt said, and fought the urge to call him 'my liege'.

Dom paced the area around the pool of fresh water while Grumpy waded through it with a spear in hand. He held the handmade spear aloft waiting for a fish to come into view, he pulled the spear back ready to throw it when Dom turned and yelled, "It's right on the tip of my mind, but I just can't...reach it!"

Lou sighed and lowered the spear. He turned and looked at Dominic, a sour expression crossing his features. "You're scaring the fish, boy."

"What?" Dom asked, his mind elsewhere.

"The fish." Lou nodded toward the water. "You're scaring them away." He trudged back toward the shore and tossed the spear into the sand. "I thought you were hungry?"

Dom plopped back into the sand and held his head in his hands. "I am, but...this is driving me nuts," he said softly. "It's like its right on the tip of my mind, but it's just out of reach."

Lou sat down next to him and shielded his eyes with his hand. He looked up at the sun and shook his head. "This is damned strange, boy."

"I know. You'd think it would eventually come back to me..."

"No, I mean the sun." he continued staring at the sky. "It's been high noon all day. You'd think the sun would move a little across the sky."

Dom looked up at him as if he were crazy. "You're worried about the sun?"

"I'm worried that your time here is limited and without a way to measure it, we have no idea how long we've been here."

Dom studied him a moment and realized just how worried his grandfather was. "How long do I have?"

Lou shook his head. "I don't know." He turned and looked at Dom, shrugging his shoulders. "Nobody ever gets an instruction book. I just…know. Your time here is limited." He stood up and brushed the sand from his shorts. "And we have to eat."

"We got bananas and coconuts and…" Dom started.

"Yeah," Lou laughed, "we do, but you need to be careful. Coconuts will give you the squirts, bananas will clog you up and those berries over there? I have no idea if they're even edible." He pointed back at the water. "That's why I was trying to catch us some fish."

Dom shoved his hands into the moist sand and squeezed again. It had such a calming effect on him and he didn't know why. Lou watched him a moment and then hunkered down next to him and pulled his hands out of the sand. Dom struggled against him, trying to drive his hands back in the sand. "What are you doing, Grumpy…stop it."

"Why do you keep shoving your hands in the sand?" he asked.

"I don't know…I like playing in the dirt," he said. "I need to…"

"That's not dirt, boy, that's sand," Lou said, still pulling at his hands. Dom struggled with him but the old man was stronger than he looked. "Stop it, boy."

"No, I need...I, I need..."

"You need to remember something and you aren't sticking your hands back in the sand until you..."

"It's not *sand*, it's *dirt*," Dom nearly snarled. The old man held him tight, his face like stone as he continued to hold his hands. "Stop it!"

"Tell me why it's so damned important to you and I might," Lou argued.

"I don't know why, it just is..." He was cut off as Lou dragged him to the edge of the jungle where the plant life was thick and used his foot to kick away the detritus to expose the rich soil below.

"You see that, boy?" he said as the deep, rich aroma of the dark soil rose up to Dom's nostrils. "*That* is dirt." Dom fought harder this time, the desire to stick his hands into the dirt almost overwhelming. He wanted to roll in it, to lay in it, to *sleep* on it. "Tell me why it's important," the old man ordered.

"I...don't know," Dom choked out, still struggling. He had to have the dirt. It called to him, it needed him...no, he needed it. It was safety to him. It preserved him somehow. It was...*important* to him. It would keep him safe. It would...

"Tell me why it's so damned important to you boy. Why do you want to stick your hands into it?" Lou barked.

"I don't just want to stick my hands into it. I want to lay on it. I want to sleep on it...I *need* to!" he cried.

Dom began to shake now, the tremors rocking his core. He could feel whatever block that was in his head start to crack and it hurt. It felt as though an ice pick were being driven through the center of his brain and he pulled his hands away from Lou's with a jerk and grasped at his head, clutching the sides in agony. "No-o-o!" he screamed as he fell to the ground, rolling to the sides, clutching his temples.

Lou fell beside him and was yelling to overcome the onrush of pain, "Tell me boy, tell your Grumpy what it is…" He got lower to the ground and next to his ear and whispered against the onrush of pain, "Tell me what it is…why the dirt, boy?"

When the wall finally shattered, the vampire's secret revealed to him, Dom's eyes flew open and he sat up, his breath coming in pants. He turned to his grandfather and slowly a smile came to his face. He chuckled at first and then laughed out loud. He pulled his grandfather into a hug and squeezed the old man to him tightly. "I know now," he said softly.

Lou pulled away from him and stared him in the eye. "Are you sure, boy?"

Dom laughed as tears formed in his eyes. "Oh yeah, Grumpy, I'm sure."

Lou sat down hard in the dirt next to him and with his hands resting on his knees, he sighed heavily and nodded. "Good. Because I was starting to worry that…"

"What?" Dom asked.

Lou snorted. "I was afraid we had run out of time and you were losing it." He sighed again and reached out and patted Dom on the leg. "You have no idea how worried I've been..." He stopped mid-sentence as the sun suddenly set and the stars began twinkling.

Both men sat in the darkness staring at the sky, an eerie oh-shit feeling shared between them. Dom looked at his grandfather and said, "Suddenly I'm very thirsty."

"Yeah...I imagine so," he said cautiously. "Look, Dom..." Lou began, turning to him urgently. "I may not have much time left with you, so I want to ask you to do something for me, okay?"

"Anything, Grumpy, you know that," Dom said, suddenly afraid that he'd disappear as quickly as he appeared.

"When you get back, please, tell Grammy that I miss her. Let her know that I meant to come home and spend the rest of my life with her," he said, tears forming in his old weather worn eyes. "Tell her...I love her."

"Grumpy," Dom began, his chest tightening and his eyes misting, "she already knows."

The old man nodded sharply and sniffed back a few tears. "I figured as much." He looked up at the stars and breathed deeply of the cooling night air. "Heart of gold, that one."

"Yeah, you picked a winner with Gram," Dom said. They both sat silent for a moment before Dom sat up and got to his feet. He stuck his hand out to help Lou up, but he was already gone. The only indication that he was ever there was the impression he had left in the dirt. Dom looked around the area and stared at the spot where his grandfather had last been. Dom slowly fell to his knees, the tears flowing freely. "I never got to say goodbye," he whispered.

He fell over and rolled on to his back, the tears flowing freely and he sobbed. "Thank you, Grumpy," he whispered. "Thank you for helping me..." He pressed his eyes closed to block out the pain and heartbreak and he sucked a huge amount of air to cleanse his mind. He lay there in the dark, doing his best to control his breathing, to bring his emotions under control, to try to figure out what he should do next.

Dom allowed himself only a few moments to gather himself before he decided it was time to carry on. As much as he hurt, both emotionally and physically, he had to push on. He inhaled one more breath of the cool sanitized air and opened his eyes. He glanced around the darkness and saw the medical monitors hooked to him. The lighted numbers on the machines showing his heart rate, O2 levels, and blood pressure levels. He glanced in the other direction and saw a table with charts and paperwork on it. The lights were off in his room, but the moonlight through his window illuminated enough of the interior that he knew he was back in the hospital room in Italy.

It had all been a dream. A wild, crazy dream induced by the drugs that the Team Two members shot him up with. He sat up slowly and pulled the blankets off of him. As the leads fell off of him, the machine at his bedside registered alarms that he chose to ignore. He pushed the machine to get it away from him as his head was still throbbing from his concussion. He slid his feet out of bed and felt grit in the sheets. Pulling the blankets back further, he ran his hand across the sheet and found…beach sand? His feet and the sheets were covered in beach sand. And no matter how Dom tried to explain it away, he couldn't.

He stumbled into the bathroom and flipped on the light. It took a moment for his eyes to adjust to the sharp brightness of the overhead fluorescent bulb as it flickered to life. He glanced at his reflection in the mirror and was shocked at the growth of facial hair. He ran his fingers across his face and saw his hands in the mirror. Pulling them back, he studied them in the harsh fluorescent light. There was dark colored dirt embedded into his nail beds and thick layers of it under his nails. He held them close to his eyes and studied them. He pulled one closer to his face and held his fingertips under his nose…with a deep lung-filling sniff he smelled his fingers and the aroma of the soil under his fingers was exactly that of the soil from the island in his dream.

Dom staggered back against the bathroom wall and stared at his hands. His dirt encrusted hands… and questioned *how* they could have gotten that way.

And then he remembered…the importance of the dirt and he turned to leave the bathroom as two nurses came into his room to investigate the alarms from his monitor. "Mr. DeGiacomo, you *must* return to your bed," she said as he pushed past her.

"Where are my clothes?" he barked.

"What?!"

"My uniform? Where is it?" He stood in the middle of his room in his hospital gown and nearly growled at the woman.

She shook with fear and her eyes betrayed her as they darted to the storage cabinet on the far side of the room. The other nurse darted from the room to get security. "Thanks," he muttered as he marched to the storage cabinet and pulled his gear from the locker. Of course, his weapons had been confiscated, most likely by Team Two personnel, but at least he had some clothes. A bit ratty and torn, but thankfully someone had cleaned them.

He put them on as quickly as he could and made for the door in time to see three large security guards running down the hall toward his room. "Great," he muttered as he went back into the room and propped the door shut with a chair.

Dom looked around and made for the window. *Great, another second story jump.* At least he felt better this time. His wrist hardly hurt any more, but there was still a slight pain as he pulled the window open. He settled on the ledge and jumped to the grass below. He looked back up at the open window and made for the shadows to try to conceal himself should any more security come for him. He had to get to a safe place and contact Colonel Mitchell. He had to have him arrange for getting him stateside.

He pulled up alongside a building and scanned both ways to make sure the coast was clear. As he stepped out along the way he heard sirens approaching and knew they were meant for him. He sighed and ducked back into the shadows. This journey was going to be tough enough, but now he had unlocked the secret that was nagging at his mind and he had to get it to the Monster Squad. For whatever reason, he felt it was important. It might, in fact, be the key to bringing down the Sicarii.

From the desk of Heath Stallcup
A personal note-
Thank you so much for investing your time in reading my story. If you enjoyed it, please take a moment and leave a review. I realize that it may be an inconvenience, but reviews mean the world to authors…
Also, I love hearing from my readers. You can reach me at my blog: http://heathstallcup.com/ or via email at heathstallcup@gmail.com
Feel free to check out my Facebook page for information on upcoming releases:
https://www.facebook.com/heathstallcup find me on Twitter at @HeathStallcup, Goodreads or via my Author Page at Amazon.

The Monster Squad Series

RETURN OF THE PHOENIX   WAYWARD SON
FULL MOON RISING   OBSESSIONS
COALITION OF THE DAMNED   SPECTERS
BLOOD APOCALYPSE   AWAKENINGS
HOMECOMING   RECKONING

Mankind always suspected that he wasn't alone at the top of the food chain. Since time immemorial, he has had an innate fear of the dark, a fear of the unfamiliar, a fear that something evil lurked just outside his field of vision. Once the sun set and the moon lit the sky, an unfamiliar snap of a twig or rustling of a bush could make the deadliest of men's blood run cold. Something was out there.

Humanity had spent its time enjoying a peace that can only be had through blissful ignorance. For centuries, stories of things that go bump in the night had been told. When creatures of the night proved to be real, the best of America's military came together to form an elite band of rapid response teams. Their mission: to keep the civilian populace safe from those threats and hide all evidence of their existence.

Caldera

For years, the biggest threat Yellowstone was thought to offer was in the form of its semi-dormant super volcano. Little did anyone realize the threat was real and slowly working its way to the surface, but not in the form of magma. Lying deep within the bowels of the earth itself, an ancient virus waited.

Recently credited with wiping out the Neanderthals, the virus is released within the park and quickly spreads. Can mankind prevent a second mass extinction? Can humanity survive the raging cannibals that erupt from within?

Whispers

How does a sheriff's department from a small North Texas community stop a brutal murderer who is already dead and buried? When grave robbers disturb the tomb of Sheriff James 'Two Guns' Tolbert searching for Old West relics, a vengeful spirit is unleashed, hell bent for blood. Over a hundred years in the making, a vengeful spirit hunts for its killers. If those responsible couldn't be made to pay, then their progeny would.

Even when aided by a Texas Ranger and UCLA Paranormal Investigators, can modern-day law enforcement stop a spirit destined to fulfill an oath made in death? An oath fueled by passion from a love cut down before its time?

Forneus Corson

Nothing comes easy and nothing is ever truly free. When Steve Wilson stumbles upon the best-kept secret of history's most successful writers, he can't help but take advantage of it. Little did he know it would come back to haunt him in ways he'd never have dreamt... even in his worst nightmares.

With his life turned upside down, his name discredited, his friends persecuted, the authorities chasing him for something he didn't do, Steve finds himself on the run with nothing but his wits and his best friend by his side. When a man finds himself hitting rock bottom, he thinks there's little else he can do but go up... unless he's facing an evil willing to dig the hole deeper. An evil in the business of pitting men against odds so great, they risk losing their very souls in the attempt to escape...

Flags of the Forgotten

What do you do when you've devoted your life to working for the government, then that very same government turns on you?
You take the fight to them.

It's just another day at the office for Bobby Bridger and his co-horts when they are used as scapegoats. Follow along as this rag-tag group of operators attempt to stay one step ahead of their pur-suers.

From the heart of Texas to Pakistan to the very bowels of the CIA, these boys know how to play hard, fast and dirty.

Hunter Trilogy

Born of Viking stock, careered into the Swedish Navy, Sven Ericsson finds himself in the fabled New World. Away from the restraints of society, the young Northman is dragged into long nights of debauchery; nights that lead him into the waiting arms of a dark beauty that will change his very nature forever. Fighting his new unnatural status, Sven steers clear of humanity, skulking along the fringe of society, and filling his inhuman need with the blood of the outcasts or the easily forgotten. A shadow among the shadows...until extraordinary events, centuries later, force him to emerge from the dark. A mishap of his own making pits Sven Ericsson into a moral quandary that will remind him what it means to be a warrior.

He is a killer. A fighter. A Hunter of his own kind.

Sinful

AUTHOR OF THE MONSTER SQUAD SERIES
HEATH STALLCUP
SINFUL

Charlie Johnson is your average American teenager. He's a good student, he's a good son, his girlfriend is the love of his life. He's a nice kid. Charlie also murders people for their sins. A serious car accident leaves Charlie comatose and when he comes to, he suffers from visions of unspeakable horror that keep him awake at night. He soon discovers that when he touches people, he can sense their evil and see their greatest sins. Some crimes are too terrible to describe. Some crimes are too terrible to go unanswered. Some crimes can be averted...but only if you're willing to step into that world.

For a refreshing change of pace, check out JJ Beal's exciting Young Adult Zombie thriller.

Lions & Tigers & Zombies, Oh My!

The cold war has heated up again. This time the battle will be fought in every street of America.

Trapped in a major city, hours from their small town country home, a team of young girls find themselves cut off from everyone they know and left to fend for themselves as the world spins out of   *control.*

With nothing but their wits, their softball equipment and their friendship to hold them together, they face incredible odds as they fight their way across the state. Physical, emotional and psychological challenges meet them at every turn as they struggle to find the family they can't be sure survived. How much more can they endure before reaching the breaking point?

ABOUT THE AUTHOR

Heath Stallcup was born in Salinas, California and relocated to Tupelo, Oklahoma in his tween years. He joined the US Navy and was stationed in Charleston, SC and Bangor, WA shortly after junior college. After his second tour he attended East Central University where he obtained BS degrees in Biology and Chemistry. He then served ten years with the State of Oklahoma as a Compliance and Enforcement Officer while moonlighting nights and weekends with his local Sheriff's Office. He still lives in the small township of Tupelo, Oklahoma with his wife. He steals time to write between household duties, going to ballgames, being a grandfather and the pet of numerous animals that have taken over his home. Visit him at heathstallcup.com or Facebook.com for news of his upcoming releases.

www.devildogpress.com

Indian Hill Series

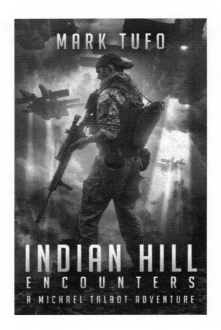

All That Remain By Travis Tufo

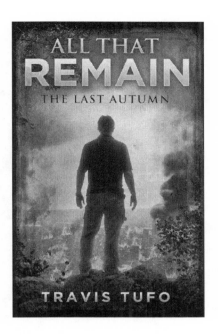

Prey By Tim Majka

Vodou by Brandon Scott

Redemption & Revenge by Nicholas Catron

CUSTOMERS ALSO PURCHASED:

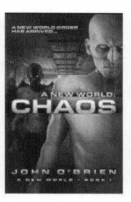

SHAWN CHESSER
SURVIVING THE
ZOMBIE APOCALYPSE

WILLIAM MASSA
OCCULT ASSASSIN
SERIES

JOHN O'BRIEN
A NEW WORLD
SERIES

ERIC A. SHELMAN
DEAD HUNGER
SERIES

HEATH STALLCUP
MONSTER SQUAD
SERIES

MARK TUFO
ZOMBIE FALLOUT
SERIES